The characters and events portrayed in this book are fictitious. Any similarity to real persons, living or dead, is coincidental and not intended by the author.

ISBN: 978-1-63684-795-5 (hardcover)
ISBN: 978-1-63684-809-9 (epub)
ISBN-10: 1477123456

Cover Concept design by: Thomas P Craig III
Cover Art design by: Arzie Gashi l AGstudio
Library of Congress Control Number: 2018675309
Printed in the United States of America

RETURNING TO HALONAWA

PROLOGUE

The wood was weathered, grey overtaking a few areas of the once polished walnut. Despite over two centuries of aging, the wood was still strong and securely holding the old double barrel steel that lay on top. Perfectly crafted and balanced, it curved downward to form a handle. Below the two gooseneck cocks on either side were two brass plates that held illegible prints that once read Ketland & Co. surrounded by what appeared to be engraved floral patterns. The brass was very worn and extended from the side plates down into the handle. The same floral patterns on the brass plates ran the length of the 9-inch barrels.

There were two soft lights flickering on opposite sides of the partially dark room causing shadows to dance on the walls. The pungent odor lingering in the air was from weeks of trash building up in an open can, mixing with body orders, cigarettes, and the latest TV dinner that was recently cooked in a microwave.

A man paced back and forth next to a table, mumbling to himself as he snuffed out a cigarette that was burning at the filter. His fingers were stained yellow from the tar, hands were calloused from manual labor and traces of dirt, oil and a bit of blood were under his fingernails. He paused in front of the table and took in the contents laid out carefully before him. He sat down and started the process he had done several times before.

As he packed the barrel and prepared the flint in the cock, he got up and walked around his victim that lay lifeless on the floor. He rolled her over and stared at her with his head tilted to the side. She had some fight in her, but not enough to last the series of malice acts he put her through over the last few days. A grin slipped onto his face as he raised the pistol taking aim at her heart. With his arm fully extend, he gently pulled the trigger and a second later the flint served its purpose igniting the powder and sending the ball of lead into her chest. She got what she deserved. As far as he was concerned, they all got what they deserved.

CHAPTER 1

The Coroner briefed us on the strange circumstances of the body that was found in Sweetwater Creek State park near the Sparks Reservoir. It was in fact the missing girl from the news, which had been one of our open cases for about two weeks. She was assumed to be abducted on the outskirts of Mableton, GA on her way home from High School. She was only sixteen, beautiful, popular and just starting to plan for college. Life was just beginning for her and then it was over.

The coroner described how she was apparently malnourished, beaten several times, repeatedly bitten, some leaving deep teeth marks and bruising, violated, and ultimately suffocated before being shot postmortem by what appeared to be an old gun. The Coroner suspected that once he examined the lungs, throat and nose, he would find inflammation from the ether used repeatedly on her.

This was the fourth victim in a six-month period that fit this pattern, each horrific case gradually getting closer together in time. This one was only a month after the last. Clearly the killer was escalating his need for more and was not going to be a letting up anytime soon, unless stopped.

I was recently given a case of a missing 14-year-old girl in Douglasville, GA, close to where I lived. We all hoped she was not caught up in this killer's pattern, but it would be too much of a coincidence if she wasn't. I spent several days interviewing family, friends, neighbors, teachers and shop owners between her school and home. After getting a lucky lead from shop cameras, I tracked down a person of interest from a van that frequented the girl's path home. I decided to take Andy with me to check this guy out.

The house was about 10 miles west of D'ville, off a dirt road tucked in the woods. As we pulled up to the dilapidated old house, the scene gave me chills.

Tall trees shading the road, rusty roof, the old grey patina wood walls with a wrap-around covered porch. The weeds were growing high and the grass had turned wild. An old stripped-down car was off to the left side of the house in the far yard next to the tree line. Weeds growing through it and consumed by rust, it must have been there for a decade.

I stopped about a hundred yards shy of the house to not make any noise. I took a moment to allow Andy to sniff the girl's shoes the mother gave me two days earlier.

"Smell." I said to Andy as I opened the brown bag which held the tennis shoes. Andy did as he was told.

As we got out of the car and approached the porch, I told Andy, "find the smell." Off he went around the right side of the house, the direction I was pointing.

I did not see the van and there were no indications that a car could have made it to the backyard. No garage either. As I stepped foot on the porch, a rough looking, very thin, pock-filled face man in his late 40's opened the door.

"This is private property and you are not welcomed here. Please go."

"Yes sir. I'm Detective Abrams with Mableton PD, and I'm following up on an Amber alert in the area. Have you seen this girl before?" He barely looked toward the direction of the photo in my hand before saying 'no'.

"Can you please take a closer look before I move on?" At this point, he had taken a step forward out of the door frame to look at the picture. He smelled of cigarettes and beer, among other smells I cared not to try to identify. He mumbled to himself and looked at the photo. "Nope, never seen her."

At this point, I heard Andy start barking, which only

meant one thing.

The man looked startled and his eyes darted from me to the side of the house and then back to me before making a move to re-enter his home quickly. As he spun around, I grabbed the back of his pants and belt stopping him in his tracks. We began to wrestle each other to the ground before I had the upper hand and was able to cuff him to a cast iron bench that was on the porch.

Unsure what I would find as I ran around the house to Andy, I called for backup and an ambulance.

Andy was still barking as he stood in front of an old shed in the backyard. I surveyed the area for others and then gave Andy the command to watch my back. He went silent and turned to face the house. The grass was so tall that someone in the yard or house would not be able to see Andy, which gave him the upper hand.

I had my gun drawn as I used my asp to break the old padlock from the chain on the shed door. As I opened the shed, it must have been slightly over a 100-degrees inside. I felt the heat hit my face as it escaped the 8x8 area and then the smell of bile buckled my knees.

There she was unconscious, cuffed to a metal worktable, bruised from head to toe. Clothes were dirty and torn apart. I quickly checked for a pulse and then uncuffed her. Before I knew what I was doing, I was cradling her telling her it was okay, she was safe now. I was full of anger and there was a knot forming in my stomach. How could someone do this to another person, a child, an innocent carefree child?

She wasn't moving. I could barely feel her breathing. Sirens crept in from a distance. Andy was still at the door facing the house.

As I looked her over again, I noticed the bruises had disappeared and she was waking up. Without even thinking about it, I had healed her in minutes, righting any physical wrongs that had been done by her capture.

She started to scream and wiggle free as I said, "it's okay,

I'm the police, we got him. You're safe now. Can you hear the sirens? You're going home."

As she started to calm down, tears and confusion came over her face. She whimpered words that sounded like "he did bad things, painful things to me."

I told her the nightmare was over and asked her if she could stand and walk with me to the side of the house where we could see the police and ambulance. We stood together and she saw my detectives shield on my belt. She hugged me and said, 'thank you'.

As I hugged her back, I had one hand on her upper back and the other on the back of her head. She was a little more than a foot shorter than me, so it felt like the right places to put my hands. As she hugged me, I felt the warmth travel through my hands and her knees buckled a few times before we began our first steps out of the shed. I think I know what I had just done, but only time will tell.

As we came around to the front yard, the first officer was already approaching the porch when I yelled out that the house was not cleared yet, but the backyard was covered by police K9. Andy still stood guard outback. The second police car arrived with the ambulance shortly thereafter. The first officer came out and yelled, 'all clear'. I whistled for Andy who appeared seconds later.

As the paramedic took the girl's hand and led her to the back of the bus, I went to advise the other medic that she appeared to be physically okay, but being trapped in the heat had her weak and delirious.

Fortunately for the victim, but unfortunately for physical evidence, my healing powers erased traces of sexual assault. We clearly had him on kidnapping, and a few other charges. However, word would get out what she claimed he did to her and the favor would likely be returned onto him once he was in the system. Jail justice or Karma as many call it.

I just felt terrible that her words and experience would not be substantiated with evidence, leaving her to feel like people would not fully believe the full horror she experienced.

From about 6:00PM to 11:30PM that day, I placed the man from the porch in custody back at the precinct, spent time at the hospital to ensure the girl and her parents were doing well and then back at the precinct filling out more paperwork, including the hospital findings.

It had been a hell of a day.

Entering my home, Andy, the departments 7-year-old Australian Shepherd K9 police dog and my recent somewhat faithful companion, followed me in gently nudging my knee with his nose. I knew he was hungry, but he thought it best to remind me.

I placed my gun in the side table drawer next to my chair and went to the kitchen to fill his bowl. I felt bad that I had not picked something up for him earlier in the day, but we were both so busy.

On days like this when he is at home alone, the dog door allows him to come and go as he pleases, and he has been known to go to neighbors for playtime or a bite to eat.

Both immediate neighbors know him well and adore him. They also know I go out on jobs at all hours. I sometimes take him on jobs and today was one of those days.

He is no ordinary Aussie. Andy has built up quite the resume over the years. We have been together for 3 years, but have known each other for about 6 years. His previous owner was a close friend of mine on both the Phoenix PD and then Atlanta PD before being taken from us in the line of fire. For months after the incident, Andy would not respond to any other police officer, so they called me in to see if we would be a fit. He instantly responded to me.

It took a while to train me on the 15 commands and 6 different whistles that sent Andy into action. He is experienced in search and rescue, detection of many different items, an excellent retriever, guard dog, companion, and judge of character. Well, he is an excellent judge of men, but he loves most women. Not sure what his deal is there.

Andy finished eating and curled up on the couch.

Andy had eyes of two different colors, a white chest with blue and brown patterns covering the rest of his coat that had a few black spots mixed in and he had white feet that looked like socks. There was a multi-colored blanket on the coach that he blended right into.

Quiet. I was finally surrounded by peace and quiet. This was one of the main reasons why I chose this location when I was house hunting a few years ago.

I was in the middle of relocating from Phoenix to Atlanta and feeling a bit rushed to find a place before my first day on the job. I actually stumbled upon this duplex for the reason that I wrote the address down incorrectly. I was nowhere near where I was intending to be. When I realized I may have written down the wrong address, I pulled into this nice duplex on the edge of town.

A very pleasant elderly lady, Anita Banks, was outside pulling weeds from here flowerbed. Anita and her recently late husband had been running the eight-unit duplex together for many years. Turns out she owned the duplex. We struck up a friendly conversation that entailed a few self-inflicted stabs at my navigation skills that made her laugh. She was kind-hearted and took pity on my situation.

Anita mentioned she had a vacant unit joined with hers and without any background checks, offered it at a discount on one condition. With ample notice, I had to help her with a few "things" on the weekends. Since that day, I have become a self-proclaimed expert plumber and carpenter. I'm smart enough to not touch the electrical problems.

Anita is the perfect neighbor. Quiet. That is exactly what I needed after the night I just had. It's late in the evening. I just poured a scotch and sat down in my chair in complete darkness. As I took a sip, I thought to myself how the evening went from bad to worse.

"Shit." I whispered. Who's going to hear me? Andy? He doesn't mind.

"Shit!" I said loudly as I exhaled and swallowed the rest of the Scotch. Andy lifted his head to look at me before flopping it back down on the couch.

There will be questions tomorrow. Questions I don't want to answer. Questions from people that thought they knew me...until now. What could I have done differently? What will they ask me? What did they notice? Jesus, I need another drink. I need to clear my head and think through what just took place a few hours earlier.

Perhaps my time is up here, and a new city is what I need. My thoughts were erratic and I'm tired, extremely tired. I just need to lock the door, turn off the phone and get some sleep. The answers will come in the morning. God help me if they don't.

I walked over to the front door and set the locks. After having a second drink to help calm the nerves, I settled back into my old leather lazy boy recliner and allowed myself to fall asleep. I wasn't asleep for more than 20 minutes when I heard a scream.

The second scream had me out of my chair and grabbing my 9mm Glock from the side table drawer. As I left the house through the backdoor in the direction of the screams, I noticed Ms. Banks coming out in her bathrobe.

"Please stay inside Anita. I will check it out." I headed towards the pool area. The duplex had 8 units; each unit with two houses joined together, all surrounding the tree covered courtyard that encircled the pool area. You had to get through your backyard to make it to the courtyard and community pool. There were light shrubs, a moderate collection of maple trees and a few pines between my backyard and the pool. I was cutting through the trees making a straight line for the pool instead of taking the winding walking path. A clear sight of the pool was still obscured, but I could make out a few figures and hear someone saying,

"Stop it!" Don't!" Clear pleads from a woman.

"Time to go!" A man shouted.

I had not realized I was running in just my socks until I stepped on a pine cone. Normally, I'm pretty light-footed, but this hellish object was designed to take down the swiftest of barefooted night runners. I tucked in my right shoulder and went into a controlled roll, popping right back up into a run. When I broke the line of trees into the pool area, I quickly realized this was a case of stupidity, not violence.

My gun found its way to my lower back and into the waist band. Andy appeared at my side. The gentlemen I assume said 'time to go' was in the process of throwing a young lady into the pool. There were two gentlemen. The other was retrieving beverages from a cooler with his back to me. Another fully clothed young lady was already in the pool cussing at the man standing poolside, now laughing at his ingenious handy work.

"Real mature asshole!" Shouted the brunette, who must be victim number one of the proud prankster. She was pulling herself up the ladder quite impressively as she was still wearing high heels. From the looks of her, she was dressed up and probably coming in from a night out with her girlfriend, who, unfortunately was not having the same luck getting out of the pool.

"Oh, come on, lighten up. You said you were hot. Now you're not." He said with a grin and somewhat of a chuckle. The man at the ice chest tossed a beer and said, "Here you go Brad." Brad caught it with ease and popped it open as close as possible in front of the young ladies' face. "Chill Michelle. We are just having fun. Just like you and Lacey were tonight at the club...without us." The tone in his voice went from stupid prankster to anger and jealousy.

I don't think anyone noticed me walk over to the step ladder to help out Lacey. Andy put himself between me and the gentlemen who were about 15 feet away. "Hi, can I help you out?" I stuck out my hand and she gave a head nod as she reached for it. She stared into my eyes for a moment and made an inquisitive face.

Ah, my eyes. My eyes seem to be the topic of many conversations and subjected to many stares. They are bright royal blue, almost glowing next to my tan skin and black hair. I am one-half Native American, Zuni to be specific, and one-half Dutch. Which does not totally explain the phenomenon of the eyes, nothing does.

The light from the pool magnified the glowing affect in my eyes. She broke her gaze and I caught a smile forming on her face.

Somewhat out of breath she whispered, "Wait a second. I have to get these damn shoes off first." With one hand holding mine, she arched her back and reached behind her to slip off her heels. I had to shift my weight back a little or she would have pulled me in with her.

I could not help noticing how beautiful she looked. Perhaps it was the effects of the soaking wet clothes that helped outline her body or the perfect complexion the water seemed to give to her skin.

Scandinavian popped into my head as I looked over her straight blond hair, strong facial features with a proportionately round face, wide shoulders, almost athletic build, and a modest bosom which was heaving inches below my face.

I turned to look at Brad as her eyes came back to my face. Crisis averted. Nothing beats a 'hello, let me size you up'.

As I turned back to her, our eyes met again, and she offered her other hand. I heaved her out swiftly and gently. Again, I could not help looking her over. This time I played it off by saying, "are you okay?" as I looked her over.

She was wearing a black leather mini skirt that made it half way to her knees and a very thin tan blouse that left nothing to the imagination when wet, which it was not intended to be when designed. Out of the pool and next to me she must be about 5'10.

I was still holding both of her hands as she said, "Thank you. Other than a ruined outfit and ego, I'm fine. This evening has gone from bad to worse."

"Funny, I was telling myself that exact thing a half hour ago before I heard screams" I said with a genuine smile.

"Oh no, I bet we woke up all of our neighbors. I'm so sorry..." She was cut off.

Brad was walking over saying, "Who the hell are you? You're the maintenance guy, aren't you?"

"I've been known to fix a few things around here." I said politely. I was about to ask what was going on, even though I already had a good idea, but Brad felt it wise to send me on my way.

"Nothing here needs fixing, so why don't you go back to bed." Brad said harshly as he looked me over.

"Hey look, I'm not looking for trouble. I just heard screams and thought I would check it out." By now I let go of Lacey who stepped back towards Michelle. Brad's friend was already at my right side. Andy forced him to create a bit more distance between us with a little growl that was just enough to catch his attention.

Both men looked to be in their mid-twenties, well-built and unfortunately slightly inebriated. Now I'm thinking I should have let Ms. Banks handle this. She is a much better negotiator than I.

"Everything looks fine here, so I think I will be leaving now." I said with a cool head. I knew these guys were looking to let off some steam as it appears things went south with their girlfriends this evening. From what just occurred and the obvious distain between the two parties, there would be an unlikely reconciliation in the future.

"That's smart man. Go on home now." Brad's friend said very condescendingly.

Usually I keep a cool head in these situations. Two scotches and a gun in my back waist band, I'm not thinking straight tonight. Too late for doing the smart thing.

To their surprise, I walk directly to the ladies and said, "On my way home, may I escort you to your door so you don't trip into any more pools or bushes?"

Lacey immediately said, "Yes, thank you." with a little hint of a laugh in her voice. I like her spirit. Much like mine, she can appreciate well placed attempts of humor.

Brad was already quick stepping towards me saying something like, "you must be stupid" and Michelle was already defending my intelligence by telling Brad off. What I thought would be funny and kind of the right thing to do, obviously provoked the two gentlemen. Honestly, I knew what I was doing. They were being assholes and did not deserve the courtesy they were receiving. I figured my size and my dog would have been enough to make them think twice about starting something, but I guessed wrong.

I saw Brad's right hook coming and easily side stepped it. With his overzealous missed punch to my head, he was off center and heading towards the pool. I helped him out with a little nudge to his right shoulder sending him pirouetting to the deep end.

Brad's friend was two steps behind him and cocking back to release his barrage of punches when a high heel caught him square in the nose. No time allowed for either Andy or me to act, the shoe stopped him hard in his tracks.

Instantly, blood was coming out of both nostrils and a cut on the bridge of his nose. He spun around holding his nose and cussing. His eyes were already watering up causing blurry vision.

Brad came up for air cussing and asking for help from his friend who seemed preoccupied with the blood gushing from his nose. I leaned over and picked up the high heel and turned to Lacey and Michelle.

"Shall we go now?"

Lacey smiled while I handed her shoe back to her. Michelle did not say much as she led the way down the windy walking path to their house.

Andy seemed to drag behind us to ensure no further interactions occurred between us and the two gentlemen. In the short walk, I learned from Lacey that they had lived here for 6 months. "Almost odd that we never crossed paths before now." I casually slipped in. Such a small community and we never saw each other. Perhaps our jobs had us on opposite schedules.

"I've seen Andy around plenty. We should figure out why I never see you with Andy over a cup of coffee tomorrow" Lacey said as they approached the door to their home.

"I would like that, but tomorrow is not a good day for me. Do you mind if I get your number and call you?" I knew tomorrow was going to be a long day and unsure what it had in store for me. The last thing I wanted to do was to make promises I couldn't keep.

"That will have to do. First, does our hero have a name?" Lacey asked as Michelle entered the home and left her their alone with me on the half porch.

"Lusio Abrams. But my friends call me Lou"

"Okay, Lou, why does a maintenance man have a gun tucked in his backside?" She asked with such indifference, like it did not bother her or she was not afraid of the weapon.

"Habit. Hear women scream, grab a gun. Well, that and I am actually a Mableton Detective" I said.

"Wait a second; I'm still digesting what I just heard. You're a detective? No wonder we never see each other. You probably work all the time."

"Now don't start talking yourself right out of a good cup of coffee." I said taking a step back from the porch. A tactic to see if she was truly interested or just being nice. She stepped forward to keep the distance equal to what it was a second ago. I started to feel a wave of warmth travel all over my body. I think she is actually closer than before. She is really confident and beautiful and seemingly interested in me.

She lowered her voice to just above a whisper. "I'm not talking myself out of that coffee. It is the least I can do for our hero of the evening. Plus, you must have a ton of interesting stories. It won't be boring, right?" She said almost telling, not asking.

"No, I promise it won't be a boring coffee date" I said before realizing I used the word 'date'.

"Well good, no boring dates." She riddled her words with a smile that hooked me as she drew out the word 'dates.'

She's quick on her feet and knows how to put someone at ease. I feel like we have known each other for months and are sharing a playful intimate moment before foreplay starts. Wanting more, but knowing timing is everything, I willed myself to smile and step back.

"Lacey, it was my pleasure to be awakened by your scream tonight. I now bid you a farewell. As you said, my hours can be brutal and I must catch sleep when I can." Giving her a playful wink and gesturing an informal goodbye solute I started to walk away. "I'll call you tomorrow."

"Wait a second" she said as she went inside for a brief moment. She came out wearing a shawl that now covered her top and was holding a pen and paper. "There will be no excuses. Here is my number and if you would not mind, please give me yours. If the two assholes try coming around to bug Michelle, I want to know that we have a friend nearby to call."

"Why only Michelle? I thought they were both your boyfriends or ex-boyfriends?" I asked while handing her back the pad with my cell number on it.

"God no. I knew they were trouble 3 months ago when Michelle first started dating Brad. I kept my distance. I was an innocent bystander caught up in their childish antics tonight. Enough about them, we will catch up over coffee, right?" She said as she placed her number in my hand and then quickly leaned in planting a quick kiss on my cheek.

"Right...thank you..." I stammered as I slipped her number in my pocket. She caught me off guard. Smooth reply. Lacey waved as she closed the door. As the click of the lock sounded, Andy and I started on a different path home to avoid the pool area. I figured the knuckleheads were nursing their egos and still drinking. They were probably planning the next encounter. As long as we did not hear them tonight, I did not care. I want to go to sleep. This day needs to end. It's late and the lazy boy is calling me.

CHAPTER 2

Morning came too hastily, just as I thought it would. All my life I have awoken at first light. No alarm needed.

I remember when I was 12 years old, I learned things about myself that most 12 years would not be equipped to comprehend or deal with in a normal healthy way. I had endless amounts of energy in the Spring, Summer, and Fall. Winter was slightly different. Some days felt normal and other days seemed to carry unexplained anxiety. One thing was consistent; I always woke up at first light.

I grew up in a western suburb of Albuquerque, New Mexico. Admittedly, the majestic mountain scenery and picturesque sunsets were wasted on me during my youth. Now, it is hard to forget the spectacular mountain ranges mixed colors reaching up and touching the pink and blue skies in the evening. Winters were equally beautiful from a distance, but at times harsh conditions to live in.

I recall a summer day, around age 12, when I was riding my bike with a friend of mine, Lolotea. As usual, I was showing off riding wheelies to get her to laugh, when the front wheel came down wrong it sent me straight into a curb. My knee met a bolt on the bike, which inflicted a gash that bled hard for a few minutes.

I held my knee tightly, wincing in pain. As I applied pressure with my hands, Lolo sat with me telling me it would be okay. After about 5 minutes, we checked it out and it had stopped bleeding. We walked our bikes home, me using mine as a crutch of sorts. No one was home at the house, so we decided to attempt to clean the wound on our own. This was the moment my life changed.

After I cleaned the dirt and blood away, there it was. A pink scar as if 2-3 weeks had passed and it had healed. We both were speechless, but our eyes were saying so much as we kept starring back and forth at my knee and each other's faces.

After a few moments, I begged Lolo not to tell anyone. She agreed wholeheartedly. I remember her hugging me and saying, "I don't know what to say except I'm glad you are okay."

I remember it was a month later when Lolo approached my mom and me to go on to the Zuni reservation for fishing with her father and uncle. She lived in the city with her uncle, but they both spent weekends on the reservation with their people, our people. My mom is Zuni as well and my dad was Dutch.

It was about a three-hour ride west of Albuquerque to the Zuni reservation. They are a secluded and private tribe of about 10,000. Although I am half Zuni, my mom raised me away from the day to day traditions and language. Hearing my dad always refer to the Zuni as 'they", sort of brainwashed me to think of the Zuni as 'them' and not 'us'. The Zuni don't let many outsiders in and even though my dad was married to my mom, he rarely went to the reservation when he was around.

My dad used to travel overseas for a construction company. We last saw him when I was eight and that was after he relocated to Belgium due to the business he conducted in Europe. My Mom and I used to visit the reservation during weekends to see our relatives and stay connected. It was tough not having a dad around. We all had a very hard time with him passing away at such a young age and away from us. They say he died from stress, but my mom was convinced it was from a lonely heart. She used to pray he would quit and return home. But he never did.

My perception was always that the Zuni did not have much and really depend on living off the land. I mistakenly would compare the city life to the Zuni life and draw this flawed conclusion. I do remember that the fishing and hunting was great on the reservation. At my age, I saw these trips as camping trips and was somewhat oblivious to my surroundings and the culture.

This memory was different though. The second night on the reservation with Lolo we were summoned to participate in an old ritual of sorts. I was not informed exactly what would be taking place, only that we had front row seats.

There were about 50 elderly and about the same number of adults my mom's age. No kids except for Lolo and myself. We were inseparable at that age. There was a bonfire and we all sat encircling the flames in silence.

One of the councilmen spoke in Zuni for a few moments gesturing to the sky, the fire, someone across from us and in our direction. I thought nothing of it at first. Then I recall my mom leaning over and saying to me, "Lusio, be at peace with your heart and head. There is nothing to be afraid of. A woman needs help and the council wants to see if you can offer assistance."

"I don't understand." I said to her at the time.

"Just follow Motuka and lay your hands on the woman's back. If nothing happens, no one will blame you for trying. Please do this."

I remember looking at Lolo with disappointment, anger and fear as she mouthed the word *sorry* to me.

I remember looking back at my mother with fear and frustration, she knew in that moment I had no idea what to do. It was too late though.

The councilman Motuka had appeared at my side and extended his hand to help me up. He walked me over to the elderly women and she turned her back to me. People started to chant something softly in unison. I remember how weird it became and I had the urge to run back to my camping tent.

Just then Motuka lowered the shirt off the woman's shoulders to about halfway down her back. There was an awful collection of deep cuts and bruises. I learned later that it came from a horse accident. The horse was spooked by a snake and dragged her backside over rocks, cacti and thorny shrub. Infection had set in.

Motuka continued chanting with the crowd and gesturing for me to lay my hands on the woman's back. I remember gently rested my palms on her back and closing my eyes. After a very long minute, I opened them to see nothing had changed. Everyone was still chanting.

I kept my hands there and started to think of my accident and the pressure I put on my knee. I focused on that moment in time and what I had been feeling, the pain, the fear, the pulse of my heart. How I wished it would stop hurting.

The pain had started to feel real again. I felt the fear and the pulse, but it was not mine.

The chanting continued and so did my thoughts of healing. Her back felt hot from the infection. My hands felt on fire and she moaned in pain. *Don't stop. Make the pain go away. Make her pain go away.* I remember chanting to myself.

A moment later, the moaning stopped. The burning sensation and fear subsided and I could not hear the chanting anymore. I opened my eyes to find her back covered with scars, not open wounds. Then I passed out.

I woke up in my tent with Motuka, my mom and Lolo at my side smiling. "How are you feeling?" My mom had asked me.

Motuka said something to my mother in Zuni and then put his hand on my chest. "You are special and live up to your name Lusio. Thank you for saving my sister from a painful death. You honor our Gods and people with this gift and we will cherish you in our hearts for many lifetimes." He left the tent and had taken Lolo with him.

"What is he talking about?" I had asked my mom at the time.

My mom explained the Gods to me again and how religion and myth can be intertwined to make sense of the unexplainable. My name "Lusio" meant 'bringer of light' and that can be related to Apoyan Tachu, Father Sky.

I was born at dawn and awakened every day of my life at dawn and drew my energy from the Sun in more ways than one. No one could tell me what to expect, it was a journey of self-discovery. I have learned a great deal over the last 20 years and I can imagine I have not learned everything about my gift yet.

I made several trips to the reservation in my teens to help the sick and meditate with the elders hoping more answers would come. They never did come in that form. They typically came from experiences.

For example, when I moved to Phoenix to attend ASU for my Criminal Justice degree, I was the victim of a drunk driver running a red light and smashing into my driver side door seriously injuring me at the time.

I was hospitalized for two days with doctors and nurses tending to my fractured leg, broken ribs, arm and wrist. I also had a few facial lacerations. During the first night, I knew my face was healing quickly under the bandages, so I had to purposely keep reopening the wounds to not draw attention to my quick healing.

No laying of hands needed at this age to self-heal. It was on auto-pilot. My wrist and ribs fully healed in about 12 hours. By the second day, I knew my broken leg was better.

Between nursing shifts, I slipped out of the hospital to avoid suspicion and the likelihood of becoming a lab rat. I had a hell of a time removing the cast. Sneaking out raised plenty of questions, but my mom called and explained she moved me to the Zuni reservation and that was the end of that discussion.

Over the years as a police office and detective, I have had several instances where the job put me in situations that landed me in the hospital and each time it was a chore to slip out before my healing was discovered. The scars are a reminder of my gift and curse.

I have been constantly paranoid people would find out and my life would be over. Freedom was paramount. Staying 'normal' in the eyes of others was a constant shell game. As I grew older the healing became quicker. It also became a constant guilt trip. I could give up my life of somewhat normalcy and wonder the earth laying hands healing the sick. Not knowing why, I had this gift or if others were out there with this gift haunted my dreams.

I have had similar nightmares all my life. I lay in a bright white room with tubes running in and out of me. Fluids being pumped into me, while blood is drained out. People in lab coats coming and going from the room. They were probably synthesizing my fluids in mass production for cures all around the world. No thank you.

Perhaps part of my gift is seeing the possible future in my dreams and this is what is in store for me if people find out. Thankfully, I did not have that dream again last night.

I was up, so I went for a jog on the trails behind the duplex. The trails ran through the woods along a creek that led to a lake about 2 miles down.

Andy loved the morning runs. Birds and squirrels would distract him at times and send him into a chase. He would always catch up moments later. This jog would help me think through the events of the evening.

My concern today was regarding follow up questions based on what the girl told authorities about my time with her. There will be questions. My jog cleared my head and I convinced myself that it will all work out, just play ignorant and skeptical to any mention of the healing and no one will be able to make the logical connection without losing credibility. It was settled.

CHAPTER 3

"Hey Lou, nice job yesterday." The front desk officer, Mike, had the news and dirt on everyone and sometimes knew details he shouldn't. He rarely called you by your given name unless he was trying to tell you, 'Look out somebody wants your ass in there'.

Childhood friends called me Lusio, but most people knew me by Lou. I felt a sigh of relief that Mike was not warning me. Could mean nothing. He doesn't know everything that goes on around here.

I sat down at my desk and locked my gun in the drawer. Detective Royce "Roy" Cable sat across from me smiling. "What Roy?"

"You're early and I hear you made a new friend"

"What are you talking about?"

"The Amber alert girl, Tammy, is asking for you. They let her go home early this morning and she has called three times asking for you. Watch out, hero complex could be in your future."

"Give her a brake Roy, she is thirteen and probably just wanting to say thank you." I knew there would be questions. To be honest, I would rather take them from a thirteen-year-old victim than from my Captain or Internal Affairs. Christ, what if she talks to the news?

"Why is it that you land on such high-profile cases all the time Lou? You're like a magnet for this shit." Roy said as he leaned back in his chair as if about to place his feet on the desk.

"Simple math really" I replied.

"How's that?" Roy said coming back to a sitting position in his chair showing interest in the explanation.

"Well, there are only 4 detectives here. By process of elimination...you are old, slow and try to only put energy into finding the best coffee of the day during the 2 hours of work you manage to put in each day. John and Nick are spitting images of you, because you trained them a hundred years ago. The three of you work mornings in order to get your afternoon nap and 9 holes in before your 5 PM dinner and 7 PM bedtimes. That leaves me to close cases. The good state of Georgia would be elated if the three of you just retired and let me run the show solo for a huge savings to our tax payers."

Roy looked me over with this hard look that broke many of suspects into giving "it" up and then burst out into a deep laugh.

The truth is Roy was quite well known in Georgia for solving many high-profile cases over the last 20 years. The rest was pretty accurate, but he still closed many cases. Granted most were easy cases of missing cars, petty theft, assault, and others like this that did not require much follow up. All three of them worked early days, which left me to cover afternoons and evenings when something came up.

"Abrams!" Our moment of teasing each other was over as our Captain was shouting my name.

As I entered Captain Hershel W. Whitmore's office, he could not have looked more upset. One time, Roy had super glued all the Captain's pens and pencils to the desk, drawer and cup they sat in. He looked more pissed off now than when the prank was pulled on him. The only prank, I might add. "Close the door behind you Lou."

"What's up Cap?" I might as well get the first question in.

"It hasn't been more than 12 hours since you brought that piece of crap into my house and the D.A. is already bugging the shit out of me. I have this phone that won't stop ringing. The Media, parents, and the kid 3 times, the Chief, more media, and the D.A. think I have nothing better to do other than be your fucking messenger service. Why aren't you here fielding these calls?"

"Captain, its 9:00A.M., I'm three hours early."

"Perhaps you should have been 5 hours early in anticipation of the glowing response from the community and to prevent pissing me off. Everyone else got up with the Sun today except for you." He said pointing at me.

I started to explain, but he had other plans that did not involve listening to me.

"Go call all these people back before any of them call my phone again...or it's your ass. We clear?" he said, now pointing to the door.

"Crystal" I replied as I turned for the door.

"Lou"

"Yes sir?"

I half turned to shield myself in case he was throwing something at me, but only caught a slight grin on his face as he said, "Nice job."

Roy sat smiling as I returned to my desk. He was acting curious, but I know he already had the answers. "Anything left of your ass? Wow. I thought he was going to throw something at you. What's going on?"

"I have to call back some people before Cap gets anymore calls. You want to help out?" To my surprise, Roy called back the D.A. and handled the line of questions as if he had been there, occasionally looking at me for confirmation to avoid embellishing.

He also called back the media and told them to back off as the child needed space, and any details they wanted could potentially hurt the case or disturb the family.

I called back the Chief of Police to receive his thank you and then called the parents.

It was not at all what I expected. The mother answered and I quickly identified myself. She was so appreciative, just like she was the night before when she hugged every cop near the hospital room her daughter was in. She gave me praise and gratitude and promised to stop by soon with an in person thank you.

I asked how Tammy was doing and she said, "Considering what she went through, she is doing remarkably well. She insists on talking to you right now and is pulling the phone away from me. Thank you again Detective Abrams."

I heard the phone being fumbled with and then Tammy's voice came on, "Hello, Detective Abrams?"

"Yes, Tammy, it's me. How are you feeling today?" Roy leaned in closer and batted his eyes at me. Prepared for the less than professional gesture, I launched my pen at his chest sending him backwards in defense.

"Funny you should ask. I'm hoping you can tell me what happened yesterday." Oh, great. I'm glad this is over the phone and not in person. "What do you mean Tammy?" I asked innocently.

"I remember everything up to the point where the man took me inside his house a few days ago, but nothing after that. The hospital said you were the first one to find me. My clothes were a mess and I was really dehydrated. I don't remember anything from the moment I entered his house until the moment the doctors gave me sniffing salt to snap me out of a daze. I was hoping you could tell me something."

I could hear her mother saying something to her like, "I thought you just wanted to say thank you. Why are you asking him these questions Tammy?"

To prevent a fight in their household, I diverted her attention back to me. "Tammy, I found you in the shed where you clearly were fighting to free yourself. This explains the clothes and mess. The heat was bad those two days and it could have done things to your memories, possibly even caused hallucinations. You were lucky. I'm glad I found you when I did."

"Oh. That explains it. It's weird not knowing where two days went, but my mom says it's a blessing. I want to thank you again Mr. Abrams."

"Call me Lou the next time we see each other Tammy. I'm proud of you. You are a fighter and your strength and determination inspire me. Take care and rest up."

"Thank you again. Bye." She said as she hung up on her end.

We would likely meet again in a couple of days for a press conference the Chief had mentioned.

Roy looked at me and gave his approving nod.

It was just past ten o'clock and I had a few moments to myself. I picked up the phone and called Lacey. To my surprise she answered the phone. "Hello?"

"Hi, Lacey, this is Lou." There was silence for a few seconds. "Lou from last night." I said unsure of myself now.

"I know silly. I'm surprised you are calling me already. It sounded like you were going to take a few days to call me... with your busy schedule and all."

"Yes, well, uh, in the spirit of not sounding desperate, I have some unexpected free time today and was wondering if you were still open for that coffee?"

"In the spirit of hearing a couple of good stories, I will make the time. How does the cafe at the corner of Higgs and 4th street sound in 45 minutes?" she said with enjoyment in her voice.

"It's close to the precinct, I know it well." I answered.

"Good. See you then Lou."

I arrived at the coffee house ten minutes early to find an umbrella table on the front patio. It was close to the lunch rush and I wanted to ensure we had seats. I just ordered water and claimed my table when I saw her walking up the sidewalk towards me.

To my surprise, Andy was right at her side with his leash in his mouth. What the hell?

My eyes were back on Lacey. She was wearing this smart

outfit that had my heart racing. Simple and classy gets me every time. She was wearing a white tailored butterfly collar shirt with cuffed sleeves that stopped short of the elbow. The shirt was slightly open, and her curves were highlighted by the expert craftsmanship of the shirt maker and likely a little help from Victoria's Secret. She wore khaki shorts and what looked to be sandals with heels. In the light of day, she was strikingly tan against her white shirt, white tipped nails and what now looks like more white than blond hair.

She caught me and smiled. I waved her over and she gracefully slipped past the two tables and came to my side. I was already getting up from my chair as she placed her right hand on my shoulder and came in for a light casual half hug greeting. I reciprocated and could not help noticing she smelled of coconut. My senses were on fire now.

"I brought Andy along. I hope you don't mind. He comes and hangs out with me when I read and sunbath in the mornings. We gossip and then go our separate ways most days, but today I invited him along." She was sitting down, and Andy was still at her side.

What the hell is this? I think Andy was trying to tell me something, probably that we need a lady in our life.

"Perfectly fine. Sunbathing and gossiping huh, this I need to see." I said with a smile.

I put my hand down by my side, palm facing Andy. It was a quiet command to instruct him to come here. He looked at my hand then at my face and then started to lick Lacey's calf. Oh my God, this dog is messing with me. I chuckled.

"Me sunbathing or Andy gossiping with me?" Lacey said bring my attention back to her. My dog is clearly trying to distract me.

"Both. I mean either. I, uh...that didn't come out right. As much as I would love to share a sunbathing moment with you that would be very forward of me this early in our coffee date." Andy was still licking her calf. You are killing me Andy!

Lacey reach over and tapped my hand softly. “Is this normal behavior?” She said as her eyes directed mine back to Andy.

“I have only had him for a few years, but apparently he is more of a Hound dog than a Sheppard.” I replied, as I leaned to the side and told Andy to stop.

She laughed and pushed his snout away gently. Andy still staying by her side slowly laid down next to her.

“What are you feeding this dog that he is acting like I’m not even here?” I had to know. Whatever it was, I am never buying it for him.

“Ms. Brown feeds him all the time. I, however, only chat with him. He truly likes me for my intelligence and witty banter.” Lacey said as she looked past me to the coffee bar. “Shall we order coffee now?”

“Absolutely, tell your dog to stay and let’s go order.” I said to her jokingly. She turned to Andy and said ‘stay’ and he did what he was told. Unbelievable, the trained professional is totally whipped by this beautiful lady. At this point, I’m not sure if I’m referring to Andy or myself as I follow Lacey to order coffee.

I put my hormones in check and had a great coffee date with Lacey. She is an extremely intelligent paralegal working for two lawyers that are brothers of a local firm. I always see their ads on TV. I have actually met one of them before at the precinct and also in court. Straight shooters, older, happily married and apparently cherish her legal talents.

She told me modestly that they have commented on several occasions she does the work of the last three paralegals combined and can come and go as she pleases. They pay her well and she works from home as much as she does in the office. They don’t mind.

It turns out that she has been teaching Andy a thing or two about law poolside. As far as I was concerned, we could have sat there all day and enjoyed each other’s company. She was showing no signs of needing or wanting to leave.

An hour had gone by and I had to get back to work before the others decided that their lunch made them tired and they had to call it a day. I decided to make my move.

"I have to get back to work, Lacey. I really enjoyed this get together. I had a rough day yesterday and meeting you set things right. Before I go, I was hoping you would agree to a date with just you and me, Andy free. Perhaps dinner?"

"I really enjoy your company too." She said smiling and placing her hand on mine again. "Seeing how I did most of the talking this time, you owe me a story or two at dinner. How about my place two nights from now, Friday. I cook while you tell stories. Does 6 PM sound good?"

I was pleasantly surprised at her response and invitation. "I think I have a public relations matter Friday at 4PM or 5PM, can we push it to 7:30PM?" I am fairly sure the Chief said the event would be in a couple of days and late afternoon press conferences took forever.

"Sounds good. Are you allergic to anything?" She asked plainly.

"No, I'm not. At least I have not found anything yet"

"Great. Come with your appetite. I love to cook"

Thank God she didn't ask me to cook. It would be a terrible date. As we started to part, we hugged again and I felt a warmth of energy spread down my spine and the hairs on my neck and arms started to stand up. "Hey, I'm going to take Andy to the station with me."

"Honestly, Lou, he is no trouble. I can take him home."

"Well, since he is here, there is this matter he witnessed yesterday and I want his full statement on record." I said with a smile. She laughed and did not press the subject. She patted Andy on the head and said goodbye to us both. Andy whimpered.

"We are going to have a talk at the station buddy." Andy snorted and dropped his leash next to my shoe.

On the way back to my office, I had Lacey on my mind. It's amazing how you can just cross paths with someone that just instantly makes sense in your world. She impressed me on many levels, but there is something about her I can't put my finger on. I seem to feel this energy when around her. It is unexplainable.

At first, I chalked it up to feeling very attracted to her. However, when she walked away this time, I made note of the feeling and could sense the warmth subsiding the further she walked away.

CHAPTER 4

Lars Bowman had been an outsider all his life. The high school years were his toughest years and probably set his course of recent events. Those were a very cruel 4 years. His drunken dad did not help, and mom left long before then.

Dear old dad berated Lars about everything. It takes a strong person to find light in their life when they are surrounded by darkness, hatred, negativity, and lack of compassion. The kid could do nothing right in his life, even if he wasn't wrong.

People couldn't see it then, but sometime in his youth, his humanity switched off and predator switched on. Back then, he was small, weak and could not defend himself. Now, in his late twenties and filled out, he could handle himself quite well.

Lars Bowman's father was Tanner Bowman who was arrested for kidnapping a thirteen-year old.

Tanner was only guilty of being a stupid, aggressive drunk that had no clue his son had already kidnapped, raped and killed four teenagers and was well on his way to killing another before Detective Abrams got in the way.

After putting two and two together during the 6-hour interrogation last night, Tanner knew his entire life had amounted to nothing more than creating a rapist and murderer and he could not live with this disappointment in himself and his monster of a son. Strange how 15 years of being a drunk and abusive father did not raise concern to his conscious, but his son being a monster was too much to bear.

At lunch, in his holding cell, Tanner took the plastic fork that came with the food and he splintered it. Then he proceeded to wait for the guards to walk away for a few minutes, curled up in the corner and tore at his own jugular until he made a large enough tear that it only took 30 seconds before he passed out and died 2 minutes later.

When I arrived back at the station, the noise level had risen to deafening. Everyone seemed busy, some shouting at others, phones ringing, including my cell phone, and the Captain screaming at two officers in his office with the door still open.

I looked at my phone and saw that it was Roy calling me. I saw him at his desk with the phone to his ear. When he saw me approaching, he slammed his phone down and said, "I've called you 3 times. You are missing one hell of a shit storm here."

I was about to ask what was going on when I heard Mike yelling at a camera crew to shut off their cameras and leave. The media was flooding in behind him and he was furious that he had to corral them like kindergarteners at the end of recess.

"The rapist killed himself with a spork. Can you believe that? A spork!" Roy chuckled with distain. "Those poor saps in there are probably going to be reassigned to some shit detail for years. For what? The Chief called the Captain minutes ago and said something that set Cap into a fury." Roy motioned to the Captain's office where the two officers on holding cell duty were lowering their heads and leaving quickly. The Captain looked my way and motioned me over.

"Just got back from lunch, Captain. I'm caught up. How can I help?" I wanted to be on the offense and sympathetic to the situation.

He took a deep breath and asked me to go address the media. He knew I did not need a script as I was well versed with giving little and still pleasing the media.

I tapped Roy on the shoulder as I walked towards Mike and the media he was still trying to shuffle out to the lobby. Roy got up slowly and followed me to the media. I got their attention by advising them I would give an update and take a few questions outside. Mike looked very relieved to have them all out of his area.

Once outside, I gave them a very high-level recap of the events as I knew them. Keeping details safeguarded and answering questions with the standard "we are still ascertaining the details of the events and will have more information later or tomorrow for you."

Cameras were rolling and I figured this would make the news tonight. When the press was somewhat satisfied, I made my way to my desk and gave Tammy's parents a courtesy call to give them a heads up on the events.

CHAPTER 5

Unbeknownst to me, the Chief had been in conversation with the regional FBI office most of the day and in light of recent events there was about to be a change in the pecking order at our precinct. It was just after 4pm when two suits walked in and went straight to the Captain's office.

The other detectives had already gone home for the day, so I had no one to make a scoffing comment to. After a heated one-way discussion lead by the Captain, the two suits sat down. One was a tall gentleman who seemed to be leading the now civil discussion with my boss. The other suit was a taller than average height woman with brunette hair, pulled in a tight ponytail. She seemed to be stoic during the discussion.

As I observed them, she slowly turned her head towards my direction and met my eyes. I was not backing down. After an uncomfortable stare-down she casually turned her attention back to the Captain, stood up and waved them both silent. She said a few words to the Captain, who seemed very attentive at this point. He nodded a few times and then leaned back in his chair and pointed towards my direction.

I was already getting up from my chair when the Captain barked my name. As I entered the office, the Captain introduced me to Special Agent Jones and Shah. Special Agent Jones extended his hand for introductions, but Shah turned to the Captain and asked for a briefing room. I stepped to the side as the Captain lead Shah and Jones down the hall. She was kind enough to give me a head nod as she passed by me.

As we entered the briefing room, Shah made it very clear

that she would waste no time with her expectations. She laid out how she wanted the room set up with whiteboard, all case files on the deceased and survivor as well as a debrief with the detectives within the hour. That would not go over very well with the grumpy old men.

However, they all showed up just over an hour later. As they walked into the briefing room, we already had the board covered with pictures, a map of the area showing the locations of discovery, last known area victims were seen, and their homes, creating a triangulated pattern.

Roy looked 20 years older as he came in and fell into a chair without saying a word. He looked like a grandfather in sweats that had just been awakened from his late afternoon nap. I walked over and handed him a coffee, black. He smiled as he accepted it.

John and Nick walked up to the Captain and expressed their displeasure. He dismissed them and pointed to two chairs.

"Listen up." Agent Jones said as he put down a folder and turned his attention to the rest of us.

"Special Agent Shah and I are from the Behavioral Analysis Unit of the FBI and have reason to believe that Tanner Bowman's son is in fact our primary suspect for these murders." Roy sat up and looked at me for a reaction. I gave none as Jones continued.

"Our database and team of analysts notified us of this pattern and when we heard of Mr. Tanner being in custody and then killing himself, it did not add up. Serial killers like this are driven by hatred that does not stop when caught." Jones said as he pointed to Lars's picture on the board.

Roy finally chimed in. "Why the task force? Why not just call us and tell us he is a person of interest and we pick him up?"

Special Agent Shah stood up and addressed Roy's question. "As we put out an APB and BOLO, we had a Sheriff's Deputy that was close by stop by Lars' apartment as soon as we heard the news of Tanner Bowman's arrest and suicide. There were signs of Lars' quick departure, but no luck picking him up. Local PD, Sheriff's Department and Highway Patrol have the manpower and we are here to help aid and assist in locating and bringing in Lars for questioning."

"Aid and assist or order and observe?" Roy shot back.

"Look detective, we know how tough it is to work these cases. We do it for a living too. Special agent Jones will share our suspect's profile and motive, along with how his escalating pattern will lead him to his next victim if we don't find him first. We are on the clock and any minute Lars is going to be looking for his replacement victim or attempt to go after Tammy again. This is why we have to eliminate her as one of his options. Your Captain has already stationed officers with Tammy 24/7 until we find Lars." Shah said as Jones was already handing out a list of behaviors and likely next steps of Lars Bowman. It was pretty comprehensive.

I had this eerie feeling that we missed something at Tanner's house. "I would like to head back over to Tanner Bowman's house and give it another thorough search."

Shah looked at Jones and said, "I will join Detective Abrams, you work with the other detectives to coordinate the efforts of the search."

I got up and the Captain gave me his nod of approval. Shah followed me out to my desk where I retrieved my gun and Andy. Lacey saved me a trip home to get Andy. Lacey was still on my mind but fading fast after that briefing. The day seemed to be going so much better 7 hours ago. I would like to go back to that moment, as I could use a coffee break and good company right now.

As we got into my car, Shah broke the silence. "What's the story on your dog?"

"He's not mine, he just follows me around. Kind of like an unwanted mascot."

"A sense of humor, nice." Shah said, without prying for

the real story.

I explained Andy's background and experience so that she did not feel Andy would be a nuisance at a crime scene. She seemed okay with it, although it would not have mattered. Andy was coming in with me whether Shah liked it or not. I trusted him. The jury is still out on Special Agent Shah.

"Well, you met my partner. How long have you been partnered or working with Special Agent Jones?" I asked.

On the ride over she informed me that they are not partners and that they are in fact in different Behavioral Analysis Units. All part of the FBI's Critical Incident Response Group (CIRG), their units were part of the National Center for the Analysis of Violent Crime (NCAVC) designed to provide behavioral-based operations support and multi-agency coordination between all law enforcement agencies, including Interpol. Jones was part of Behavioral Analysis Unit 3 (BAU3) which specialized in crimes against children. Shah was in BAU4 specializing in the apprehension of violent criminals. She has been doing this job for over seven years. Atlanta is her home, but the job has taken her all over.

Twenty minutes later we were at Tanner Bowman's house. The porch light was off; the house was dark and yellow tape still everywhere. We exited the car and went up to the front door ducking under the yellow police ribbon. As we entered the house, I turned on the light. Police officers were out here hours ago and there were no signs of activity.

As we entered the house it smelled of dirty laundry, stale beer and cigarettes. The place was a mess. No organization. I had to admit, it is hard to believe this man could have planned anything and not have been caught immediately.

The old gun was still unaccounted for as well. No signs of blood, struggles or someone being held against their will here.

Shah went out the back door and I entered the kitchen. I looked in the refrigerator, cabinets and drawers for anything unusual. I even moved the refrigerator.

As I stood there taking it all in, I looked down at the kitchen mat next to me. I kicked it away and saw the trap door to a basement that was not reported on the search report. I tried to open it quietly, but was met with immediate resistance. It was probably nailed shut or locked from inside.

Shah stepped back in and we both said at the same time, "I've got something." I was pointing at the latch and she nodded.

"Come outside, I think I have the other way in." She informed me as she led the way.

As soon as I stepped outside, I found Shah shinning a light at an ivy bush. She was already stepping into it with her gun drawn. I came up beside her with mine drawn as well. She handed me her flashlight and reached down into the weeds. I heard a metallic sound as she found a handle and slowly started to pull the cellar door upward. It was dark inside.

I handed the flashlight back to her and took mine out. Andy was by my side awaiting orders. I locked eyes with Shah and held my hand up showing her to stay put. I then pointed at the black hole and whispered to Andy "Attack." He leaped into the hole in silence.

I opened the other latch and we both descended side by side with our lights crossed over our gun hand. It reeked of cigarettes and other unkind odors. At the bottom I quickly spotted a light switch on the wall and turned it on.

Andy stood alert in the center of the room. The area was slightly bigger than the kitchen upstairs. On one side of the room was a desk in the corner, a bed next to it, sink, small refrigerator, and microwave.

On the other side, closest to me, was barren tile floor, a drain in the center, chains on the wall and floor, and plenty of blood on the chains and around the drain. This was quickly shaping up to be a horrific place of torture.

Something embedded in the tile close to the drain caught my eye. I knelt down to take a closer look. It appeared to be a bullet buried into the tile. Shah broke my focus calling me over to the table. She walked me through what seemed to be the gunpowder, flint and possible lead balls for an old pistol or musket.

"You smell that? It smells like someone was smoking in here earlier. Jesus, he was right under our noses." I said in frustration.

"They usually are. I don't think I would have spotted that latch in the day. My light barely caused the reflection of a small piece of hinge at least two inches beneath the ivy." Shah said, in hopes to comfort me. It was not working. Someone should have moved the mat in the kitchen.

Shah was now looking through whatever personal items were left behind, pausing at each momentarily, studying them closely. Occasionally picking up a book, a knife, a cup and closing her eyes as if taking in and imagining the subject using the items.

She broke away from her pattern and said, "He has to be on the move now and knows we are looking for him."

I was immediately on the phone now calling in forensics and notifying the Captain on what we found. Shah was updating Jones.

We were back at the station updating the board with new information. Dinner had arrived and we all worked as we ate. We missed the opportunity earlier to get Lars's picture on the 6 o'clock news and that really bothered me. It would however make the 10 o'clock evening news. Every policy officer in Georgia had his picture now, but we did not know what he was driving or where he was. It was another long day and about time for Andy and I to go home.

◆ ◆ ◆

The media had plenty of time to make the 6 o'clock news to broadcast the dirty details of Tanner Bowman's suicide in his jail cell. Lars watched with a sense of pleasure and fulfillment of a vendetta that he knew he himself could have never pulled off. No matter how scary of an individual Lars grew up to be, he still feared his dad.

"Abrams" he said out loud as the TV mentioned the detective's name that brought his dad in. Lars could care less that his dad just killed himself for his demented actions. His sights were now set on the man that took his prize away.

Lars had a small apartment in the city, but spent most of his time in his dad's basement in the woods. When his dad was not at the bars, he was passed out at home. His dad never went down into the basement anymore, as it was once his wife's sewing area. When she left, he never set foot in it again.

There was an entrance from the kitchen floor under the kitchen mat, that the police did not know to check for, as well as a cellar door in the backyard hidden by bushes that detective Abrams could not see. It was well covered with ivy and unless you had blue prints to the house, you would not know it was there. There were no windows in the basement. There was nothing to give its existence away from first glance when walking the property.

Lars had turned the space into a true dungeon of torture, well sound proofed, and with ample amenities for the truly deranged psychopath that he had become.

"Abrams" he roughly mumbled as the news posted a picture of the detective showing him as a hero. He took a long drag on his cigarette and then a sip of whisky. Four hours earlier he had packed up what he needed from the basement and left the rest behind. His next stop was his apartment where he did the same. One suitcase was filled and he was gone within the hour. He was now changing the game. He sat at a bar surveying the crowd as if they were the Happy Hour specials.

CHAPTER 6

She was about to light her cigarette when the gentleman offered the favor. They struck up a conversation and seem to be hitting it off when her friends and coworkers decided to leave. She waved them off and stayed behind.

She never saw herself as beautiful, so when the man paid her the complaint, she was hooked for the evening. It didn't hurt that he was paying for the drinks too. She was enjoying his company so much she had lost count of the drinks they had together. She also lost count of the last hour or so. She blacked out and it probably had more to do with what the man slipped in her drink than it had to do with how many drinks she'd had.

She woke up confused, tape on her mouth, hands bound, cramped up in a ball in a small space. It was dark and smelled of gas and exhaust. She just realized she was in a car when the trunk opened revealing moonlight and the outline of a man.

As the man reached in and easily lifted her out of the trunk of his car, she started to cry. She was confused, head throbbing, and fear consumed her. *Was it the same man that she was enjoying the evening with earlier? If, so, why? What is he doing? Oh my God, I'm going to ...*

"Hello beautiful. Vanessa was it? I have to admit, I don't know what to do with you yet." Lars said as he positioned her for another lift.

She wept more as he heaved her up and draped her midsection over his shoulder, holding the back of her thighs as he closed the trunk with his other hand. He stood there for a few seconds taking in a few deep breaths. She started to wiggle and that frustrated him.

"Stop that. Don't make me hurt you." He left off the word 'now' as he did not want to escalate the begging and attempts for freedom just yet.

She could make out that they were in an alley between two buildings. It was dark and the streetlights were not on in this area. She had no idea where she was as he opened a door and entered what seemed to be a large empty warehouse.

Just then she could feel his hard, calloused hand slow sliding up her inner thigh. She started to wiggle and scream under the layers of duct tape. But it was no use.

Both his hands quickly slide to behind her knees, his grip tightened, and he whipped her off his shoulders slamming her backside and head into the concrete below. That was the last thing she felt as the bright lights consumed her vision before everything went dark. The lights would never turn back on again. Nothing would.

Lars looked down at Vanessa and was fascinated by the pool of blood forming around her head. He lit a cigarette and watched with amusement as her body twitched a few times and her lung compressions become slower and less frequent. When he was done smoking, he straddled her at the waist and sat down on her pelvis. He slowly removed the tap from her wrist and mouth and gave her a long kiss as if expecting her to reciprocate with equal passion. It was as if he stole her last breath from her. The damage to her brain was too traumatic and it shut down.

He lay on her for a few minutes taking in her smell and occasional feeling her warmth and repositioning her arms. She became his personal life size doll. He placed her arms around his body and felt a peace come over himself. He moved around a bit to curl up with her, and then fell asleep with her still warm corpse in his arms.

When Lars woke up the next morning, he removed himself from her cold corpse on the floor. Covered in her blood, he calmly walked into a janitor's closet with his backpack and proceeded to strip down. There was an industrial tub for cleaning mop buckets and other things. Using the hose that was attached to the facet in the small tub he started to clean himself.

He then retrieved a battery-operated electric razor from his pack and shaved his head bald, then did the same to his eyebrows. He picked up the hose again and rinsed off his head.

After the rinse, he took out iodine he had grabbed from his apartment medicine cabinet and poured it onto a nearby rag and rubbed his bald head. As he wiped it on and then off a few minutes later, the iodine had stained the whiteness away from his head giving him a more yellow worn bald look. It wasn't beautifully bronze but would do in a pinch he thought.

He put on some fresh clothes and then wrote something on a piece of paper. As he gathered his belongings and started to head out, he stopped by Vanessa's body and tucked the note into her blouse. On the way to the car he stole yesterday, he tossed his bloody clothes in the dumpster outside the warehouse.

Minutes later he was deep in thought as he drove down a dirt road that lead to an old cabin in the woods. He had only been there a few times before and that was over fifteen years ago when his dad was slightly sober and still into fishing.

When he arrived, he could barely recognize the structure. There was so much undergrowth, the grass and weeds must have been inching towards four feet tall. Part of a tree had fallen into the roof. Vines had taken over the walls.

He pulled the car around behind the cabin and quickly parked it. He got out and shuffled underneath the vehicle and started pulling weeds and grass out of the ground that were touching the catalytic converter. No need to start a fire and advertise his whereabouts. He then covered the car with debris, weeds and shrubs that pulled easily from the surrounding area. Satisfied with the camouflage, he entered the old cabin and surveyed his new hideout for the time being.

He sat in an old rocking chair and continued to fight with the conflicting urges he had. He had not planned to kill Vanessa so quickly and was really looking forward to having his way with her as she begged and struggled for mercy. His disdain for Detective Abrams clearly got the best of him and he lost his temper with Vanessa.

He was troubled, but it was not by guilt of his atrocious acts. He could not seem to decide if he wanted to complete his unfinished urges Vanessa could not partake in or figure out how to take someone Abrams loved away from him before killing him.

CHAPTER 7

I woke up the next day at sunrise and headed out for a jog with Andy. There was a thin layer of morning dew on the grass and plants that lined the trail by the creek. Andy was darting left and right off the trail in search of imaginary creatures. He was picking up so much moisture from the leaves, that he would have to stop every few minutes and shake off his coat. I chose to cut the run short as I knew today would be another long day.

Before I left the precinct last night, Special Agent Jones had been running over some protocol with the FBI Atlanta Field Office for coordinating a Major Offender Task Force today. It consisted of the local FBI, Sheriffs, Atlanta PD and Mableton PD. The meeting was this morning and the debriefings along with the coordination of tasks to ID and capture Lars Bowman were going to be daunting.

I stopped a mile short of where I usually turn around and gave Andy a whistle to reel him in. As I stood waiting for him to leap out of a bush or tall grass with both joy and disappointment of not catching a squirrel or rabbit, I thought I noticed a figure down the trail from where I had just come from. It was a windy trail in thick forest. It could have been someone on a jog and turning around to return, just like I had just done. What are the odds? They were gone now and I did not give it much more thought. Andy had silently appeared at my side and startled me by shaking water all over me.

It was about 7 A.M. when I finished my morning routine and had breakfast. I was making coffee and deciding what to do for the next two hours before going in to work. The briefing would start around 9 A.M. and I was thinking of getting some morning sun with coffee and a newspaper. Andy was already napping on the coach as I slipped out the door and headed towards the pool.

Normal doses of sunlight acted like a good meal or a shot of steroids for me. Even now in my early thirties, I still find it puzzling and even hard to understand at times. It gave me an instant lift of energy that lasted for hours, sometimes days. Feel the flu coming on, lie in the sun and feel better. Twist an ankle on a jog, a dose of sun would speed up the healing from an hour to about one minute.

I had learned little about what I was or how I became this 'gifted' person. However, I did learn how to harness the sun for instant healing or storage for later. The rush of a long bake could last for days and act a bit like drinking an energy drink all day and night. Sometimes the hairs on my arms would stand for hours or goose bumps would appear and hang around.

I proceeded to remove my shirt and lay down on a pool lounge chair. I held the morning paper to my face, catching up on news outside the city and country. Half a cup of coffee and two sections of the paper later, I was feeling charged, for lack of a better description.

I sat up just in time to catch Brad and his buddy walking past the pool on the way to the parking lot. They were dressed for work and both looked over my way before focusing back on the path to their cars. I have a feeling we will be meeting again, but not now.

Those two were the least of my worries right now. As I folded my paper in half, the front page brought me back to the priority of the day. The headline read 'MAN HUNT' with a picture of Lars Bowman and an article describing his pattern of killing along with some details of his unfortunate upbringing. There was also a paragraph about me and the FBI's involvement. I decided to head in early.

As I was walking up the back-porch steps, Ms. Brown poked her head out to say hello. I caught her up on the events from two nights ago and she mentioned that Brad and Steve were up for a lease renewal in a few weeks and she may just give them notice. She has had other complaints in the last month about them.

"So, what do you think of Michelle and Lacey? Sweethearts, right? They remind me of my daughters. I talk to Lacey all the time at the pool, she is really smart and a great cook. I love her Quiche. I can put a good word in for you, if you like." Ms. Brown said with a look of anticipation.

"Wow. Uh, as it just so happens, I have a dinner date with Lacey tomorrow night. So, your match making services will not be needed, but I thank you for thinking of me."

"Oh, I think you will really like her. She is so down to earth. There is something about that girl that just makes me feel happy when I'm around her. She has good energy, almost euphoric personality." Ms. Brown said.

She hit the nail on the head. "I know what you mean Ms. B."

Before I went inside to get ready for work, she told me she had read the newspaper this morning and asked me to be careful, but not without adding, "Catch the S.O.B. Lou."

I entered the briefing room 30 minutes before the scheduled time and found a civilian looking over the board. She was tall, with long black hair, wearing a white blouse and fashionable blue jeans that enhanced her tall, model like physic. It didn't matter how good she looked; she had no business being in here.

"Excuse me, but there are no civilians allowed in here. How did you get in here?" Catching her attention.

As she turned around, I was shocked to find Special Agent Shah smiling back at me, "Is there a problem detective Abrams?"

"Yes Ma'am. I mean no, no problem Special Agent Shah. Sorry, you look totally different." I said. It was a failed recovery.

"I look different?" She said as if I said something wrong.

"I mean in a good way."

"Oh?" She said, allowing her smile to return.

Oh, crap, this is getting awkward. I started to hear footsteps approaching. She must have noticed the panic on my face and decided to let me off the hook before I found a way to stick my foot further in my mouth.

"Lighten up Lou. I do have a sense of humor, too, you know. Can I call you Lou? I feel like I know you after reading your PHX and ATL case records and profile earlier this morning. You have a very impressive track record."

"Lou is fine. I have files? Why were you reading my files?" Everyone has files, but perhaps I should have come in early today to stay ahead of the game.

"I always research our lead investigators to see who I am dealing with or how I can best work with their strengths. Since we are on a first name basis, mine is Arya." She said as she walked towards me.

"Arya...is that Indian?" I asked.

"Very good, my father was from Mumbai."

"That's on the west coast, uh, the Arabian Sea, right?" I said more as if testing myself rather than trying to impress her. I enjoyed geography all through high school and into college. However, I never traveled across either of the big oceans.

"You are starting to impress me." She said with a smile. "I had to Google your name to find out that Lusio in Zuni has a possible meaning of 'bringer of light'. You must tell me some time how your mother came to see that name for you. You have such an interesting background" she said as Jones and Roy walked in.

"Roy, she Googled me." I boasted as I leaned back and interlocked my fingers across my chest.

"Oh yeah? I bet she found a picture of a donkey." Roy fired back. Arya laughed as she walked towards me. I pretended to look offended from Roy's comment, but Arya just gave me this look of 'you got what you deserved.' I hope I didn't ruin the moment, but sometimes I can't stop my little attempts at humor.

She had totally transformed from the agent I met yesterday. If I had my choice though, it would be working with this version of Agent Arya Shah. She sat down next to me and noticed the goose bumps on my arms. They were still there from the sunbathing earlier. She looked around as if trying to pinpoint the source of the possible chill I was experiencing and looked tempted to ask if I was cold.

"Good morning Special Agent Shah" Jones said, as he made his way to the front of the room.

Roy just gave Arya a head nod and then slapped me on the shoulder as he sat down on the other side of me.

In walked the Captain accompanied by the Sheriff of Cobb County and six of his deputies. The other detectives and about 7 officers followed after the deputies. It was now standing room only.

Apart from Agent Jones and Shah, everyone knew Sheriff Richard Connelly. Sheriff 'Rick' was a good old boy from the South and did not have to campaign very hard to be reelected for his terms. He was generous with his deputies' time when duty called, never failing to respond, and enjoyed making his rounds to keep up relations.

He was sitting in front of me and a Deputy Smith was sitting on the other side of Arya. Agent Jones addressed the room and caught them up on what was released to the reporters and then debriefed on the details of Lars Bowman. Deputy Smith leaned over to Shah and whispered something. She either did not hear him or was purposely not acknowledging him keeping it professional.

Jones paused for a second and then announced, "I would like to turn the rest of the briefing over to Special Agent Arya Shah." Arya stood up and walked to the front. Deputy Smith let out a sigh and said, "Shit" under his breath. Arya went into an in-depth description of Lars's mental state, urges, upbringing, tendencies, the need to stay close to home, and showed photos of what he would look like if he altered his appearance and even describe the gun, an old flintlock pistol.

She then stressed the urgency of bringing the public into the manhunt using his photos and asking for bystanders to not approach the subject, but to send in photos or recordings via cell phone if they believed he was near. It was a social media tactic the FBI had used successfully before. It enhanced the public awareness and left very little places for the subject to hide.

Arya ended her briefing with, "He is a very unstable individual, willing to die, and willing to kill anyone, with an out of control urge to stay the course of kidnapping and killing woman at random possibly more than just weekly now. Almost daily if the circumstances present themselves. We decrease these odds of another death and his capture exponential with your coordinated efforts and the social media teams filtering data as it comes in live. I want to thank you all for the generosity of your resources and team work. Sheriff, the room is yours."

Sheriff Rick gave a quick overview of how his deputies would liaise with FBI, local PD and media. Deputy Smith was positioned with Mableton PD as a liaison, which meant he would be working closely with me, Agent Jones and Shah to coordinate local deputy support as needed.

There were about 50 roads that could lead away from Mableton, but more than half met up with other main roads that fed Interstates and highways. The Sheriff's Office and Highway Patrol already had check points set up. Short of hiking through the Appalachian Mountains to escape, it would be very tough for Lars Bowman to move very far in Georgia.

The room cleared out slowly as law officers went back to what they were trained to do, keep the public safe. Deputy Smith was having a few words with Sheriff Rick as I went over to Arya to see what the earlier exchange between the two held. She just finished talking to Jones and turned to find me approaching her.

"Lou, I hope you don't mind that I spoke with Captain Whitmore earlier and requested to ride with you today. Jones is going to stay at the station with Deputy Smith and others to coordinate intelligence and check points." Arya said.

"I welcome your company. Perhaps you could bring your personnel file for me to have some light reading when we break for lunch?" I said jokingly. She knew she had the upper hand and that I would be prying for information to even the field.

"It's bugging you, huh?" She said with a smile and led me out of the room.

It was bugging me a little, but I would get over it.

As I was unlocking my desk drawer to grab my gun, the Sheriff deposited Deputy Smith at Roy's desk across from me. The two introduced themselves and as the Sheriff started to leave, he gave a small nod to Agent Shah.

Deputy Smith had this look of shame on his face and dared not look our way. Seconds later Roy was advising Smith he could sit at my desk since I would be out on the road all day. I could care less, since I only had two personal items on the desk; a picture of Lolo when she was 18 years old before heading off to college and a picture of my parents from when I was 4 years old.

Arya tapped my back as she started to head out towards the front door. I holstered my gun and caught up with her outside. I pointed to my car which she was already heading towards. As I put myself behind the wheel, I paused before putting the keys in the ignition.

"I get it. Researching me to see my methods, my weaknesses, what I could have missed. I would do the same in your shoes. However, I'm not riding around with you all day unless you spill the beans on who Arya Shah is?" I said. I then started the car and pulled away from the Precinct.

"But first," I said as I drove down the street. "What went on between you and Deputy Smith?"

"Fair enough, but just remember, I'm the expert at psycho analyzing here." She joked.

We headed out to interview Lars's coworkers at the McCormick Wood Mill as well as neighbors of his apartment. I waited a whole ten seconds, and then broke out with my line of questioning.

"Let me guess. Only child, collected bugs growing up, full soccer scholarship, BS in Psychology and then went on to Master in Criminal Psychology, top of your class and recruited by the FBI." I announced proudly.

"Wow, that was impressive, Lou. Did you work on that last night?" She said with a hint of sarcasm and fun she had asking the question. I was definitely off by a little.

"It was butterflies and ballet up until College. It was a science scholarship, not my athletics that paved the way to the FBI. But you pretty much nailed the rest." Arya said as she looked out the window. There was obviously more she was not telling me.

"Do you still have your tutu?" I asked with a slight laugh, which earned me a soft backhand to the chest. That got rid of the goose bumps.

When Arya backhanded Lou, she immediately felt a hot surge travel though her wrist and arm. For a split second, she thought she hit him strangely and hurt her wrist, but the heat traveled past her arm through her chest and into her stomach. She sat up straight and put her hands on her stomach as she looked out the window trying to catch her breath. She was not one to get car sickness, but perhaps this is what it felt like.

We did not get any leads or beneficial information from

coworkers or neighbors. Lars clearly leads a double life and had his act down.

People described him as helpful at work, did his job, gave overtime when asked and rarely called in sick. Neighbors agreed that he kept to himself, said 'hi' in passing, and were all shocked to hear the news the day before. No one had seen or heard from him in days. His old Chevy pickup truck was still in the lot out back. It would be impounded later as evidence.

We just picked up a couple of sandwiches from a local deli, when a call came in over the radio. We were about 5 minutes away from the location passed on to us. If I recall correctly, it would put us in the warehouse district. On the ride over, I asked Arya, "Are you going to tell me what Deputy Smith said to you in the briefing this morning or not?"

"Will it end your line of questioning with me today?"

"Yes." I replied as I turned down the road that led to the address. I could see the warehouse and a few police vehicles out front.

"He said...'I will keep you safe darlin', which I think the Sheriff overheard."

"Oh shit. Sheriff Rick is a good old boy, but he does not tolerate his deputies stepping out of line. To use such condescending language to FBI's Special Agent Arya Shah, A.K.A. "Tippy Toes", I'm sure Deputy Smith will be on desk or jail duty for a while." I said as we turned into the parking lot.

"You are going to milk that bit of information for every bit you can, aren't you?" she said smiling and shaking her head as she looked down at her lap.

"Seems like the right thing to do." I shrugged as I put the car in park and got out. An officer was already approaching us and I asked, "What do we have here officer?"

He informed us of a 911 call from a realtor that was meeting a potential client for the property. Nothing was touched. The building had been vacant for about a year. She noticed a forced entry and expected vandalism, not a homicide. She had still been asked to stay for further question, but she didn't have anything new to add for us so we released her minutes later.

After entering the warehouse, we found ourselves almost immediately looking over the body that would be identified later as one Vanessa Morris. The medical examiner showed up a few minutes after us and went to work. Arya was right at his side observing and exchanging thoughts and observations.

An officer escorted me over to the utility room where he believed some activity took place. As I looked around the room, I noticed a few small patches of hair around the maintenance tub. What really caught my attention in the room was the smell of iodine. Above the faucet on the wall tiles was a splash of the brownish substance with "U R Next" wiped into the stain. If the words were an attempt at being prophetic, they just came across as creepy. Perhaps that was the purposes.

I rejoined Arya and the Medical Examiner. Arya quickly pointed out the tape residue on the victim's hands, ankles and mouth. The cause of death was believed to be from the blunt force trauma from a high impact fall she experienced at almost the exact spot she was laying. Seeing no apparent places to fall from, she must have been slammed to the ground headfirst.

The odd thing about this scene was the disturbing smears of blood around her as if someone had attempted to revive her or moved her with little success.

It wasn't until the examiner saw a faint pattern in the blood on the floor that he suggested someone lay with the woman for quite some time causing the blood to dry outlining what seem to be a jean pocket and shape of an arm behind the women.

She was on her side in somewhat of a fetal position with one hand free and the other tucked under her cheek as if sleeping peacefully. Clearly, she was positioned this way. Then there was the possibility someone lay with her for hours. This went from creepy to utterly disturbing.

The checkpoints had not produced anything yet, which gave us hope Lars was still local and would be tracked down soon. The flip side was he could be looking for his next victim versus his escape route. Hours later, the Medical Examiner informed us he had more information to share. As Arya and I entered the room, we found ourselves staring at Agent Jones and Captain Whitmore. Neither looked pleased to see us. What did I do now?

"Lou, we have an unanticipated problem." The Captain said. He rarely calls me by my first name unless I'm on the receiving end of bad news he rather not be delivering.

It made me think of the time two years ago when he informed me Lolo had called looking for me because my mother was sick and hospitalized. Ever since then, my mother has lived on the reservation in New Mexico, cutting herself off from the outside society and 100% in the care of Shaman. No phones, no letters. I fly back three times a year to check in on her. The Captain had that same look now that bad news was imminent.

"Lou, we believe Lars killed this woman and sent you a message. He left a note on her body addressed to you." He said pointing to the table left of me. Arya joined me to read the note through the evidence bag.

ABRAMS TOOK FROM ME. HE WILL FEEL WHAT I FELT. THEN HE WILL DIE.

Arya showed true concern on her face as she looked over to me. Then she addressed Jones and the Captain. "He is clearly delusional, and I doubt he will allow us to catch him alive. He is probably beyond psychiatric help and has manifested a level of culpability in Detective Abrams for saving Tammy. We need to rework our analysis on him to help refocus our search efforts and manpower."

She turned to me. "He could be stalking you or people close to you. We need to consider possible protection details for your friends, neighbors and significant other. Do you have a signif...?" I waived her off to avoid the need to answer the question that was coming.

"Look, before we all start worrying about me and the people around me, which by the way is mainly you all, how about we address the fact that he has most likely changed his appearance and is now killing adults too. The hair shavings, the iodine, we are looking for either short hair or even a bald description of our subject. Do we have someone working the computer- generated picture of his possible profile?" I asked.

Jones chimed in, "Once you and Special Agent Shah relayed the info from the crime scene, we started the facial reconstruction options and had them sent the agencies and media. I also notified BAU2 that his pattern is loose and adults are now in the scope. They specialize in crimes against adults and will be helpful in our new analysis"

"Detective, we have to consider this threat real and imminent" the Captain said as he took the note from me and handed it to the Medical Examiner. "Until further notice we are positioning two patrol cars at your residence and contracting 3 security guards to walk the premise 24/7. I already spoke to a Ms. Brown, the landlord, and she is being very understanding. You will also be accompanied by an officer or Detective 24/7."

"Captain, is that really necessary? We can't afford the manpower to be diverted from the search." I protested.

"It's not a suggestion." He barked.

Great, all I needed was an old detective complaining that he had to baby sit me or worse, a young cop trying to impress me 24/7. I would not wish this assignment on anyone. The Captain knows I'm perfectly capable of watching out for myself. I've been riding alone for years plus I have a trained attack-dog, this is ridiculous.

As I headed out of the room, Arya stayed behind to defuse the Captain. I'm sure he was not pleased with me just leaving the room, but better to do so than to say something that could damage my career.

Arriving at my desk, Deputy Smith looked as if he'd made my desk home. Was he going to move or would I have to move him? I think he noticed the pissed off look on my face, and decided to get up and move. Even though the look was not intended for him, it served the situation well. I flopped into my chair and leaned back looking at the ceiling for a sign that this was all going to get better. Focus, Lusio, focus.

Just then Arya walked up to me as if reading my mind. "You ready to catch this guy?"

"Yep" I said as I sat up. Smith looked confused, like he wanted to follow us but also was waiting to take my chair over again. Poor guy. Serves him right though.

Roy handed me a piece of paper with the address of the bar Vanessa was last seen the night prior. Once she was identified, he immediately started calling around and lining up witnesses for interviewing. A few coworkers were already showing up for questioning, but the bartender was in the middle of his shift. So, we figured we would go talk to him and look around for any other useful information.

As we both headed back out to the car, she handed me a couple of photographs of what our killer could look like with no hair.

CHAPTER 8

It was about 5 o'clock now as we arrived at the Bar where Vanessa was last seen. As we entered, it was much larger than I had anticipated it to be. There was an entry way that led out to a 10x10 platform overlooking the lounge area below. Stairs on both sides of the platform descended to two long bars on the right and left walls.

Glowing glass shelves illuminated the hundreds of bottles of liquor the bartenders used. With the variety of shapes and colors each bottle had to offer, it was quite an eye- catching site. Mirrors were behind the shelves creating a false sense of more liquor and space. The place was already hopping for happy hour.

We split up and each took a bar looking for a John Curtis. It wasn't long before I found him mixing drinks for two young ladies at the end of the bar. I waited until he was done and caught his attention by flashing my badge. He told the other bartender to cover for him for a few minutes and came around the bar to meet up with me. Arya arrive a few seconds later.

"Hi, John, I'm Detective Abrams and this is Special Agent Shah with the FBI. Thanks for making a few minutes with us.

"The FBI! Shit, what's this about?" sighed the bartender.

"You had a young lady in here yesterday that you were observed serving and we have a couple of questions" Arya said.

"If I served her, she was 21. I always card." He said defensively.

I chimed in and said, "We are more concerned about the

gentleman she met." I showed him a picture of Vanessa and our rendering of Lars.

"Oh, I remember them. He was here first drinking alone at the end of the bar. He looked pissed off and the other bartender, Mike, was serving him. She came in around 6 P.M. with four other ladies for happy hour. I was serving them until around 7:30 P.M. when her friends settled up and left. That's when I noticed he had come over and was talking to her and started buying her drinks. She was into him." He stressed.

"Did you notice anything out of the norm before or during their departure? Did she leave of her own free will? Was she drunk and needing his assistance?" Arya asked.

"I think they had three drinks each. She looked fine when she went to the restroom and that was when the guy settled up and left. He paid cash and I went on to the next customer." He answered.

"Hey, what's this all about?" he asked.

"She was murdered last night and we believe this person was the last to see her alive." I said.

"Jesus!" Exclaimed the bartender.

I asked if he had any security cameras inside or outside and he replied they did. I asked him to call his manager in early and get the tapes or CDs to us immediately today. He assured me he would go do that right away.

"Thanks for your time. If you can think of anything else that would be helpful, please call us." I handed him my card and Arya did the same.

"Let's look around a bit." I said to Arya as we stepped outside.

She agreed and we started a grid search of the bars parking lot. After about 30 minutes, I came up empty. Arya found an earring and a used roll of duct tape close to each other towards the far side of the lot. She had it marked off and was on the phone with Jones relaying the information.

As I walked up, she was taking pictures with her phone and sending them over to Jones. The Crime Scene Unit would be out shortly to try to lift tire tracks and possibly give us a possible make and model just in case the cameras did not catch this corner of the lot. I took a few orange cones from my trunk and cordoned off the area until they arrived about 30 minutes later.

It was getting close to 7 P.M. and Arya wanted to grab a bite to eat before heading back to her hotel to work her new information into the analysis. We grabbed some Chinese food to go and then I took her over to the Best Western where she and Jones were staying. I parked close to the lobby and started to walk her in.

"Hey, I think we work well together. I just wanted you to know that. I really appreciate the support you and Jones are lending to our department." I sincerely said as we entered the lobby.

"Thank you, Lou. It's not easy always being the outsiders. Before we say our goodnights though, would you mind waiting here for a few minutes?" She asked.

"No problem. I'll be over here checking out those 'welcome' cookies on the table."

She laughed and disappeared down the hall. A few moments later she reappeared with her overnight bag and laptop bag.

"What's this?" I asked.

"Guess who gets to protect you tonight?" She said

"You have got to be kidding me. With two patrol cars out front and 3 security guards walking the grounds, the Captain still thinks I need someone staying in my house? What does this say about my self-defense abilities? No offense to you, of course." I sounded slightly perturbed.

"No offense taken. I would have told you sooner, but I had a feeling you would not be pleased and I did not want to have that hanging over our heads all day." Arya said. I could tell she was expecting this reaction from me.

"I'm not even sure my house is up to code. You have a

hard hat packed in there?" I said to lighten the moment.

She smiled and said, "There it is, the humor in the uncomfortable moment."

"No, I'm serious. I can't recall the last time I cleaned. You may need my protection in there." I said as we left the lobby.

"I'm not a neat freak and just so you know, my two older brothers conditioned me for many levels of a man's idea of clean. I doubt you will even come close to what I might find as offensive living habits." Arya said with laughter in her eyes.

As we got back into the car and headed to my place I asked, "Who did the Captain tell to stay with me? I know it wasn't you."

"You are not going to like this. After you left the medical examiners room, he went through five people that adamantly protested the assignment before I couldn't take it anymore. I volunteered to speed up the process so we could all get back to work." She said as serious as can be.

"Now you're messing with me." I said.

"No, I'm serious. I'm pretty sure they were in the process of choosing the shortest straw to decide, before I intervened." She added.

"Alright, alright, your humor is killing my ego. Thank you for stepping up."

She gave off a small chuckle as she opened her Chinese food and started to eat an egg role. The smell awakened my stomach instantly and it growled loudly. She clearly heard it and handed me one as we drove down the street.

As we pulled up to the duplex, the police presence was obvious. One patrol car at each entrance, one officer in each car and a third was walking up to us as we parked.

"Hi Detective. We are personally checking each car that enters and exits. Please pop your trunk, this will take 2 seconds." The patrol officer was already walking to the rear of the car before I could even say 'Hi" back.

I pulled the trunk release lever and he closed it almost as quick as it opened. I pulled forward and parked the car. It was dark now, but the parking lot and walking paths were well lit. I was carrying Arya's overnight bag over my shoulder as she followed me to the front door. I noticed a guard off to the right heading toward the backyard and pool area.

As we walked through my door we were immediately greeted by Andy. "Hey buddy, how are you?" I said as I rubbed his head and side. Andy gave a little whimper as his tail became more out of control with the excitement of a visitor.

Arya took a knee to properly greet Andy at his level. "Hi Andy, do you mind if I hang here tonight?" she said as he sniffed her and then started to lick her hand. "I will take that as a yes."

"I'm going to put your bag in the spare bedroom over here. The kitchen table should be clean enough for us to finish our meals on and there is beer, soda and tea in the fridge." I called out as I disappeared into what would be her bedroom for the night. I heard Arya say 'okay' as I quickly looked around the bedroom. I removed one of Andy's blankets that lay in the middle of the bed and threw it on the closet floor. Everything else seemed okay.

I had only been gone for 60 seconds, but Arya had already served the dinners on plates, silverware and chopsticks set, and a beer next to each plate. She was also in the process of refilling Andy's water and food bowl. I was amazed how fast she took the lead. I was thinking of something witty to say, but only one thing came to mind.

"Thank you, Arya."

"No problem. Everything seemed to be easy to find, so it made it very easy to help out. Shall we eat? I'm starving." she said as she plopped down.

"Absolutely." Even though we were both famished, we managed to eat at a reasonable pace and kept the topic of conversation away from work.

I had asked Arya to tell me about her favorite places she had been. She shared her top five, but two destinations stuck out as she really seemed passionate about their locations, history and how they touched her personally.

One was Croatia and its lovely beaches and islands. The other destination she described was St. Barts in the Caribbean. She could have been a travel agent the way she recalled it to me.

It had the most peaceful areas, rich in French, Caribbean, Arawak Indian history with a ton of long white sandy beaches and crystal-clear water. There were rocky coves and cliffs, short and tall palms everywhere, French deco houses, harbors filled with magnificent yachts and boats, and little quaint beach front villas at every turn. She explained how she almost stayed there indefinitely after college, caught up in learning French and really enjoying the island life.

"I'm sold," I said. "Just as long as dogs are allowed on the beach. Just a few months ago, Andy almost ran himself to death chasing seagulls on Tybee Island beach."

"I know that beach well and several others on the Georgia and South Carolina coast. When I retire, it will be the beach life for me." She said as she raised her beer to toast the proclamation. We tapped bottles.

"How about you?" she asked.

"I love the sun, so beaches are a nice destination. I really enjoyed Saint Martin and Saint Lucia Islands. I spent several weeks on both islands. *J'ai appris un peu le francais en France.* Both places were beautiful and rich with history. My favorite destination has to be..." She cut me off with excitement.

"*Vous parlez francais. Qualle merveilleux!*" She said with enthusiasm.

"Well, not really. I know a few lines. I have probably over played that phrase. I can understand the language better than I can put together a complete sentence. I should probably stop saying that I know a little French." I said truthfully.

"Don't sell yourself short, Lou. Understanding the language is tough enough, but speaking it comes with practice. You spoke it perfectly and you understood what I just said. I'm impressed." She said as she finished her last bite.

"Sorry I cut you off earlier. What is your favorite destination?" She asked.

"Oh, uh... Graceland." I said deadpan.

"Get out of here." She said, obviously not believing me.

"No, it's true. Nothing grounds me more than a few days with Elvis impersonators, fanatics and old groupies taking in the shrine of the divine musical genius that gave us all 'Hunk of Burning Love.'

She laughed so hard she instinctively covered her mouth and nose with both hands to muffle her outburst. I chuckled as I stood up and cleared the table. Arya then excused herself and took her laptop into the spare bedroom. She had a sense of grace as she glided through my living room to the bedroom. Andy was hot on her heels. A moment later I heard Arya call out,

"Do you mind if I change into my sweats?"

"No worries, I think I will do the same." I replied as I headed to my room to change.

We met back up in the living room a few minutes later. She was plugging in her laptop and getting comfortable on the couch when Andy jumped up next to her. She scratched his cheeks and then just held his head gently in her hands as she starred into his eyes for a few seconds. He was mesmerized and sat there perfectly still. Then she released him and he curled up next to her.

"Were you two just having a moment there?" I asked inquisitively.

"It was nothing. I was just admiring his different colored eyes. The blue and green, he is beautiful." She said.

◆ ◆ ◆

However, it was something. She was extremely good at her job for many reasons; dedicated, intelligent, great collaborator, patient, extremely analytic, a superb problem solver, and a bit clairvoyant at times.

That last skill was not officially registered on her FBI resume and she had never spoken of it with people she knew in fear of not being taken seriously. She sometimes saw things when holding objects or people's hands, other times the visions came from positive or negative energy around her.

Sometimes they were past events which came through much clearer than future events. When she saw something that had not yet happened, it came in puzzle pieces like a highway mileage marker, but no clue of the highway or state. Or like when she held Lars's knife in the basement, she saw a vision of him driving on a road alone and then a quick glimpse of him fishing.

When she looked into Andy's eyes and held his head, she could see him sitting next to a woman's leg and looking at Lou. Then she saw him chasing someone in the dark. She did not know if these were past memories or future events. It was also the first time she saw something through an animal. This took her by surprise, and she hid it well.

There were plenty of cases where she wished she could harness the skill to develop clearer visions. It was something she has spent her whole life secretly researching and experimenting with.

She had taken many discreet trips and vacations to attend sanctuaries or classes designed to facilitate the growth of her clairvoyant abilities by learning to harness her intuition, read energy, and piece together the mental pictures that came to her.

Arya had even called in a few renown Mediums on a few cases to not only get their assistance, but to study them and ask questions about their technique. The FBI doesn't frown on outside help, but they only recognize a handful as consistently 'helpful' Mediums, which made it nearly impossible to get their help when needed.

These highly respected Mediums are extremely busy

using their gift to help others, while trying to balance a regular life with friends and family. She did have the pleasure to work a case with the renowned Allison Dubois. Arya was amazed to see Allison recall a vision during the case as if it were a movie she just saw. Already 32 years old, Arya believed it may take her a lifetime and she still may never fully develop these abilities.

She came back to life after apparently in deep thought for a moment.

"Lou, your eyes, I hope you don't mind me asking. Are you wearing contacts? I've never seen eyes so alive with that bright grade of blue." She was now sitting with her legs criss-crossed on the couch leaning back with the computer in her lap.

"I wanted to feel normal in college and decided to where brown contact lenses to avoid the stares and questions of how my eyes were freakishly blue." I shared before continuing.

"I never got use to putting them in and finally came to terms with it. These are the real deal. The question doesn't bother me anymore and neither do the stares. I think of them as a gift so unique that at times needs to be explained. However, I'm left with no explanation other than, I'm different." I shrugged.

She put her laptop down and walked over to me. I was sitting in my old lazy boy. She stood right between my feet and leaned over, putting her hands on my arm rest. Her face was about twelves inches from mine and she looked right into my eyes as if to study them closer.

"People stare...people ask, because they are so beautiful and so rare, like blue aurora borealis." She said with a soft, caring voice.

I felt the hairs on my arm start to stand up.

"That is a unique perspective and one hell of a compliment. Thank you." I said as I made an attempt to swipe down the hairs that stood before she noticed.

But it was not just the arm-hairs at work. I could sense a magnetic like force pushing and pulling between us, like two north poles of two magnets being forced closely together, at odds in their attraction, but constantly looking for the slightest movement to off center their position causing them to immediately crash together with such lightning speed and force.

It seemed Arya felt it too as she pushed herself off the arms of the chair and took a step back.

"Well, I call it as I see it and you're welcome." She said as she reached under her long black hair and rubbed the small hairs down on the back of her neck. She took a deep breath and went back to the couch.

That was strange, she thought. She felt an enormous amount of positive energy around him and it overwhelmed her. Positive energy is good and typically something she can read very well, but the pushing and pulling between them caused her to be almost weak in the legs and become momentarily thoughtless. As she sat down, she cleared her throat.

"I think if I can get this program going and make a few updates. I can develop a more comprehensive analysis to assist us in his next move and travel patterns." She said.

"That's great. What can I do to help?" I asked.

"Just being here to bounce thoughts off of is a big help. The majority of the work is technical jargon between me and the program questions and formulas."

As she sat on the couch typing away, I took a good look at her profile. I'm about 6'2 and when we walked together earlier, she was only a few inches shorter than me, probably putting her at 5'10.

Her hair was straight, black, and about eight inches past her shoulders, but her bangs were just below her chin slightly curving in, framing her face. If she wore makeup, it was so little that it could not be detected. Her Indian complexion gave her a young, vibrant face and her skin a slightly tanned appearance. Her jaw was smooth and round from ear to chin and her nose was long, thin and proportionate to her face.

What fascinated me was how round her eyes were and how much white showed, which was accentuated by dark eye lashes. Surrounded by her dark hair and tan complexion, her eyes stood out even more. When she was face to face with me, I was lost in the light hazel colors that sparkled at me. She was beautiful and I caught my self-imagining her dancing to Tchaikovsky.

She looked over at me, catching my gaze and asked, “Are you staring at me?”

“I was just imagining you dancing to Tchaikovsky.” I said honestly.

“I do not have any ballet gear and haven’t for over 10 years. Also, I was a contemporary ballet dancer, not classical. You are incorrigible, you know that, right?” she said without lifting her face from the computer.

“I do. I bet you had a hell of a time keeping the boys away in college and at the academy.” That comment did not come out exactly the way I heard it in my head.

“Did you just pay me a compliment?” She said looking up at me with a surprised look on her face. Wow, her eyes were gorgeous, inviting me in.

“Just stating the obvious, but yes, that was a compliment.”

“Could you be more specific please? I want to know just how sincere you are being.” She said with this interrogation look on her face now.

“Now you are just trying to make me feel uncomfortable.” I replied a little too quickly.

“No, not at all. I was just searching for the specifics to see if it was a sincere compliment or you just poking fun at me. You can be hard to read at times.” She said as she turned her body to face me.

“Fair enough. You obviously have a very athletic figure from the years of ballet and the discipline has stayed with you and... you have very attractive eyes." There, now I've done it. She will probably ask Jones to work with me tomorrow.

"You really think so? My eyes, I mean they are so uninteresting." She said with a hint of bashfulness, reserve and curiosity.

"Stay there for a second. I want to get something really quick." I said as I headed to the bathroom to retrieve my 8x8 shaving mirror. When I returned, I approached her from behind the coach and asked her to sit back.

"What are you going to do?" She asked as she put her computer on the coffee table.

"Trust me. I want you to see what I see." I said as I took to one knee behind her and brought the mirror around to about a foot in front of her face.

"I want you to look at your eyes as if they were someone else's. Really look at the different light brown and green flecks in your iris and how round and white your eyes are when you open them up with different facial expressions." I said.

"Is this some sort of introspective exercise?" She said.

"This is no exercise, Arya. I want you to see something no one has ever shown you and you had no reason to look for it. I'm going to bring my face in behind your left ear and reposition the mirror so that you can see my eyes, but don't take your eyes off of your irises, okay?"

"Okay" she said unquestioningly.

As I leaned in, I slightly moved the mirror so our eyes could meet, she kept her focus on her own eyes and watched in amazement as the light brown and green flecks started to give way to blue flecks as well. My eyes were stirring an ocean of colors in hers that she never imagined existed before. Her eyes grew bigger with excitement as the colorful display continued to move around in her iris.

"That is amazing and beautiful" she whispered, as she stayed glued to the mirror. "Did you notice all of that in the few seconds that I leaned over to pay tribute to your eyes?" she said as she spun around to meet up with my face again.

The hairs on my arms and neck were at full attention and I could feel the pushing and pulling sensation even more now. I wonder if she felt the magnetic tug of war.

As if struggling to breathe, the words "I did" softly slipped out of my mouth. We were so close to each other. Still looking into her eyes, I slowly slid the mirror down the cushion of the couch next to Andy.

"You are something else Lusio Abrams" she whispered as her right hand found the back of my neck and gently pulled my face into hers. Our lips met and my body was instantly on fire.

I think we stood simultaneously as I found myself standing, seconds later she was over the couch and in my arms. The kiss became more passionate as my hands began to slide up and down her back side pulling her in closely. I could feel her bosom pressing and heaving against my ribs. Her right hand was still on the back of my neck as her left hand was exploring my side and back.

Still holding each other tightly, I pulled gently away from our kiss and manage to say, "Should we be doing this?"

"Probably not" Arya said between breaths staring at my lips and about to reconnect.

"Should we stop before we..."

"Lou, don't you dare let go of me. I can't feel my legs right now." She said as she started kissing me again.

I bent my knees a little allowing my right hand to reach past her butt to lift her left leg up to my hip. She knew exactly what to do as she gave a little leap off the right foot and wrapped her legs around my waist.

Next thing I know we were down the hall, into my bedroom and falling sideways onto my bed. I immediate got up and shut the door to keep Andy from getting nosy.

As I turned around, the light from the pathway out back crept through my blinds on the other side of the bed offering a wonderful silhouette show of Arya taking off her shirt. I could make out her plentiful round breasts and slim waist as I walked towards her. She was on her knees meeting me at the edge of the bed, helping me lift my shirt.

She was kissing my chest as I removed the shirt over my head and onto the floor. As she worked her way up, our lips met again, and we kissed deeply and slowly enjoying each other.

I gently pushed her down on her back and slid her sweatpants off and then removed mine. I hadn't had sex in a while, so I started out slow and in control. There was a great deal of hands exploring each other's body, enjoying the physical connection.

"You feel wonderful." She whispered. Moving as one and staying connected, I rolled over positioning her on top allow her to be in control. She arched her back as she held my hands to her chest. I could feel myself losing the war on self-control.

I sat up and told her she was driving me crazy. She knew what I meant and said she was close too. Moving my hands to her back and pressing her close to me, I lay back down with her chest resting on my chest. We both enjoyed the final moment before having a passionate climax together.

After we caught our breath, she propped herself up on one arm and held her hair on the right side of her face back behind her ear and smiled at me.

"That...You were incredible" I said.

"So were you." She said grinning.

"I have to tell you that this is not something I do very often." I felt it was important to say as I did not know where this was going and did not want her thinking I was a hound dog always on the hunt.

"Neither do I, but it seems we both needed it, wanted it. That was kind of electric. I feel amazing right now." She said as she moved off my hips and to my side.

I could try to explain why she felt like she could go run a marathon right now, but I chose to keep the secret of passing my energy on to others.

I adjusted onto my side to face her. She locked her eyes on mine and was still smiling. I was too.

"I would describe it as magnetic." I said.

Her mouth open and eyes widened as if shocked at what I just said. "Yes! Good description." She slapped my chest, gave me a full kiss and then hopped out of bed.

"Where are you going so fast?" I asked while watching her nakedness search around for her clothes and then head to the bathroom.

"Like I said, I feel amazing. I can't explain it, but I am going to use it to my advantage right now and finish that analytic work up." A moment later she was out of the bathroom with her clothes on and heading out the door.

She paused and asked if I would like something to drink. I told her I would be out in a minute and would grab something then.

Well, that was interesting to say the least. I took a moment to reflect on the past few days. My powers were pulling fast ones on me. I had never wiped someone's memories away, Lacey had a spell on me I could not explain, especially the heat I felt when she was close to me.

Arya had this magnetic attraction I had never experienced before that had us switch from professional to bed buddies in a matter of minutes. Also, I have never had sex with a woman leaving her anything but equally exhausted, at least that is what I would like to believe. Yet here is Arya feeling like the energizer bunny afterwards.

Am I out of control or just being introduced to things I will learn to control? For now, I will enjoy the moment Arya and I just had and rejoin her in the living room. I was thirsty. Dressed and on my way to the kitchen, I fetched us both a water and noticed it was only 9:30 P.M. Arya had plenty of time to work her analysis and we both would be able to catch a good night's rest, if the magnetic forces allowed it.

CHAPTER 9

The trail was normally empty at this hour of the evening, but not tonight. He had stumbled upon it while trying to take a roundabout approach into the duplex without all the authorities taking notice.

It was pitch black where he was, but the lights from the duplex acted as a beacon. He was now in the shadows of the trees just on the outskirts of the pool area observing a guard walking down a lit path.

It seems the police were taking his threat seriously. He didn't care though, as he was hell bent on getting his revenge. As the guard disappeared behind a unit, another one appeared from his left carrying a flashlight and pointing it into dark areas of the community area.

The pool light was on, creating a large area of exposure if entering the duplex area from the backside. He knelt behind a bush patiently, observing the pattern the guards took around the common grounds. He desperately wanted to rush in shooting or stabbing anyone that got between him and detective Abrams back door. The urge to kill tonight was almost uncontrollable.

A moment later, two men approached the pool area and sat down at a table. They were obviously residents as they started to chat and drink. He didn't feel like waiting around any longer. As he backed away and found the trial again, he became obsessed with violent thoughts.

He was a hundred yards down the trail when he became blind with rage and could not stop himself from turning back.

This time, he left the trail, cutting through the woods to avoid the pool area. He came out in an area close to a path that led to what he believed were the two back doors of the duplex detective Abrams could be found in.

He sat there for a few minutes waiting for the guard to appear and pass by before making a mad dash for one of the doors. The porch lights were on and he felt totally exposed. A rush of adrenaline overcame him as he jimmied with the doorknob. There, the click sounded and he slid inside a dark room.

He didn't consider himself suicidal, but he often found himself lost in vivid thoughts about a bystander trying to be a hero as he took a girl right off the street and what he would do to said bystander.

He planned his moments well, but one can never plan for the unexpected. He almost relished the thought of unplanned events and how he would rise to the occasion to defend himself and his prize.

Alone in this dark room, he could make out a couch, chair, TV, kitchen table and the glowing numbers on the microwave. 11:05 PM.

Just then a light came on beyond the hallway and he found himself quickly crouching behind the couch. As he peeked over it he could now tell it came from one of the bedrooms. He was up and moving quickly through the hall towards the room. He passed by another bedroom door that was closed and dark inside. That room was not the priority right now.

As he entered the room with his hunting knife ready for action, he noticed the bathroom door was closed and the light was on, otherwise the room was empty.

He walked slowly over to the bathroom door and stood in front of it waiting. He could hear some rustling and then the sink faucet running briefly. He tightened his grip on the knife as he tried to keep himself from opening the door. He knew if he stood his ground, he would have the advantage of the darkness while his victim's eyes were still adjusting from the well-lit room.

The door opened as the bathroom light was turned off. She almost walked right into him but the thrust of the knife into her abdomen stopped her and forced all the air out of her lungs. She stood there in fear and shock as he abruptly pulled the knife up towards her sternum. She fell quickly to the floor and let out a moan as she grasped at her wound.

He quickly came down on her chest with his knee, knocking out what little air she tried to gather for a scream. He dropped the knife and wrapped his large hands around her thin neck and choked the remaining life out of her in a matter of seconds. Her eyes were wide open, staring at him. He looked down at her grinning as he released his grip.

As he picked up his knife, he made his way to the second bedroom. Pausing just outside of it, he stood there smelling his hands. There was a scent of lavender that transferred from her neck to his hands and he stood there enjoying the aroma contemplating whether to enter the room or not.

He stepped back and slowly walked towards the back door. Before exiting the way he had entered, he looked out the blinds and waited for the guard to appear and disappear again. Moments later he was strolling down the dark trail pausing every hundred yards smelling his hands as he looked up through the trees towards the night's sky. It could not have gone any better.

CHAPTER 10

I woke up for my morning run and found Andy curled up next to me sound asleep. He was not who I fell asleep with and I was disappointed that Arya was not still tangled up with me like she was when we passed out last night together.

For the first time I can remember in my life, I slept in. It was 7:30 A.M. and the sun had been up for well over an hour. I didn't think anything of it last night when I went to bed with Arya. However, now, sitting in my room feeling like I could use another few hours of sleep, I couldn't help but to wonder just how much energy I passed along to Arya last night. What the hell is happening?

I did not have time for a run. I quickly showered and dressed. As I headed down the hall I stopped by Arya's room and peeked in. There was no sign of her in the bed and the light was not on in the bathroom beyond the bed, nor was she in the living room. Perhaps she decided to let me sleep in and caught a ride with a police officer back to the precinct.

Something didn't feel right though. As I headed back to the extra bedroom to see if she left a note or something, the phone rang. I went back to the living room and grabbed my cell off the table.

"Abrams." I answered.

"You need to get your ass in here pronto Lou. We had a run in with Lars Bowman this morning on I-20." Roy exclaimed.

"I'm on my way. What happened?"

As I grabbed my gun and headed out the front door, a

security guard was standing on my porch drinking coffee. Roy explained over the phone that a Highway Patrol officer was checking out an old dirt road off I-20 and came head to head with the car Lars stole. Shots were exchanged and the officer is now receiving medical attention. Lars got away.

On the short drive over to the precinct, I couldn't stop myself from think about the time I had healed Motuka's sister on the reservation. Sometimes after new experiences, I find myself looking back on that day. The feeling is similar every time. The knot in my stomach, the extreme focus fed by the pain, sensory neurons firing all over my brain making tens of thousands of connections causing my head to pound at times, followed by the heat wave that travels to my hands and then lightheadedness. It all happens so fast that at times it is difficult to control how much energy I use or to know if I'm putting the energy where it needs to go.

I didn't mean to clear Tammy's thoughts a few days ago, but I do remember feeling her pain. Not just the physical abuse she endured, but the mental abuse as well. Perhaps just the awareness was enough for the energy to find its way to the area in need.

Which brings me to Arya and what she experienced last night. I had no awareness of a knot in my stomach, but there were definitely butterflies. She was not in any pain that I was aware of, but through the amount of touching and holding that went on, energy was indeed transferred.

I was drained this morning and for the first time ever, the sun did not wake me up. I rolled down the window and hung my arm out over the door as I drove. It wasn't much, but perhaps ten minutes of sun would alert my senses and get me out of this fog. By the time I reach the precinct I felt a little better, but still not up to my standards.

As I walked into the precinct, Mike was herding media again. I went through the bullpen and made my way to the briefing room. It was full of activity as Roy walked towards me. I did not see Arya or Agent Jones in the room.

"I'm getting ready to head over to the hospital to see how Officer Thompson is doing. I hear he took one in the shoulder and is in surgery now and should be out soon" Roy informed me.

"Thanks for calling me, Roy. I wasn't feeling well this morning and slept in, I guess. I see everyone but the FBI are here. Any signs of them this morning?"

"No, but we just got new information in that the car Lars was using was found abandoned in a busy Mall parking lot in Douglasville. It's only a matter of time before we get a call about another missing car."

Roy walked off and I walked over to the board to look at the pattern of Lars's recent whereabouts. He was all over the place. With the amount of law enforcement out looking for him, it was becoming extremely frustrating that he moved so freely. I noticed the Captain finishing up a conversation on his cell phone as he was walking towards me.

"Abrams, that was the Bureau in Atlanta. It seems that after doing some serious digging, they found an old deed on file in the Cobb County Clerk's Office for an old house a few miles down that dirt road the exchange took place this morning. Apparently, it has been in the Bowman family for quite some time, but under his great grandmother's maiden name. I need you out there to look it over. Highway Patrol still has the road on lockdown."

"I'm on my way. Any word on Jones and Shah?" I asked.

"Not sure. Why?"

"It's probably nothing, but Arya...Agent Shah was not in my house this morning and now they are both not here. I was just wondering if anyone has seen or heard from them." I tried not to sound worried.

"I'll let you know if I hear anything." He said as he opened a folder and continued to read its contents.

I stopped by the house to pick up Andy on the way out to the cabin. As soon as I opened the door, I received a call from agent Jones advising me that he would meet me out there. He was traveling in from Atlanta and was about 20 minutes out, but alone. I whistled and Andy was already heading out the door as I closed it behind him.

As I approached the turnoff to the dirt road there was one State Trooper and three Highway Patrol cars parked with their lights on. Little orange triangles were still scattered all over the place identifying shell casings from the exchange that took place a couple of hours earlier. Yellow tape was pinned to the ground in certain places as well as around the Highway Patrol car that had clear signs of bullet holes in the driver side.

As I pulled over, I noticed the State Trooper discussing something with a Highway Patrol Officer. Technically they both had rights to lead the scene, but at least for now they looked like they were keeping it civil and working together. If it were not one of our own involved, attitudes and rank might have worked their way into the discussion to jockey to take lead.

Veteran Trooper Walter "Smokey" Grime was headed my way. I got out and shook his hand hard trying to match the notorious vice grip he so proudly pushed upon everyone.

He looked like a dead ringer for Jackie Gleason, thus the nick name 'Smokey' from the movie *Smokey and the Bandit.* He embraced it and if you got a few drinks in him at one of our Law Enforcement picnics, he would nail an impression of Sheriff Buford T. Justice by telling a rookie, "Junior, get daddy a beer." It was always a crowd pleaser and usually led to more impressions and request for impressions of some of Gleason's most famous moments.

"Abrams, it has been awhile. What brings you here?" His Southern accent would have been calming if his grip wasn't grinding every bone in my hand to dust at the moment.

"I'm not planning on joining in the dance you have going with HP, but I will need to navigate through and head down that dirt road a few miles. The FEDs are right behind me and will be asking the same. It seems the dirt bag may have a cabin down there. Can you manage to create a path that doesn't disturb the scene or sends us into the ditch?" I politely asked as I visibly rubbed my hand to show him he is still the reigning hand crushing champ. He noticed and gave me a slight smile.

"Let me see what I can do." As Walter rejoined the others, an orderly effort followed to create a narrow path from the Highway to the dirt road they were blocking. I gave Walter a salute as I drove past and headed down the road.

The road took me deep into the woods where the sun became a dim light through the tall canopy covering the road. About 4 miles in, the road turned into tall grass and what appeared to be a small cabin sat in front of me covered in overgrowth.

I parked the car and released Andy to make a sweep of the area. All I could see was tall grass moving as he ran around the perimeter of the cabin. I knew he was not here, but instinctively I drew my gun as I entered the cabin. It wasn't any bigger than my living room. There was a table, chair, sink and what looked to be the remains of a cot. Andy appeared in the doorway after not finding anything outside.

I could hear a car approaching and assumed it was agent Jones. As I turned my attention back towards the sink and table to see if anything was worth examining or from this decade, my phone rang.

"Abrams here."

"Lou, it's Arya. Where are you?"

"Where am I? I'm right where I'm supposed to be. Where the hell are you?" I was glad to hear her voice, but she probably couldn't tell from my tone.

"The Atlanta office. I'm sorry I had to leave so early. I tried to wake you, but you were dead to the world and I had to rush back to Atlanta."

"No problem. I'm just glad you are okay." My voice and words were sincere and caught her by surprise.

Arya paused for a couple of seconds and then replied,

"I..." she cleared her throat. "I did not mean to worry you, Lou."

"I know you didn't. Everything is good with us, right?" I felt strange asking, but I really did not want to screw this work relationship up. Even though it's all of 3 days old.

"We are good. Thanks for asking. I have so much to share with you. For now, I really need to know where you are."

"I'm at the cabin and Jones is now standing in the door way blocking what little light we have in here." I said as I motioned Jones to come in.

"Lou, is there a table in the cabin?"

"Yes, there is one."

"Please let me know if there is anything on it."

I walked over to the table and found a silver watch that looked like it belonged to a woman. The knob was pulled out and the watch was showing 11:10.

"There is a watch." I said as Jones came over to me to see what I was looking at.

"Lou, is it silver and perhaps even stopped at 11:10?"

My heart skipped a beat. "What the hell, Arya."

"What's up Abrams?" asked Jones.

"Not sure, but this watch has some importance in our case."

Arya was talking in my ear again. "Lou, I will explain later, but for now I think you need to get back to your duplex and check on your neighbors."

A chill went down my spine as I picked up the watch with a handkerchief and looked at the back of it. MY LOVE, A.B.

"Jesus!" My mind was wild with thoughts. Anita Brown, the sweet old lady next to me, this could be her watch. God, I hoped not. Could he have already been there? How could he have slipped by all the security? Jones was showing signs of agitation trying to piece together what I was already fearfully assuming.

"Arya, I have to go." I hung up as I carefully placed the

watch in the plastic evidence bag Jones had pulled from his coat pocket.

"Jones, we need to radio the police in my parking lot to enter my neighbor's home and check on her. I believe this is her watch."

"Damn, I hope you're wrong. Let's go." Jones was swiftly moving towards his car and making a call at the same time.

Andy was on my heels as I ran to my car. We were speeding down the dirt road with our sirens on to let the troopers and patrol officers know to move aside. Walt and team had the path ready for us as if reading our urgency perfectly.

We were back on the highway and doing about 95 mph for most of the stretch, only slowing to 75 mph when other cars were around. I took lead and Jones was following me. What would have been a 20-minute drive was being cut down to about 14 minutes. I picked up my phone and went to the call log to dial Arya's number on the drive back to my house.

"Special Agent Shah speaking."

"Arya, sorry for the hang up. We are on our way back to the house to check on my neighbor Anita Banks. The watch had her initials on it."

"I was afraid of that. I know this is going to sound beyond believable, and I really don't want to get into it over the phone, but I had a hunch. Well, honestly, a vision. Almost like a day dream."

"What are you talking about?" I honestly did not see the conversation going in this direction, but I embraced it as I flew by a station wagon with two kids looking wide-eyed out the side window at our unmarked cars with sirens and lights blaring.

"Lou, please give me the benefit of doubt. I know I sound crazy. Please trust me until I can explain in person."

"Of course, I'm just a little taken aback. It's not every day someone shares this kind of...news. But believe me, I'm not judging you." I didn't know what else to say.

"You are being kind with your words and I respect that.

I will not abuse your trust and I will come clean later today when we meet up. I have said too much over the phone and cannot afford to say more at this time. Please trust me." There was almost a trace of desperation in her voice for my acceptance, but I may be confusing it with how guarded she was with the announcement or being protective to prevent others from overhearing.

It was very risky to admit such a thing in the law enforcement circle, as we can be very unforgiving with the unexplainable and supernatural. However, I was the last person to pass judgment.

"Hey, your secret is safe with me. I mean it. I did not tell Jones anything. I need to let you go as we are about to exit the highway. Are you heading back soon?"

"Yes, within the hour. Thank you, Lou." She hung up and I turned off the highway.

As we pulled up to the duplex, there were two officers standing in front of Ms. Brown's opened front door, but no signs of her. A sick feeling came over me as I parked the car and rushed over to the door. The officers recognized me and stepped aside as I entered Ms. Blake's house.

Everything looked in order as I walked in. Perhaps this was all a bad assumption on our part, and this was all an overreaction. Just then, an officer stepped out of a bed room down the hall and waved me over. I could tell from the expression on his face that I needed to prepare myself for what I was about to see.

"Abrams." Jones called out from the living room as I walked down the hall. "Let me go in. If she is in there, you shouldn't have to see her this way."

"No, I'm alright." I paused by the door taking in a depth breath and then entered with Jones right behind me. At first everything looked normal. A rocking chair to my left accompanied by a dresser, bed and two nightstands to my right and the entrance to the bathroom beyond the bed.

An officer stood on the other side of the bed close to the dresser. He looked disturbed and stood there uncomfortably, as if not sure how to divert our attention to what lay on the floor just out of our sight.

As we moved around the bed, it became clear the horror that awaited us. Ms. Banks lay in the doorway of the bathroom surrounded by a pool of blood. What was once a white night gown, now looked like a red rose with a few snowflakes. Her midsection was torn open. The force of the blow was so powerful, I could see a couple of ribs exposed.

I pressed my lips together and looked over at Jones thinking I should have taken him up on his offer. This image of my sweet neighbor and friend will haunt me.

CHAPTER 11

Just off Interstate 85, tucked away on Century Parkway, lies the FBI's Atlanta Field Office. From the outside, it clearly looks to be 7 floors of office space sitting on top of a three-story parking garage.

Only FBI or high-level clearance personnel can park in the garage. The rest of the general public, including non-FBI law enforcement agencies, park in the front or back lot. There is heavy screening and security if entering the garage or building.

This typical office building has its secrets though, one of them being the "Bull Pen." There were three additional floors underground.

One floor was dedicated to housing super computers and the highly trained guards and technicians that monitored the equipment 24/7.

The other two floors were designed for tactical response team planning, field analysis support, and a variation of a 911 operations center where FBI operators are connected to every local, state and federal law enforcement agency, as well as Interpol filtering alerts that come across their computer screens and phones.

If the alerts are deemed credible and given priority review, the Bull pen shift supervisor reviews it and determines which FBI unit will be assigned to the case. Everything takes only a matter of minutes thanks to the super computers knowing every agent's skill, past cases, applicable knowledge, assigned unit, availability, whereabouts, and case load.

Arya and Jones spent the morning in the Bull Pen working with two senior analysts running through the subject's family history, credit, banking, loans, purchases, travel patterns, etc. They caught their break when one analyst cross referenced all family maiden names with scanned archived bank notes, liens, and mortgages for the last 100 years.

Unfortunately, the break came an hour after the Patrol Officer was surprised by Lars returning to the cabin they discovered during their new analysis. Jones left immediately to meet up with local PD at the scene.

Arya stayed behind to finish up some paperwork and give Lou a courtesy call she knew she owed him after leaving so fast.

She had just filed her report and was taking the elevator up to her office to gather her personal items when it hit her. She felt a hot flash as the elevator doors in front of her became blurry. She grabbed hold of the handrail to steady herself.

A second later her world went dark and all she could see was a faint light in the distance. She slowly walked towards the glimmer. As it grew brighter, she noticed a table appearing in the light. When she arrived at the table there lay a watch. She looked around, but was surrounded by darkness. She could not even see her hand if she were to reach into the blackness around her.

She returned her focus to the watch and picked it up. It was an old silver wrist watch. She picked it up and took a close look at it before realizing how hot it was. It started to glow red hot and then in the blink of an eye she was staring into the eyes of an old lady she had never seen before.

The woman's eyes were wide and filled with terror. She was face to face with her in the darkness. The old lady started to look down and Arya's eyes followed. Arya could see what appeared to be her own hand thrusting a knife into the woman's sternum, but it wasn't her hand at all.

Just then, she snapped out of it and was back on the elevator. With one hand still gripping the handrail and the other on her chest, she fought to catch her breath.

Just then the doors opened to her floor and she gathered herself quickly before exiting. Arya landed heavily in her chair at the cubicle she was assigned on the 5th floor. Thoughts ran wild in her head. Never had she experienced such a clear and overwhelming vision. It took her a few minutes to truly catch her breath and calm herself.

Previous visions, if she could call them that, were almost like experiencing déjà vu. No clear vision, just a sense that she knew what was about to happen. Only a few times had she seen a quick flash of an object or scenery, but nothing animated as if she was really there experiencing it.

Moments later she called Lou and confirmed what she just saw was related to their case. It was an awkward call to say the least and ended abruptly.

Her subsequent call with him did not go well either, but she had the feeling an in-person explanation might restore his confidence in her.

She started to head out of the office to return to Mableton. Exiting the elevator, she turned towards the security exit to the garage, and her ritual set in. Her eyes were drawn to the three cursive words above the doors for all agents to see as they left; **Fidelity, Bravery, Integrity**. The same thought went through her head every time, 'Be brave for others and yourself, Arya.'

It started in Quantico on her first day of basic training. She saw the FBI motto on one of the walls and thought to herself how bravery would be her challenge.

Her family was concerned by the stories she shared about the training at Quantico and how the place would weed out the weak or timid. Still, against her father's wishes, she passed the background checks and was accepted into the FBI.

Even though she was recruited, that didn't mean the job was hers. More like, the job was hers to lose if Quantico beat her.

In her past life, her definition of being brave was performing in front of others, but that became so routine that she was challenged to think when she had to truly be brave for someone else or herself.

Every day for five months in Quantico, Arya was tested physically and mentally. What pushed her was her daily reminder to herself, 'be brave for others and yourself.'

After a couple of case exercises and other realistic shootouts in the streets and buildings of Quantico's infamous mock town, Hogan's Alley, her nerves settled, and she felt at home with the agency and the duties. However, the ritual stuck and not a day went by without her saying it in her head or out loud.

As she approached the exit where two security guards stood by the metal detector and x-ray machine that every person must pass through to entered the FBI building, she noticed a third guard heading towards her. He had a clipboard in his hand and was obviously looking at it and at her several times as if comparing her to a photo.

"Special Agent Shah?" he asked as he approached.

"Yes, what is this about?"

"The Director wants to speak to you."

"Okay, I will call him. I'm on my way to a crime scene."

"He was pretty direct with his instructions. I am to ensure you see him in person. I apologize for the inconvenience."

Arya turned around and headed back toward the elevator. To her surprise, the guard followed her onto the elevator.

"Is this really necessary? I know my way to the Directors office."

"Yes, ma'am. I'm just following orders."

They rode the elevator to the 7th floor. Arya couldn't recall ever visiting the Directors office.

Director Thomas Pitman Cooley was usually navigating his way through the building, popping in for updates or attending briefings in person. Otherwise, he spent the majority of his time in the Bull Pen. Everyone in the agency respected the Director. He was one of them at one time, spending 20 years in the field and part of many high-profile cases that helped his promotions. He was tall, broad shoulder with a linebacker's physique and a deep voice to match his frame.

As she knocked on his door, the security guard started to walk away.

"Come in."

Arya entered the Directors office and stood in front of his desk. It appeared he was finishing up a call as he motioned for her to take a seat.

"Agent Shah, I'm sorry for the dramatics. However, I had to speak to you in person on this matter and it could not wait."

"No problem. What's this about, sir?"

"It's about this Detective Abrams you are working with."

Arya did not move a muscle, but it took all of the will power she had to not react to Lou's name.

"I read your reports for the last two days and have been impressed with this detective. He has an impressive record from Arizona and Georgia. I did some extensive research and found him to be highly competent in field work and more importantly research. This much you probably know from witnessing him in action and reading his case files and profile. What I can't find is anything of the personal nature, like religious beliefs, hobbies, stress relievers, or strangely...family and friends."

"Excuse me, sir, but what do these things have to do with finding Lars Bowman?" Arya asked.

"Nothing." The Director answered frankly. His pause seemed like eternity to Arya and she was tempted to press the issue, but thought better of it.

"However, if one were to find a very capable individual with very little commitments, other than catching bad guys at a highly effective rate, one might find this individual invaluable to their organization. Arya, have you ever been asked to recruit a prospect for the FBI?"

"I have not, sir." She was almost flabbergasted at the

direction this conversation was going and now clearly understood why this would not be an appropriate phone conversation.

"We ask this of agents from time to time. Jones tells me you and Detective Abrams have quickly developed a rapport. This is good.

She felt her muscle tense again and her heart started to race as she thought of last night's intimate moments. "He is easy to work with and that is refreshing considering what we typically face when we come in to someone else's house."

"And you stand by your assessment of his abilities?"

"Yes, but how...I mean, what is protocol for recruiting a law enforcement officer?"

"Look, I would like for you to continue to partner with Abrams on this case. Think of how you were recruited. Casually ask the questions that fill in the blanks and make further notes on his aptitude and potential in this organization. We had a few transfers recently and lost 3 great agents in the Highlands Park raid last month. I could use a few good prospects. It seems DC, New York, Miami and other East coast offices are getting all the recruits these days. We need to mark our territory when it comes to prospects before those high-profile offices get their claws in them at Quantico. Are you up to this?"

"I believe so. Is there a clock on this?" she asked.

"The sooner the better, but I understand that timing is everything. I trust you will handle this right. If this works out, it will look great in your file. If you will excuse me, I have to make some calls." With that, Arya was dismissed.

As she left the office, Arya felt like there was more to this request than just recruiting 'Detective Abrams'. She buried that suspicion and refocused on what was just asked of her. Her approach had to be genuine with Lou to avoid putting their newly formed trust and partnership at risk. Nor did she want to ruin their...connection? She shook her head and thought to herself, 'Get it together woman.' Before she knew it, she was driving down the Interstate towards Mableton.

CHAPTER 12

I stood out front as the coroner's van pulled up. The CSI team was done with the scene and the medical examiner had told me what I already knew.

Jones was 10 minutes into grilling a security officer and police officer that were on shift last night during the homicide. There is being thorough and then there is Jones. He was looking through their cell phones to see if they had any activity that would have distracted them from their duties. The only piece of interesting news he gathered was that two men used the pool area around the time in question. I must have looked distracted as Jones walked over to me and put his hand on my shoulder.

"Hey, you doing okay?" Jones asked.

"She was a sweet lady who minded her own business. I will be alright once I get over how angry I am right now. How could this happy right under our noses?" I was livid that Lars was not only stalking me but was doing so at will and through our security.

My heart went out to Ms. Brown, but I had to get a hold on this anger before I could afford to grieve. She was like a grandmother I never had.

"I'm going to go track down these two guys at the pool last night, see if they saw anything." Jones released my shoulder with a double pat and started to walk away. I was tempted to tell him they could barely tell their ass from their head and would not be much help, but kept my sarcasm to myself for once.

Arya pulled in as the coroners were closing the doors on the van. I could see the concern on her face as she approached me.

"Lou, I'm so sorry." She already had both her hands cupping my left hand, but it was her eyes that truly showed me how much she cared, how much she hurt with me, how much she wished she could have prevented it all from ever happening.

I put my other hand on top of hers and squeezed briefly before we both disconnected.

"Tell me we have a chance to stop him before someone else dies. Tell me and I will focus on that possibility. I need to hear the truth, Arya."

"These are never good stories, Lou, but with our involvement the FBI has exponentially increased the capture and prosecution rate of predators like Lars. BAU involvement leads to extremely high success rates. We will get him." Arya stated with confidence.

It was enough to settle my nerves for the moment, but the anger was still churning just below the surface.

This was not the place or time to start asking Arya about the vision she had, but I could tell she was dying to share the experience and see if I would call her crazy or appreciate her even more than I already do.

I advised her that Jones was around the corner talking to neighbors that were out last night. Before I could suggest taking a walk to the car for a private chat, I noticed Andy out of the corner of my eye making a scene.

About twenty feet to my left was a police officer talking to Lacey. It appeared she was trying to come over to check on me, but the officer was doing his job and keeping her away from the scene.

Andy seemed conflicted. He was trained to support the Blue, but being especially attached to Lacey had him barking at both of them. I turned back to Arya who was also noticing the scene unfold.

"That's one of my neighbors. Let me go grab Andy and meet you in your car. I feel like you have something to share with me that can't wait." Hoping to divert her attention away from Lacey for a moment, I started to walk away before she could reply. Arya turned and starting walking towards her car.

As I approached Andy, he immediately calmed down. Lacey looked worried and I wasn't sure anything I could share at this time would give her relief.

"Hi, Lacey. It's okay, Officer, she is my neighbor." The officer took a few steps back still holding his position. When Lacey reached out and put her hand on my shoulder, asking me if I was okay, the officer was kind enough to give us even more space.

"I'm okay. I have some terrible news though. Ms. Brown was the victim of a violent crime last night that I believe was intended to get back at me regarding a case I'm involved in. There is a killer on the loose and we are doing everything we can to catch him." I reluctantly shared with her.

Lacey's hands were now over her mouth to conceal her gasp and water was forming in the corner of her eyes. She turned away for a brief moment to wipe her eyes and gather herself. When she came back around, I could see her lips trembling.

"She was...this job...how do you do it?" She was visibly scared as she watched the coroner's van pull out. "Lou..." I could see she was about to lose it at the sight of what the van represented. The end of a life, someone we knew, someone we appreciated, a good sole lost to a senseless act violence. My anger was boiling inside now, but I did the only thing that made sense at the moment. I hugged her. She embraced it tightly.

The thought entered my mind, 'I wish she didn't have to see all this.' Just then I felt the warmness overtake my body and the knot tighten in my stomach. My hands were on her upper back and close to her neck and they began to burn.

As if we both knew what was about to happen next, we simultaneously broke apart swiftly. She had this surprised look on her face that I barely caught before she played it off. She wiped her tears away again and her facial expression was back to concern and grief.

"Are you okay, Lacey?" I took a step back to give her space. If I didn't know any better, she felt the energy I was about to use unintentionally.

Truthfully, I didn't think I had the energy to pull something off like that today. More concerning is how it was about to happen, and I didn't even have time to think about it. It was as if my emotional thought trumped any response time to reason if the action was what I really wanted to do. Where the hell is the fail-safe on this process!

"I'm okay, I think. Naturally, I'm not feeling well after hearing this news, but I will be okay. Oh my God, you said a killer is after you! What the hell Lou?"

"I can't get into details now, but this is why the extra security is here. We never would have expected this to happen with all the extra security. Is there some place you can go for a few days? I know I would feel better if you were not around this." I almost said 'around me,' but it was implied.

"I know you have to go now. I can see your partner waiting for you. I'm not going anywhere, Lou. This is my home. By the way, you're not the problem." She touched my hand and started to walk away. After about a few steps, she turned back around and said. "We should probably reschedule our dinner. I will not accept a straight cancellation, as that would be a blow to my ego. How about next Friday?"

"That's a good idea and yes." I replied.

"Will you check in on me from time to time this week? I'm not needy, I swear. I'm just worried about you."

"I will, I promise. Stay safe and stay close to Michelle." As I started to leave, I told the officer to keep a close eye on her and her roommate. They just seem like the type of distraction Lars would allow himself during his quest to kill me.

Arya was patiently waiting for me by her car. She was talking on her phone as she watched Lacey and me part ways. If she was curious about Lacey and me being anything more than neighbors, it didn't show. She hung up and put the phone back in her belt clip opposite her handgun.

"Lou, our bosses are all caught up. We have a few moments to go grab a coffee and talk, if you like?" She was already getting in to the car as I arrived at the passenger side door with Andy.

"Do you mind if Andy tags along?"

"Not at all."

Andy was already jumping from the front seat to the back when a car driving by backfired. I guess my nerves were on edge. As I was getting into the car I over reacted a bit by propelling myself practically into Arya's lap. The impact of my chest onto the middle console where the computer was mounted knocked the wind out of me, slowing my response time to recover.

"Lou. Lou, are you alright?

I must have cracked my sternum. I was really struggling to catch my breath.

"I... I'm just trying to catch my breath. Damn, my chest hurts." I started to pull my legs in the car to sit up and without warning Arya floored the accelerator sending the car forward with such force that the door closed barely missing my foot.

"Jesus, Lou, you have been shot in the back! Don't move." I felt her hand pushing on my back.

The car was already heading down the road sirens on, when the real pain kicked in. It felt like someone stuck me with a hot knife and was slowly twisting it to intensify the agony. I tried sitting up, but the pain made me instantly dry heave. The pain shot up my back and I became very light headed.

"Don't move! We will be at the hospital in just a minute. Please, don't move!"

I could hear her talking over the radio to dispatch notifying them shots fired, location..., officer down, on route to hospital.

"Arya..." I tried lifting myself off the middle console to try to give myself a fighting chance for a full breath, but my muscles gave out, sending my head into her lap heavily.

"Lou, please don't move! Your back is soaked in blood. I can't tell where the entry wound is." There was panic in her voice.

I could hear Andy whimpering in the back seat and then I blacked out.

I woke up and the car was still moving. I could hear Arya saying, "wake up, stay with me." Not sure how long I was passed out, I knew what I had to do before I passed out again. I could barely hear myself think with the engine roaring and sirens blazing.

"Arya, turn off the sirens."

"What? Why?" She was clearly confused by my request.

"Trust me. Turn off the sirens." It took so much energy to speak over the sirens. I needed her to hear me.

"Okay. We are about 1 minute away. Sirens are off." She announced.

With the noise gone, I could hear myself think for a second.

"Listen." I said quietly in between breathes. "I need for you to do something for me without question for now."

"What is it, Lou?"

"Without question, Arya. I will explain later."

"Yes, tell me."

"Don't leave my side until I wake up from surgery. Sequester all notes, records, tapes of the operating team and any doctor or nurse that is involved." She was about to say something while I was catching my breath, but I began again. "As far as the official report goes...this was a flesh wound, straight through. Promise me."

"Jesus, Lou, this is anything but a flesh wound. I'm really worried and you are asking for everyone to call it a flesh wound? I could lose my job for pulling a stunt like that. What the hell is going on?"

"I could lose much more if you don't do it. Promise me. I will explain later." I was really struggling to speak now and the light headedness was winning the battle between consciousness and unconsciousness.

The car came to a stop and my door flew open. I could see someone sliding a back board in behind me. Arya was already out of the car to allow another member of the medical team to enter to strap my head to the board. Then everything went dark again.

◆ ◆ ◆

Arya was stepping out of the way as a team of medical personnel removed Lou from the car. He was passed out now and looking very pale. She opened the back door and got Andy from the car. As the team flew through the ER doors, the first police car pulled up. She was replaying the conversation in her head and torn on what to do next. The officer could see blood on her pants and arm as he approached.

"Ma'am, are you alright?"

"Yes, I'm fine. Please inform your Captain that Special Agent Shah will be going in with Detective Abrams and will provide an update A.S.A.P." She said as she flashed her credentials.

"Yes Ma'am. How is he doing?" The officer asked. Another two police cars were pulling in now.

"He was shot from behind and I don't know if it hit anything serious yet. Can you take Andy for now, please? I will collect him later." She handed the officer her keys and Andy's leash and headed in through the ER doors.

It was a scene of controlled chaos. People were moving in every direction yelling out to each other. They already had Lou in a triage area with several doctors and nurses transferring him from the board to the bed.

Arya was able to get close enough to see a nurse cut off his shirt exposing a whole the size of a quarter slightly to the right of his spine in the middle of his back. She could hear a doctor mention massive internal bleeding as he slid an ultrasound device over the area. They were all working attentively to stop the bleeding and stabilizing him to move to surgery.

Arya started pacing close by until a security guard asked her to move away. She immediately flashed her badge and asked for the names of the ER RN, Lead Physician in ER and the Operating Room Supervisor. Instincts kicked in and she went to work on the crazy request Lou had given her.

She had the security guards keeping the local police far enough away and the curtains closed. Before she knew it, she had the major players running the ER and Operating room in her presences explaining to them the sensitivity of this case and that the status of the victim needs to follow gag order protocol, forbidding public discussion of the wounds sustained in this ongoing investigation.

Evidence gathered from the victim must be provided directly to her either in the ER or Operating room and not leave sight or custody to prevent evidence from being compromised in chain of custody.

She explained the victim is Native American and has specific religious requests that must be followed to avoid possible lawsuits. Until those arrive, he will be placed in a private room post op.

Someone from legal showed up asking if a judicial writ was on its way. Arya stalled them by lying that she is in contact with her Director and the legal documents are on the way.

She reminded them all that any medical notes, documents, transcripts must be sealed. She asked them to ensure the staff were made aware of the secrecy and protocol, as she was calling her Director in Atlanta.

Arya was kicking herself for digging such a deep hole. She had one chance to pull this off without losing her career.

As the Director answered his phone, Arya immediately cut to the chase.

"It's Shah. Do I have any favors to call in from you, sir?"

"That depends. What do you need?"

Arya explained the shooting, the request, the potential screw up of over using her authority and the position it put her and perhaps Director Cooley in. He seemed pretty calm about what he just took in.

"Shah, let me see if I understand you. I need to get a Sequestration from a Judge immediately and have it delivered to Emory Hospital to seal all medical notes on Abrams, and have a gag order for the staff?" Director Cooley asked.

"Yes sir. How much trouble am I in?" Arya asked.

"That depends on two things. First, if I can pull this off, you are in the clear legally. It's Friday afternoon. Finding a Judge that I can work with may be damn near impossible. Secondly, if he recovers and is duty cleared, you recruit him successfully. This is highly abnormal. I suppose this has something to do with his culture or religion?" He asked the question as if talking to himself.

Without thinking, Arya replied, "yes sir, he is Zuni, and they are private people. If he requested this, I assume it is to protect their ways. He said he would explain later. I trust that he will."

"Alright. Let me call in some favors myself. Hold tight." With that, the line went dead and Arya's chest felt very heavy.

CHAPTER 13

He was fuming that his emotions got the best of him. Just as he was starting to enjoy the close encounters and attention this cat and mouse game brought, he got caught up in the moment.

The hours leading up to Detective Abrams being shot, Lars had found a remote house for sale and broke in for temporary safe haven. He had been using a police scanner and listening to the chatter going on at Detective Abrams place, when he decided to get a closer look.

After watching the activity in Detective Abrams duplex parking lot from down the road, he was overcome with the urge to be a part of it all.

Reaching into his backpack, he took out the old double barrel flintlock and went to work. Minutes later he was driving down the road slowly taking in the scene, left hand on the wheel and the right hand holding steady the gun that lay across his left elbow pointing out the window. Part of him wanted to get caught. Part of him wanted to kill.

He could feel his heart racing with excitement as he pulled the trigger one last time. The crack of the hammer, the spark and then the loud explosion right in front of his face was deafening and blinding.

Smoke went into his eyes and nostrils, burning his senses and temporarily overwhelming him. He barely kept his wits and held the left hand steady for a few more seconds as he waited patiently for his eyes to recover. He was forcing them to open against their will, but finally his right eye cracked under pressure just enough for him to see he was about to veer off the road. The left eye finally opened, and he floored it sending the car racing down the road.

Arya was in the observation room overlooking Lou in surgery. When they retrieved all the parts of the lead ball that ripped through his back, she observed the nurse package and deliver it directly to her outside the operating room.

"How is it going in there?" Arya cautiously asked the nurse. She was feeling useless and cut off from the support group fellow officers provide each other during times like this, but that was her doing.

"He is doing surprisingly well for the amount of damage. This thing really did a number on him. They believe it hit two ribs, sending bone and metal shrapnel everywhere. I think they will be done within the hour. I can't go back in due to bringing this to you. By the time I scrub back in, they will be done. You will have to wait until they are done to get a full assessment." she told Arya sympathetically.

Hours had past as she waited anxiously for Lou's surgery to be done and for word from Director Cooley. The phone call came minutes before the surgery had finished. The Director came through and department heads were receiving the faxed documents in order to hold them over until the actual ones arrived later in the day.

Arya thanked him profusely. He did not remind her how deep in debt this put her with him, as he seemed more concerned with her and Detective Abrams at the moment. This is what made him a great Director. He knew just what his people needed and timing was everything. Arya was sure he would call in this favor at some point, but he would not allow for it to linger over her head like a dark ominous cloud.

Half of the police department was waiting one floor

down and Arya new she owed them an update. She called the Captain and filled him in on everything. This was her second update to him. The first call did not go very well as she had to break the news of the gag order and then calm him down. It's unheard of for the police to not receive updates on their own. She promised to give him the next update as soon as Lou was out of surgery.

She could see they were prepping Lou to be transferred to a private ICU room and started to follow the team as she gave the Captain an update. She assured him that as soon as Lou was awake and allowed to have visitors she would pass along the news. For now, he was stable and being delivered to a private room in ICU where she was going to station a guard.

The Captain still wasn't happy with the process and lack of detail but was thankful for Abrams doing okay. Arya asked the Captain to come up personally to take the evidence from her. When they met, he was very appreciative for her quick thinking earlier and gave her a quick update on the shooting.

He told Arya that Jones and a team of police officers and detectives were still at the duplex wrapping up the second crime scene in the parking lot. The Department of Transportation was lending resources to review all street camera footage and red light still shots to see if anything would come up showing the car or face of the shooter they already suspected to be Lars.

They had already interviewed three civilian eyewitnesses along with two officers who were at the scene when the shooting occurred.

All were surprisingly similar in their descriptions of a tan sedan driving slowly by when it apparently backfired. Black smoke was seen trailing behind the car as it sped back up. They both had already jumped to the conclusion that it was the same murder weapon used on the kidnapped girls, an old musket of some sort. If that were true, that would make this one of the luckiest shots consider the conditions and type of gun used. The Captain left with the evidence and Arya returned to Lou's room.

Once the nurses were done situating Lou into the private ICU room and bed and had every monitor connected to him, they left Arya alone in the room with the security guard out front. Lou had already come out of the sleep twice, momentarily, but fell back into it both times. She pulled a chair close to the bed and held his hand.

"Lou, you owe me one hell of an explanation, so you better get better quick." Arya said quietly. She looked him over and noticed the color back in his face. She wanted badly to look into his blue eyes and reciprocate a smile, that same smile that melted her last night.

Arya knew these feelings for Lou were developing faster than she was comfortable with, but they were hard to resist. A part of her did not want to resist the feelings. On that note, she stood up and left the room. Pausing just long enough to tell the guard that no one was to enter until she returned. Avoiding the police down stairs, she went one wing over and took the stairs down to the main floor. She had an errand to run.

I woke up to a quiet room and thankfully no pain. My movement was definitely limited and I had no energy. The blinds were closed, but it didn't matter as the sun had already set. There were monitors on my chest, arm and finger. I followed the IV line up to a bag, but could not read the wording. Another line ran to a machine that I suspected dispensed morphine on command.

The pain in my back was nothing like it was earlier, it was tolerable now. I lowered the covers and lifted my gown to see that I was wrapped from chest to waist.

These situations are always a little tricky, but this one

takes the cake. There was no way out of this without Arya's help. The real question was, did she already put things in motion to mask the healing I would experience over the next day or two.

The door opened and a nurse came in. I could see a guard standing out front. Hopefully that meant Arya had put plans in place to protect my privacy. The nurse explained the morphine monitor, IV fluids, and antibiotics that were connected to my arm.

"So, what's the verdict? How am I doing?" I asked.

"Honestly, I don't know. I just came on. I was asked to only explain the fluids, check your bandage and tell you a doctor will see you later. Sorry." She adjusted the bed to the upright position and leaned me forward for a few seconds.

"Looks good. Rest up and don't put any stress on your back muscles. Call if you need anything." She reclined the bed to a 45-degree angle and left the room.

Using the morphine never crossed my mind, until she leaned me forward. The back muscle felt like they were on fire now and it was not gradually subsiding. I needed to think straight before Arya or the doctor came in. Just then Arya walked in holding a vase of purple tulips. She paused at the door with a slightly surprised expression on her face from the sight of me being awake.

"Are those for me?" I asked with a slight astonished tone and a smile.

She walked over to the side of my bed and gently placed the vase on the table.

"I don't know whether to hit you or kiss you." She let out a sigh and I could see all the stress and worry she had carried these past hours.

I reached out offering my hand, hoping she would take it. After a pause that felt like eternity, she put her hand in mine and looked me in the eyes.

"Thank you, Arya. Thank you for looking out for me and trusting me." I squeezed her hand lightly and tried to sit up. If my back could talk, it would have screamed 'Holy Hell." I winced in pain.

"Jesus Lou, we are picking up right where we left off. Sit still!" She put her hand on my shoulder and leaned over. "Are you in pain? Should you hit your morphine button?"

"I'll be okay. Arya, we really need to talk." I really need to know what has been going on and to see if I had the courage to share with her my gift.

She stood back up and said, "Yes, we do. Your request created a few problems for me. I'm not sure how deep in debt you are to me yet, because I'm not even sure how deep I'm in with my Director for pulling strings. Without you being awake to voice or write your own request for privacy, I had to trump up a gag order and sequester the medical notes. Everyone is pissed at me, but they all believe this has to do with your Native American culture and chain of evidence pulled from you." Arya was getting a bit annoyed.

"Those are both legitimate reasons for what happened and for how you are handling the case we are on." This was going smoother than I thought. These were perfect reasons for privacy. Now I just need a great reason to slip out of here.

"We" she emphasized. "We are not on the case anymore. You are laid up for at least a week or two and then physical therapy starts. All of this takes months before you are cleared for duty."

"I'm a fast healer." I said with a smile.

"I'm sure you are. Listen, about that vision I had, I want to explain." She pulled the chair over close to the bed and sat down. It was as if she was lifting this huge weight off her chest when she spoke. It almost felt like a confession as more and more examples poured out of her. She gave me the full history from childhood to recent event, how she tried harnessing it and how she has chosen to hide it from everyone.

Somewhere in the middle of her tell me everything, our hands met up again. Each time she looked down while telling me more, I squeezed her hand to bring her eyes back to mine.

It was an extremely vulnerable moment for her and I wanted her to feel as comfortable as possible sharing this with me. When she finished, she let go of my hand and covered her face with her hands while saying, "That's everything." Then her hands moved up her face and ran through her hair as she repositioned herself preparing for my reaction. I knew what she needed to hear, but I wanted to deliver it in an unconventional way.

"Do you like me, Arya?" When I asked her the off-topic question, it threw her for a moment.

"Wha..what?"

"You brought me flowers. I think you really like me." I kept pressing.

"It's what one is supposed to do under these circumstances. Did you hear a word I just said? Jesus, I mean, I'm confiding in you and you are wondering if I like you?"

"I heard every word and you didn't answer me. That's okay. One curve ball deserves another. I'm glad you're sitting down for this. I think I really like you. It's crazy, right? However, the heart doesn't lie. When the nurse walked in, I was so disappointed it wasn't you. When you walked in a minute later, my heart noticeably stopped. What would you call that?"

"I would call that confusing your current state of pain and drugs for being happy to see a familiar face after a life and death situation." she rationalized as she started to stand up.

"If you don't kiss me right now Arya, I'm going to triple tap this morphine button..." Before I could finish my sentence she swooped down on me so fast that when her lips hit mine, her long hair fell all around my head hiding us under the black velvet blanket for a private, intimate moment. I reached up and held the back of her head to let her know this kiss needed to be a long one. She wasn't going anywhere as she was enjoying the affection too. As the kiss came to an end, she moved her lips from mouth to my ear and whispered to me.

"I think I really like you too." As she returned to her

chair next to me, I noticed the warmth spreading across my body. The knot in my stomach was very noticeable and my hands were on fire. Then my chest started to pound like a drum. I thought about the morphine for a second and then instinctively put my hands on my chest where the pain was. It felt like someone was digging in my sternum with a dull stick. Then it happened, right in front of Arya.

My back arched and my chest looked like I was taking in the biggest breath of air in my entire life. My hands would not leave my chest and Arya started to look concerned.

"Lou, what is going on? Are you okay?" She was standing over me now and placing a hand on mine. She instantly pulled her hand back as if she had touched a hot stove.

I managed to say, "I'm fine...Don't worry." But she definitely looked worried.

As quick as it came, it left me. My chest fell and my back hit the bed heavy, but there was no pain. My healing always came from within, so I found it very strange that I just laid hands on myself.

I started to cough, and Arya saw some blood trickle out the corner of my mouth. She immediately started to head for the door to call a doctor. I felt something metallic in my mouth.

"Wait!" I said as she was opening the door. "Arya, look at this." I took the piece of shrapnel out of my mouth and held it out to her.

She walked over and looked at it with amazement. She knew exactly what it was, but just could not believe I coughed it up.

"You need a doctor, Lou." she said as she took the piece of lead from my hand.

"No, I don't. Trust me, just like you did moments ago when you shared your unbelievable burden and gift with me. I think it's time you hear my story too." I took the same leap of faith she took with me and started from the beginning.

As I told my story to Arya, it was hard for her to believe.

She would look me over as if looking for signs that would declare me extraterrestrial and other times just stare at me with her hand over her mouth. Towards the end, it started to sink in and she put two and two together interrupting me.

"Did you do something to me last night? Did you? Is that why I felt so different? Wholly Shit! It's no coincidence that I had such a clear and animated vision today is it?" She didn't know what to do with her hands. They were moving all over her body, but ended at her mouth. She seemed to cover her mouth when she was wrestling with thoughts.

"Look, I didn't do anything bad to you. Please know that if anything happened last night, it was by accident. I was attracted to you and that was an honest moment for me." I explained.

"You can control it, can't you?"

"Yes, for the most part." Honesty probably was not the right choice at this moment for this question, but all the cards were on the table. Screw it.

"For the most part?" She was about to follow that up with something, but I jumped in.

"I have learned a great deal and have found many different ways to harness and use it for healing myself and others. However, there have been a couple of occasions where the energy just decided that the person I was touching needed healing. It happens so fast I barely catch it. I'm starting to get better at catching it though."

"Do you think your energy knew that my visions needed help? Is that how this works?" She asked.

"I'm not sure, Arya, but that is possible. Strange, but possible given my history." I said honestly.

"I think this is incredible. If what you are saying is true, well, this is just incredible. I don't know what to say or think. I'm sorry." She was probably deciding whether to be shocked by the amazing truth or shocked that I was crazy.

"Well, that is to be expected. There are days I don't believe it myself. A dramatic demonstration would be to cut myself and watch the healing in a matter of minutes. But I have had enough dramatics for a day, so why don't we just look at the wound on my back tomorrow morning? It should be healed by then."

"You are kidding now, right? You were shot and had surgery today. Do you really believe you will be healed by tomorrow morning?" Arya asked doubtfully.

"It's a lot to take in Arya. Outside of the reservation, only one person knows. I don't expect you to believe me without proof. But I am asking for you to give me the same benefit of doubt I gave you. Will you do that for me?" I was counting on her. I really needed her to believe in me and accept me.

"I'm not sure I don't believe you, but I am being honest that I am struggling with this. Perhaps coming back in the morning will give me the time I need to process this. God, I must sound horrible. You took my news so well and then I am acting so unsure of myself right now." She grabbed my hand and leaned over giving me a peck on the lips.

"If I come back in the morning and shoot you, it's because I think you are either an alien or a psychopath." We both got a laugh out of that comment.

"Thanks for not making me feel like a total freak, Arya."

"No problem. Honestly though, there is a part of me that thinks you may have a screw loose." she said with a sarcastic smile. "What a day. We both need some rest. I will see you in the morning freak."

"Right back at you." I said.

As she was about to open the door, she turned and said, "By the way, those are violet variegated tulips. I put some thought into those. Those flowers mean beautiful eyes." With that, she left for the night. Perhaps this would work out. I guess if Arya does not shoot me in the morning, there is hope. However, I still needed a plan to get back to work without raising questions. At the moment, that seemed impossible.

CHAPTER 14

In the middle of the night, I woke up in a cold sweat. The dream had returned. Only this time there were familiar faces throughout the nightmare. It was all too real. I was moved to an observation room where no one would talk to me. My wrist and ankles were tethered to the bed rails restricting my movement.

Every time a nurse or doctor would enter, I would demand answers about my release, only to be confronted with their stares and silence. They would run tests, write in their charts, check my vitals, draw blood and be on their way.

This version had a window where people I knew would come and go in pairs, not to talk to me or even recognize that I was trying to get their attention. They were there to witness what a freak I was and converse their disbelief and throw disapproving glares my way before they left.

This happened three times during the night until I decided enough was enough at 4 A.M. and turned on the TV. I was hoping to find a boring old film to take my mind off the dream, but instead found myself listening to a recap of the news story from yesterday that put me in the center of the spot light.

When 5 A.M. rolled around I called the nurse in and asked her to open the blinds. Thankfully my room was East facing and had a window. When 6 A.M. came I gathered myself and managed to get out of bed. Rolling the monitors and IVs with me, I stood in front of the window soaking up the morning rays. I turned my back towards the window and opened my gown exposing myself to any nosey pedestrian looking up into my second story window. It took a few minutes, but I managed to take all the bandages off.

As soon as the Sun hit my back, I felt a surge of heat pulse through my body, followed by immense pain centered in the area I was likely shot. It took all my strength not to fall to the floor, curl up and scream.

This went on for a few minutes causing me to sweat and tremble before the pain started to subside to a manageable level. I felt my ribs pop and release some tension allowing me to take a full relaxed unlabored breath. Minutes later, the energy started to mask any pain I had, and goose bumps started to appear on my arms.

I hung around the window for about 30 minutes soaking in the sun and thinking what my next move would be to get out of here without raising too much suspicion. My focus was blocked by the overwhelming hunger that hit me.

I got back in bed and called the nurse again. When she came in moments later, I asked for a huge breakfast. She just stared at me and reread my chart.

"This chart doesn't say much about you or your condition, but it does outline no solids for 48 hours. I'm sorry, but I can only bring you ice chips and maybe some sort of protein shake if the doctor clears it." she mentioned as she started to walk out.

I picked up the phone and called Arya.

"This is agent Shah."

"Arya, good morning, it's Lou."

"Hey there, I should be able to stop by within the hour. How are you feeling?"

"Exceptionally well, so don't bring your gun in with you." This got a chuckle out of her followed by a bit of uncomfortable silence.

"Hey, are you up for a secret mission this morning? The docs will not give me real food and I know what my body needs. Can you bring me some substance, please". I begged.

"No problem. I will see you soon."

Forty minutes later my cell phone rang. On the other end was a familiar voice I had not heard in a while.

"Lusio, can you hear me? It's Lolotea."

"Lolo, it's been awhile, how are you?" I hadn't spoken to Lolo for over 2 months. This was mainly my fault as I had been meaning to call her and catch up. We typically take turns calling each other and staying in touch.

Ever since we went our separate ways after high school, we stayed in each other's lives. She is now a Professor of Anthropology at UC Davis in California and she never stops bringing me theories on where my gift comes from. Our conversations are never mundane and she is the only one who calls me Lusio other than my mom.

"I'm fine, Lusio. Your Captain called me." I could tell she was concerned and a little upset I hadn't called her to tell her I was okay.

"Don't worry, I'm okay. It's no big deal. I'll be out of here in no time." Perhaps the honest but nonchalant approach would console her.

"I'm sure you will be, Lusio, and I'm glad to hear your confidence. Unfortunately, there is a second reason I'm calling." There was hesitation in her voice.

"What is it, Lolo? Is everything okay with you?"

"It's your mother, Lusio, she is not well. I'm flying out to Albuquerque today. Not knowing when you would be able to get out there, I thought it best not to wait for you."

I lost my father when I was a kid. He was in Belgium for business and caught the flu. Being the workaholic that he was, he tried to keep working and that became a fatal mistake. We never knew he was even sick. A maid found him in his hotel room. My mother was all I had left and unfortunately the path I chose only allows for me to see her a few times a year, a few days at a time.

"I can be there tomorrow. What's going on with her?" I asked.

"I heard through a friend that lives on the reservation but frequently gets into the city. The tribes Medicine Man has been keeping her comfortable, but the Sky People don't have answers." she explained.

The Medicine Men have a special connection with the Sky People, our Gods that guide and teach them. I respect my culture and believe the rituals and ceremonies are what keep the pueblo's nucleus intact and balanced. However, I felt angered that my mom was not in a hospital receiving the best care possible. After all, we spent so much of our lives outside the Zuni reservation, I would think she would embrace the resources.

When I asked Lolo about this, she revealed that over the last 2 years my mother had started to reject the modern ways and reconnect into the Zuni way of life. Once I left, her days away from the reservation became less and less. She had been living with diabetes almost her entire life and was now with end-stage renal disease. Lolo believes my mother's diabetes had turned into chronic renal failure over 5-6 months ago, and now refusing dialysis she is being consumed by toxin the kidneys can't filter out. I was so angry I couldn't even talk.

"Lusio?"

"I'm here. I'm just trying to wrap my head around how stubborn my mom can be. I will call you later when I have my flight plans. Thank you for calling me, Lolo, and thank you for dropping everything to be there for my mom." I said with sincerity.

"You're like my brother. I would do anything for you. I love you." She said

"I love you too, Lolo. Bye." I replied back as I hung up. I noticed Arya had walked in as we were saying our goodbyes. She had this inquiring faux jealous look on her face that was more forced for show as she exaggerated her hand movement placing her right hand on her gun while holding breakfast in the left.

"Did I mention Lolo to you yesterday when I was explaining my gift?" I asked innocently to the woman ready to draw on me.

"No, not by name." She said as she walked forward and slowly removed her hand from her gun. "Lucky for you, I'm not the jealous type and I figured she was someone close to you."

"You looked a little jealous." I said as I pointed to her gun.

"Don't flatter yourself. I can act jealous, but it doesn't mean that I am jealous. Shut up and eat this food." she said with a smile as she placed the bag on my lap.

"You are just what the doctor order, Arya. I really needed a smile right now." I said with a heavy sigh.

"What's up, Lou? Are you afraid I might shoot you if you haven't miraculously healed yourself yet? Well don't worry, I'm prepared to chalk it up to the morphine you were on last night." She pulled up a chair and took a breakfast burrito from the bag.

"It's not that. I just got a call from my lifelong friend, Lolo. My mom is dying from Kidney failure."

"Jesus, I'm sorry, Lou. I didn't know."

"That's what's bothering me too. I didn't know either. She kept it from me. I need your help to get to her by tomorrow. It doesn't sound like she has long."

"I'm sorry, but I don't see how that will be possible in your current state." Arya said sympathetically.

I was starving, so I chose to wait a few minutes for the dramatic unveiling of my recovery and dug into the breakfast burritos. I made quick work of them, as if I had just been rescued from a deserted island. She watched in amazement as I polished off two of them before she was even half done with hers.

"Hungry? God, I hope I did not just make you sick going against doctor's orders." she said.

"More anxious than hungry now. Thank you for the food. That was well needed." I started to sit up swinging my legs over the side of the bed towards her to stand and she flew out of her chair to stop me.

"Whoa there tough guy! Lay back before you ruin the nice work they did on you yesterday." She put her hands on my shoulders expecting little to no resistance as she guided me back down to a laying position, but was surprised to find a wall of resistance and an unwavering determination to stand. She went from resisting to helping, but then quickly noticed I was moving with ease. Seconds later we were face to face.

"I am putting my life in your hands, Arya. You are the only person outside of the Zuni tribe that knows my secret and I would like for it to stay that way." I said as I dropped my gown to the ground and stood there facing her with just my briefs on. She never looked down. She kept her eyes on mine as she took a step or two back.

"Wha..what are you doing?" She looked concerned, so I turned around exposing my back to her. I looked over my shoulder and saw her mouth wide open, just before she covered it with her hand. Disbelief turned into shock.

"Here, let me help you sit down. I imagine this is a lot to process." I reached out for her hand and she stepped further away, backing up to the window.

"Arya, it's me. I'm normal in every way, with the exception that I heal at an unexplainably fast rate."

"There is nothing normal about any of this. I was really hoping, I mean I was trying to, I don't think..." She was started to mumble under both hands that now covered her mouth and nose. I knew I had to snap her out of the shock but only had one stupid idea. I put myself between her and the door.

"Arya, it's me. I'm going to come to and you can either shoot me, please don't, or embrace me, and be thankful I'm okay." I tried to casually walk over to her and not look like a creepy almost naked alien she was probably making me out to be in her head right now.

"Don't, Lou." I was four feet away now. "Please stop." Two feet away and the hook came. Her right hand left her gun so fast and smacked me across the face with all her force. I spun around instantly rubbing my jaw and cheek.

"Damn, Arya. I said shoot or embrace. I was not ready for a right hook."

"I don't like to be told what to do. You left me no choice but to respond with appropriate force. Did that hurt?"

"Of course, it hurt. I said I heal fast. I still feel things. Shit, wow. You are incredibly strong." I was still a little off balance so I backed up a step and leaned my back against the window near her.

"I'm sorry, I'm confused and I felt a little pressured there. 'Shoot me or embrace me'...who says that to a woman freaking out and carrying a firearm?"

"I thought the two choices were extreme enough for you to pick the more comforting one, and we could have a bonding moment that cleared your head from the shock of the news. Hindsight, probably not the best on the fly plan I have come up with."

"I feel like my life has turned upside down ever since I met you." she said as she turned to me.

"Well, that's a little harsh." I said.

"Let me finish." She was now standing in front of me. "But somehow, you seem to ground me, even when you are the cause of it."

I couldn't help to notice the familiar magnetic pull we experienced two nights ago happening again. This is probably bad timing and I hope I am not causing this.

"I know this is bad timing, but are you feeling that magnetic pull again?"

"I'm a quick study, Lou. I will admit this healing thing has me a bit baffled. I think I am grasping it now. But this energy you speak of is something I feel connected to and need to understand." She removed my hand from my cheek and replaced it with her hand. "This is me embracing you and being thankful you are feeling better." She leaned into me, pressing her chest against mine and slowly planted a kiss on the inflamed side of my face.

I put my hands on her back but couldn't feel a thing through the bullet proof vest she was wearing. I gave her a hug anyways. I could sense her hands trying to avoid my back.

"Look, just get it over with. Touch the scars and ask the questions." I said as I turned around again.

She placed her hands on my back and examined the fresh scar. As she seemed to trace it with a fingertip, she said, "I had a vision last night."

"Really? Did you get more clues on Lars's whereabouts?"

"No, it was about us. We were flying in an FBI G5 together."

"Nice. Where were we going?" I asked

"The thing is, the FBI doesn't have its own jets. I mean, we can contract the use of them, but nothing like what I had dreamt. I have no idea where we were going." She turned me around. "I think it was a sign of sorts that is telling me to go with you or you to go with me, but I don't have any plans to travel, so it must be me going with you." she said very quickly.

"Well, I did just tell Lolo that I would meet her in Albuquerque tomorrow, but why would you go with me?"

"I don't know. Perhaps I need to go to better understand you. Perhaps there is more I need to say to you and this trip would allow me the time." She wasn't making much sense unless she just wanted to see and learn more about me and where I came from.

The Zuni are not really open to 'FBI visitors', but I could probably escort her onto the reservation with Lolo's help. We are two very respected tribe members who live on the outside and they do allow us some leeway.

"To tell you the truth, I need a way out of here that does not draw attention to me. Perhaps your vision is telling you to help me with that. Got any ideas?"

"I think we just roll with what I have already spun. Your

records are sealed; you are stable and doing well, but need a few days with your mother. When we get back, we get a different doctor to see you and clear you for duty."

It rolled off her tongue as if she had already put plenty of thought into it. I'm being played. She probably had honest feelings for me and the rapport was sincere, but she had a hidden agenda. Right now wasn't the time to pry it from her, so I went with her plan. It seemed solid enough to work.

She left and brought back a suit from my home. Within the next couple of hours she had it all planned out; plane tickets, packing, Roy taking Andy, our bosses supporting the leave for a few days. I was a little curious about how she gotten leave for herself, but when I asked, she said that she had promised the Captain to 'observe' me.

With her recommendation and a doctor's release the Captain may consider light duty upon our return. Her director seemed generous with her time, which made me believe even more that she had plans for me.

After my shooting, Lars's trail went cold, but the team was still working the case and pressing for more social media awareness and vigilance filtering through the calls and emails coming in from the county.

We were also hoping that with me out of the picture for a few days, it would give Lars pause to his next step. He seemed to be hell bent of snuffing me out, but now I'm off the grid and that will take some time for him to figure out when and where I will pop up next. To him, hopefully the game is a foot and I'm still his focus.

CHAPTER 15

After some small talk about my mom and stories of me and Lolo, I could tell Arya was still holding back something. Somewhere over the panhandle of Texas, I turned to Arya and said, "Come clean with me."

She looked at me, unbuckled her seat belt and moved the armrest up so she could turn and face me.

"I feel terrible that I have not told you yet. My Director read up on you and was very impressed. So impressed that he is allowing me to accompany you on this personal trip, but not just to 'observe' you to make sure you are okay. I was asked to recruit you." She admitted.

"Recruit me? That sounds exhausting." I said.

"Are you going to make this difficult for me?"

"Oh, yes, very much so. Do they give you a budget for such things?" I asked jokingly.

"On a serious note, this is important to my Director, thus important to me. I'm not a great sales person, but I figured I could at least walk you through it on the plane ride and answer any questions."

Over the next hour Arya discussed with me the ins and outs of Quantico, the training, the places the job has taken her, the different people she works with and the variety of work that keeps things interesting. The pay was a little better, but similar.

She mentioned her Director was looking for me to be part of the Atlanta office and then tip-toed around possibly relocating closer to the city for convenience.

The job and Agency did sound interesting and the career path options were endless. I was impressed on how professional Arya remained during the entire discussion. I almost anticipated a little flirting, slight touch of the hand to the arm, solid eye contact or just over selling it to me. However, she looked almost apprehensive about the whole conversation and it was definitely unrehearsed. I wasn't sure what to make of this.

"Arya, I won't string you along, so I will tell you now that I am interested. That's not a 'yes', but you have me on the hook in case you need to report back to your Director on progress." I said.

"Fair enough. Do you have any questions?" She asked.

"I do." I paused for a second. "Would you want to continue this partnership once I'm in your department?"

That caught her off guard. She could never play poker as her tell is too noticeable. Her hand went to her mouth and I could tell she was taking in one long breath. Then she turned to me again and I could see water building in her eyes. This was unexpected as she turned the table on me.

With a slightly shaking voice Arya replied, "Lou, do you fly often?"

"About three to four times a year to see my mom. Why?" I was honestly confused on where this was going and why she was getting worked up about my question.

"I..I am a very disciplined person. You have to be to work at the FBI. My grasp on assessing chaotic situations calmly for conflict resolution is top notch." She professed.

"I wouldn't doubt it. Where is this leading?"

She started to whisper "I have been sitting next to you for three hours, less than an inch away, fighting urges to climb on top of you, every minute of this flight, Lou!" She quietly repeated herself as she wiped a tear away. "Every minute of this flight."

"I didn't know. You hid it well. What can I do, should I move?" I felt bad. I have been feeling the magnetic pull off and on again, but didn't think to ask Arya how she was doing.

"Don't you dare move. We need to figure this out, Lou. I would like to continue this partnership, but we can't compromise each other. We really need to figure out how to work together and keep our focus. I mean I need to figure it out." She said.

Unfortunately, it was a full flight and the man sitting next to me pretending to sleep was probably hearing all of this.

"Look, we both need to figure this out." I leaned over and whispered to her, "I have been having the same feelings, urges too."

"What happens now?" She whispered backed.

"I don't know Arya. We will figure it out." I said as the pilot announced our decent.

As we walked up to the baggage carousel, I saw Lolo leaning against a nearby pillar scanning the crowd. When she saw me she pushed herself off the pillar and starting to walk in my direction while raising a hand. I waived back and headed her way. Arya didn't notice me veering off to the left to give Lolo a hug.

Lolo mentioned she wished we were meeting under better circumstances and then slapped my shoulder for not caller her sooner. When we caught up to Arya at the carousel, she was a bit surprised I had someone with me. I did not know Lolo was meeting us at the airport, but I should have.

"Arya, I would like to introduce you to my long- time friend, Lolotea Manooe." I said as we walked up to Arya. Lolo extended her hand and they smiled at each other as they shook hands.

Arya was still a little surprised by the introduction and took a second before responding, "Very nice to meet you, Lolotea. Lou has told me a great deal about you. All good of course."

"Probably not nearly enough and the stinker has not

told me anything about you. Typical of Lusio and he will pay for this." Lolo said as she tucked one arm under Arya's and started to escort her away, but not before saying to me, "You can handle the bags, right? We have some girl talk to attend to."

Oh, this is going great, I thought to myself as Arya looked at me over her shoulder with a smirk. Those two are going to be trouble together, I just know it.

Lolo wasted no time with Arya. "I knew by Lusio's childish grin and absolutely no mention of you until now, that you have to be someone he cares about. Do you know he has only had two serious relationships and neither time did he tell me about them until he just showed up with them one day out of the blue?"

"I did not know that. I think there is a lot I don't know. Although I will not deny there is something building between us, even though we have only known each other for 5 days." Arya explained.

"I knew after one date that I was marrying Roberto, my husband of eight years. We just clicked. I don't say that with any hidden implications, but chemistry is chemistry." Lolo commented.

"What if you were unsure of what ingredients were in the chemistry?" Arya asked.

Lolo stopped and turned to face Arya, "That's a very strange question. What do you mean?"

"It's just...there are times...I don't feel like I'm in control of myself when I'm around him. He has this...well, I think I'm more confused than anything. I'm sorry if I'm not making sense." Arya said.

"Arya, I know everything about Lusio. What do you need to know to help you sort out your feelings? I can be a little pushy, so tell me to stop prying if that's what you want." she said compassionately.

"No, I need someone to talk to about this." Arya said.

"I have a PHD in Anthropology, BS in Psychology and other areas of study that I don't care to bore you with, but I know I'm at least a great listener and on accession give good advice when asked." Lolo said with a smile.

Arya hesitated for a moment, "I assume you know about Lou's gift?"

"Okay. That's not where I thought this conversation was going to go. Wow. He told you? He has never told anyone and for good reasons." Lolo said quickly and quietly as her voice started trailing off to a mumble. She paused for a second and then came back with, "Are you thirsty? I could use a bottle of wine right about now."

"As great as that sounds, I think I just need some quick reassurance and encouragement. Perhaps some details that make me feel safe instead of reserved and unsure half the time I am around him." Arya confessed.

"Fair enough. Lusio has retrieved your bags. Let's figure out a good time to talk today. I don't want to make you wait any longer." Lolo suggested.

I walked up and they were obviously talking about me still as they clammed up upon my approach. "Alright, I figured this would happen and I actually thought of something very unlike me." I said. "I suspect Arya may want to talk to you about my healing and energy. Do you two want to meet up with me later at the hotel?" I looked at Arya to see if I guessed right.

"You wouldn't mind?" asked Arya.

"Not at all." I said to Arya, then turned to Lolo. "Tell her everything, even your crazy theories. I will meet up with you two in a couple of hours for dinner and then we can plan our visit to the reservation for the morning."

"Finally!" Lolo exclaimed. "I have been waiting for years to speak to someone other than you about this, Lou."

"This should be very interesting. See you later, Lou." Arya said as she took Lolo's arm and her bag and headed off to the parking garage.

With that, I was left alone to catch a cab to the hotel where I might hopefully soak up some sun before it set for the day.

Later at the hotel, during my bake in the setting sun poolside, I had time to think through how tomorrow would go.

Although my mom was being extremely stubborn against modern medicine, I knew once I saw her, I could convince her to let me heal her. She wasn't even 60 years old and has more wonderful years ahead of her. I have no intentions of standing by and just saying my goodbyes to her.

The rent-a-car was set up to be delivered at the hotel in the morning. We would have breakfast, pack up, and head out to the reservation for a day or two.

Arya and Lolo should be getting back soon to meet up for dinner, so I shaved and jumped in the shower. About halfway through the act, I heard something in the bedroom.

My first instinct was to grab my gun, but that would be pointless sense it was laying on my bed. Not smart and very unprofessional of me. The bathroom door slowly opened, and I could make out a tall figure through the etched glass of the shower door.

"Lou, can I come in?" Arya asked.

"Sure, I'll be out in a minute if you need to use the bathroom." I said.

The shower door opened, and Arya walked in with only a smile on. "That's not what I meant."

I was covered with soap as she pressed herself against me taking us both back a step under the shower. Her hands were slowly rubbing the suds off my skin.

"I thought about waiting for you in the bedroom, but I couldn't wait any more." she said as her lips found mine.

There was no denying the passion that erupted between us as we made love in the shower. There were several times we would slow down and just kiss or catch our breath as we held one another and just stared into each other's eyes.

Very few words were spoken as we explored each other in the light. We both had our scars but did not ask what they were from.

Arya had two scars parallel to each other, longer than 6 inches on her back that ran from her left shoulder down to the shoulder blade. They were deep and were clearly not from surgery.

Most of my would-be scars disappeared when healing, but I let a few wounds take the natural course to see if I could control not using my power. She found those on my arm, shoulder and mid-thigh. We just touched them and smiled as if telling the other 'you wear them well.'

After leaving the shower and drying off, I walked over to her and said, "I don't know about you, but I feel like ordering in and having more time with you alone."

"Do you think Lolotea would find us extremely rude for not making the time with her?" she asked, but I could tell she was wanting to stay in too.

I picked up the phone and called Lolo's room.

"Hello" Lolo answered.

"Hey, it's Lusio. Would you mind if we met for breakfast instead of dinner? This is the first time Arya and I have had a few moments to ourselves to sort some things out." I explained.

"No problem, Lusio. Say goodnight to Arya for me. She seems like a lovely person so don't screw that up. Okay?"

"Yes, Ma'am. Goodnight." I said as I hung up the phone.

Arya walked up to me, "Sort some things out huh?"

We ordered some room service and spent the night enjoying each other's company. Later in the evening some light conversations took place regarding the manhunt followed by what Arya and Lolo discussed over wine.

It seems Lolo is a fast talker and shared every detail of my past and every theory she ever ran by me on why I am the way I am.

Arya seemed to take it all well and shared she was more fascinated by Lolo's theories than freaked out by them. One in particular really caught her attention. Arya shared that Lolo spoke of her research on one particular theory involving Zuni Gods that descend from the sky to mate with Zuni females and years later come to claim the children.

I recalled this theory in detail, because Lolo seemed to personalize this one for me by telling me that before the God could come down years later to claim me, my mother moved away from the reservation and hid in the city where she met my father.

It was getting late in the evening and I was enjoying the bonding with Arya. She had a room down the hall, but since I left notice at the front desk for her and Lolo to have access to my room, she was able to get a key earlier and decided to stay with me.

We were lying in bed together talking for a while about these theories Lolo shared before I changed the subject to her.

"How did you get this?" I asked as my hand found its way to the scar on her back.

"Would you believe me if I told you it was from a Bengal Tiger?"

"I would have guessed you got it on the job, but tiger sounds more interesting and intense."

"I was around 18 years old and visiting a family about 100 miles south of Mumbai. They lived in a rural area on the edge of some jungle. Farmers had been destroying jungle, replacing it with fields of crops. There were a few tigers in the area. Some moved on claiming new areas, but apparently one was boxed out."

"Boxed out?"

"Yes. Tigers live alone and are very territorial. One of the tigers could not go deeper into the jungle without fighting through others, so it was boxed out and took the path of least resistance. Unfortunately, I happened to be in its way one day."

"That had to have been terrifying."

"It was and I was very lucky to escape death. Unfortunately, I can't say the same for the tiger. He was hunted down later that week. It wasn't the tiger's fault, and it was heartbreaking to hear the news from my hospital bed. They are such beautiful creatures."

"I did not mean to upset you by asking."

"No, it's okay. It was a lifetime ago."

"We should probably get some sleep" I said, hoping to take her mind off of it.

"Lou, about recruiting you for the FBI..." she started to say.

I cut in, "You're not going to continue your pitch now are you?"

"No. I just want to say that whatever you decide, I will respect your decision. "However..." She put a leg in between mine, lifting herself over me reaching for the light on the table next to me. She turned it out and then positioned herself laying half on half off the side of my body. I could feel her hair on my chest as she kissed my cheek and lay her head on the pillow next to mine. "Either way, I think I want to make this work between us."

"I want that as well. To know what you know about me and to not want to distances yourself from me, makes you special in so many ways. It doesn't hurt that you are gorgeous, smart and hunt down bad guys for a living either." I added.

She pinched my chest and said, "Don't ever lose that sense of humor. It's the only thing that keeps me hanging around you."

"Touché." I said as I kissed her and pulled the sheets up

to our shoulders.

There was a knock at the door. The sun was up and we had obviously overslept. This has happened again, the sun not waking me up when Arya and I have shared an intimate evening together. This was a very strange side effect, but one that I can easily overlook with the help of an alarm clock. Arya jumped out of bed immediately started to get dressed as she went to the door. I was a bit slower in my response.

"It's Lolotea" she said as she opened the door.

They were chatting while I got myself presentable for breakfast. When I came out, Arya had already left to go change and meet us downstairs.

"I see you two worked things out." Lolo said as we left the room.

CHAPTER 16

People were locked on to their lists and no wiser to their surroundings other than the fact that they were in the aisle for a certain item.

The Roanoke Walmart, just south of Douglasville, was advertising discounted electronics and attracting bargain finders from beyond the local population of 6,000.

As Lars strolled towards the Pharmacy to pick up eye ointment and burn cream for his cheek, it seemed no one cared to notice the wanted rapist and killer walking casually among them.

Bearing the simple disguise of a hat and sunglasses, he felt above the law as he said hello to the older gentlemen behind the counter. Moments later he had the medical supplies he needed to subdue the sulfur that left his eye with a constant burning sensation.

As he walked through the crowd judging people for their mindless obsessions of having to have the newest version of tablets, phones and laptops, he stopped dead in his tracks at the sight of a familiar face.

In a sea of people moving about, Lars stood tall like a statue staring at a woman 20 feet in front of him. She was looking at a laptop, but not one of the new ones. She was smarter than the average bargain finder. Her attention was on the slightly older model that was practically being given away.

He laughed out loud as he started to walk her way. When he was only a few feet from her he remembered where he had seen her before. Lars could not help himself as he smiled at her. She barely noticed his presence as he slowly walked past her.

As if stopping to smell the roses, he paused for a second to take her in. As his nostrils flared, hoping to catch a whiff of her body lotion or perfume, he was disappointed with his irritated sinuses from the gun powder mishap. He gave off a muffled grunt of disappointment. Her body moved slightly forward giving him room to pass by in the crowded aisle.

Lars's insidious impulses were spiraling out of control these past few weeks, especially the past 5 days. He didn't care much for planning any more. He was running on pure evil as he changed his direction in the store. Circling around to keep an eye on her from a distance, only one thought was running through his mind...Torture. He was starting to get excited and a bit ahead of himself.

The salesperson finally found her, and they were talking about the computer. As he escorted her to the checkout counter, Lars walked away and left the store.

She walked out of the Walmart thankful she decided to drive out of her way to take advantage of the clearance sale. Although she could have afforded the newest version, why pay $800 more for something that basically has the same functionality and speed, but a few more gigabytes of storage that she would never need.

The merchandise was boxed well and in a plastic bag to protect it from the rain that just moved in. She was almost to her car when the rain really started to come down. She pushed the button on her key fob to unlock the car as she approached. Circling around to the front, she placed the computer in the back seat and then climbed into the driver seat. It only took seconds and she was soaked. Had she known the storm was on the forecast, she would have brought her umbrella in with her.

She started the car and began to slowly back out before noticing a truck blocking her exit. There was a car parked in front of her, so pulling forward was not an option. She waited patiently for the truck to move. Just as she thought it was about to pull away, it appeared to have lurched forward and then stalled. Just her luck she thought as she grabbed her umbrella and stepped out into the rain to see what the problem was.

The rain was heavy and brought a refreshing scent down with it. She was thinking how the hot day turned cool in a matter of minutes and how she didn't mind getting a little wet if it meant some relief from the heat.

As she approached the truck, she felt an agonizing pain travel up her side that crippled her instantly. As she fell to the ground, she barely had the strength to twist her body to land on her backside. The back of her head hit the side door of the truck as she collapsed to the ground. She heavily blinked a few times and noticed a large man standing over her holding her umbrella to shelter her from the rain.

As he bent down to check on her, he reached out a hand to help her up. She tried to lift her arms but it was no use. Then she noticed this stranger was not there to help her as his hand went towards her mouth. She was slightly disoriented from the pain and the fall. As his hand covered her mouth, she noticed the rag and the foul smell. Panic was already setting in. She attempted to fight off what was coming next but she quickly passed out.

As she opened her eyes, she continued to feel disorientated and her head was throbbing. It was dark outside and she was lying on the back seat of a moving vehicle. Still wet and cold, she could not move her arms and legs. As she tried to speak, the tape over her mouth kept her lips from moving.

This was a bad dream and she immediately started to think how she had landed in it. Her memory was still a little foggy and she could barely remember getting out of her car to check on the truck that was blocking her in. What happened? Why am I tied up? Just then a voice came from the front seat.

"I know you are awake back there. Just sit tight as I pick us up some food." The man said as the truck slowed down.

She wanted to yell, "What the hell is going on?" All that came out was a muffled response that could barely be heard.

"Tell you what. If you are a good girl and lay still without making any noise, I will let you eat in a little while. However, any noticeable movement or attempts to make noise, I will cut you slow and deep making you wish I killed you. Choice is yours." He calmly said as he stopped the truck and got out.

Her thoughts were racing now. This might be her only chance to escape. She moved her elbow over to her side and tried to prop herself up a bit to see out the window. She could barely make out some lights from a diner and a few cars around her, but nothing looked familiar.

She inched herself towards the door handle near her foot and tried to position her toe under the handle to flick it open. After a couple of attempts she noticed the lock was set. It was an older truck, and the lock knob was up by the window, making it nearly impossible for her to unlock the door without her hands.

There was nothing left to do except kick at the window, but she did not have the positioning to do so. The task could take too long to try to throw herself out onto the ground. However, the scene she makes could save her life. Perhaps it would be the last thing she ever tried to do. As she quickly thought it over, she came to the horrifying decision that she wanted to go out fighting.

She prepared to kick the window with all her might. As her legs extended quickly in a short burst, one foot slightly caught the door slowing down the impact to the window. The thump was loud, but the window did not break. She quickly repositioned herself for a second kick.

The door by her head flew open and a knife was at her throat. He was pressing it hard against her neck almost choking her with it.

"Is this where you decided to die? Right here, right now, like this?" He whispered in her ear. She lay perfectly still waiting for the knife to start cutting. She wanted to fight back but could not make a muscle in her body move. Just then his hand replaced the knife and he started to squeeze her throat with such force she instantly started to see black dots and then passed out.

She woke again to an even worse headache. She had never experienced a migraine but this had to be what they felt like. The pressure in her head was unbearable and the light that hit her eyes was so painful it made her sick to her stomach. She tried to look around but was overwhelmed with sharp pain in her head that she began to dry heave.

Hours must have pasted. There was nothing in her stomach to give up as the knot continued to try to displace her stomachs empty contents.

"Welcome back, princess." She heard from a distance. She kept her eyes closed and took in the smell of BBQ and a hint of fertilizer. Fertilizer? She was more disoriented than she thought. She could tell she was now lying on a cold cement floor, but could not for the life of her place where she was.

"You are more beautiful than I had imagined earlier." he said as he walked towards her. Almost standing over her he reached up and adjusted the light to face away from her. The relief of the light not aggravating the headache came at a price.

She opened her eyes and realized she was stripped down to her underwear. She was spread eagle on the floor with two 100-pound bags of fertilizer lying on her elbows making it almost impossible to move her arms. Even worse, her legs were wide open, slightly elevated and tied with rope securely fastened to stacks of heavy fertilizer bags.

He stood between her legs looking down at her. She started to shake in fear and then the tears started to well up and trickle down her face.

He was holding something in his hand. Her sight was blurry and she was having a hard time processing her thoughts. Her emotions and sensitivity seemed intensified. The thought finally came, he had drugged her with something.

"It says hear that your name is Lacey. Lacey, things have not gone my way lately and I feel like you were a gift presented to me to right the wrongs brought on to me by another." The man was clearly out of his mind. She tried to think of recent cases she worked on trying to place criminals that did not get there way from the lawyer's she worked with. Her mind was not cooperating. Could this be a deranged criminal on a war path of revenge? The answer was "yes," but she would find out soon enough it had nothing to do with her job.

He tossed the object to the side and knelt down between her legs and lay on top of her. His mouth was next to her ear and he slowly whispered, "Lacey, you smell good. You are a bit older than I prefer, but your beauty makes up for it. I'm not going to lie to you. I will enjoy this much more than you will."

Her eyes got wide as she knew what was coming next. She tried to move, to squirm, but his weight was too much for her.

He slowly slid his hands and then his head over her breast coming to a rest on her stomach. He moved his head to the right allowing his ear to rest on her belly for a moment as if listening for something.

Her breathing became erratic as she knew something horrific and painful was about to happen.

He waited patiently for what seemed like eternity watching her chest heave and fall, exposing her lower ribs. Without warning she felt a vice clamp down on her lower right rib. She was screaming through the tape as the pain intensified to the point she heard and felt the cartilage separate between her ribs.

The air left her chest and refused to reenter. Her lungs were burning for air, but the pain was so awful she could not draw a breath.

His smiling face reappeared above hers as she was begging for her lungs to work. He was whispering something as she fought with her diaphragm. The battle for air seemed hopeless as she started to see black dots again.

Then he smacked her hard across the face and the adrenaline caught her by surprise. Her nostrils flared open as her lungs took in the now pungent odor of fertilizer.

As Lacey winced and whimpered uncontrollably, she thought to herself, "Oh, dear God, what did I do to deserve this?"

Lars thought he had his perfect victim and planned to enjoy himself all night.

CHAPTER 17

Arya sat in the front passenger seat with sunglasses on taking in the odd rock formations and colors as we drove to the reservation. We had been driving for a while and apart from the occasional car on the road, had not seen any signs of civilization.

It was peaceful and barren, and Arya was obviously allowing her mind to wander. Lolo was in the back and had finally taken a break from preparing Arya for what she would see and hear on the reservation.

Most people had this image of adobe huts, teepees, horses with war paint, buffalo, people wearing Native Indian garments and feathers in their hair living off the land. Arya was smarter than that, but Lolo wanted to prepare her nonetheless.

Lolo described the Zuni Pueblo as a very dispersed community with a centrally small town, houses, some adobe and some shacks and even trailer homes, no fancy lawns or yards, mostly dirt, cars, mostly old cars, goats, a few horses and a few cows.

The population of 10,000 was very spread out over 450,000 acres. There was a small lake just south of town towards Black Rock and even further was a small dam. Although the dam was only 80 feet long and 10 feet high, it served a crucial role when rain came. There were long stretches of drought and water meant life for people, livestock and crops.

There were two main grounds where spiritual gatherings took place: Black Rock and Dowa Yalanne Plateau. There was intense history linked to both going back hundreds of years involving battles with the Spaniards, American armies conquering the West and other Native Indian tribes on their quest for dominance. Depending on the time of the month or schedule of events, there may or may not be any gatherings over the next few days.

Arya could not help but to think what it would be like to work longer with Lou. She was really hoping for some clairvoyant clues and even thought about how to channel Lou's powers with hers to help in the process.

She was in the middle of daydreaming about holding Lou's hands and feeding off his positive energy to receive clear visions to help solve the Lars case, when Lou said, "We are here."

She snapped out of it and looked around. Even though Lolo prepared her for the arrival, she was taken aback by the remoteness and absence of the suburbs feel she had grown accustomed to in Atlanta.

Perceived poverty seemed to touch more than a fair share of households, but the people were resourceful. There was not a large concentration of homes in one traditional place like in city. There were only a few main streets, a few hundred homes and a couple hundred trailers. After passing by the school and then a rather large and beautiful Cultural Center, Lou pulled over to a house on the edge of town. Arya was trying to imagine these two people as kids growing up in this town, when not in Albuquerque.

"What do you think?" I asked Arya. I could tell she was still taking it all in.

"Even with the tutorial on the way out here, it is still surprisingly small and...I'm sorry, it's just..." She was trying to find words that would not offend us.

"Don't worry about it, Arya, our people have different

priorities. We must. It is a bit underwhelming to an outsider, but we mainly see people, tradition and memories. The environment is not something we feel we have to build up, but rather preserve and respect."

Lolo chimed in, "It's neglected, but not from the people." Arya knew she meant the government. As a government worker, Arya did not take offense and knew Lolo was not looking for an argument.

"But you know, others around here would tell you this is by choice and that living off the land with no "keeping up with the Jones'" attitude looks like this." she followed up.

As we approached the door an elderly man opened it and stepped outside.

"Welcome to Halonawa" he said as if addressing Arya. I remembered that Halonawa was the Zuni word for our Home, our Pueblo.

"Thank you" replied Arya.

Lolo opened her arms as she approached the man. They embraced for a moment and then Lolo formally introduced Arya.

"Alimon, this is Arya and you may remember Lusio. Alimon is one of our oldest and more importantly, wisest Shamans in our pueblo." Lolo announced.

"Nice to meet you, Arya. Lusio, it has been too long. I was expecting you. We have much to discuss." He waved them inside.

As Arya walked into the Shaman's home, her eyes immediately gravitated towards a beautifully crafted bear. As a center piece on the table, there was a large hand carved shallow wooden bowl, filled with a variety of beautiful turquoise stones that surrounded the ten-inch stone carving of a bear standing as if posturing before attacking.

She was amazed by the detail, as if every hair on the bear could be seen in the craftsmanship. The time, patience and skill it had to have taken was spectacular.

She would later find out from Lolo that the Zuni are master stone carvers and have many varying beliefs that revolve around their stone fetishes. It is said that the beholder of the stone fetish exudes the character and traits of that fetish. The Bear was a symbol of health and strength, fitting for the Shaman and his role in the community.

Alimon walked over to the table where Arya still stood admiring the masterpiece. He offered his hand and she took it. Alimon was smiling as he looked her over.

"The eagle is strong in you." Alimon said.

"Excuse me? I'm not sure I know what you mean." She replied.

"You see things others don't. I will have to ask my grandson to carve you an eagle fetish. When you return, it shall be here for you." He motioned her to the sitting area where Lou and Lolo were talking.

She could not help but to think he was referring to her clairvoyance. Perhaps the Shaman was gifted as well.

Lolo wasted no time catching up Alimon on my recent developments and special connection with Arya. Alimon did not say much. He mostly nodded and mumbled affirmations.

Alimon looked at me for a moment before saying, "Answers will come soon enough, but this is not why you are here is it, Lusio?"

"No, it is not. Can you tell me how my mother is doing?" I asked

"She is strong, but her battle with Simoqueis will end soon. Simoqueis has his reason."

Lolo explained that the God of Sickness, Simoqueis, lays his hands on the chosen ones to test their faith and others close to them too. He does not make them sick to punish them, but to rejoice in their beliefs and join them with family in the afterlife. Some are chosen early to spare them from a painful life, others later in life to strengthen the faith and human bond.

It did not make it any easier for me, but I appreciated the delivery.

"Can you take me to her today, please? I really want to help her or at least hear from her why she would refuse my healing." I asked.

"Yes, I will take you. Lusio, some people in the pueblo believe you to be a demigod. Half man half God. Your acts have been witnessed by many and stories have been told and written for future generations to talk about." Alimon said as he made himself more comfortable in his chair.

I was about to speak, but he continued. "Most people believe the God's are harmonized, but this would be untrue. They question why one contradicts the actions of another all the time. Imagine what they think when a man, whether a Shaman or someone that possesses God like powers, interrupts their plans or actions? Your mother's beliefs are strong and her faith even stronger. She wants the best for you and would not forgive herself if you interrupted the God's plans and they forsook you."

"I understand what you are say, Alimon, I do. However, I will not forgive myself if I do not try to help my mother." I said.

"Your help can be given in many forms, Lusio. It does not have to come from your powers. You are your own man and I never get in between family. I merely provide perspective. If you want more help than that, you have to ask for it. I'm here for you and your mother." Alimon said as he stood up.

Arya leaned over to Lolo and whispered, "Did he just imply that Lou could be a demigod?"

Lolo smiled at Arya but did not answer her. They stood up and followed Lou and Alimon out of the house. Alimon was obviously giving Lou the directions to where his mother was staying when a group of people starting approaching the front yard. They started gathering around Lou and were speaking

Zuni. Lolo started to translate for Arya.

"They are welcoming him home and asking the Shaman to lead an impromptu spiritual gathering in honor of Lusio. Thankfully Lusio will not let this go to his head". She said with a chuckle. Arya joined in the laugh.

"Actually, I think they are hoping Lusio can lay hands while he is here. This might be more difficult for him than I anticipated." Lolo said.

"What do you mean, Lolo?" asked Arya

"If his mother refuses his healing, but others are asking for it, his internal conflict could grow stronger. Dowa Yalanne is a very powerful place in its own right. Add these charged emotions and his healing powers to the mix and he could struggle." Lolo explained.

"Dowa Yalanne is the plateau you mentioned earlier, where the old pueblo was located and spiritual gatherings still take place." Arya recalled.

"Correct. There are still a few people that live up there. A Shaman and his family along with a few others that like the old ways. Some of the skilled fetish carvers are up there too. It is a place of learning and upholding tradition. No outsiders have ever been invited in." Lolo added.

Alimon addressed the growing crowd and obviously said something they liked. The crowd responded with a yelp followed by smiles as they started to break up and go their separate ways.

"Looks like the pueblo will be gathering tonight." Lolo said as she caught up to Lou. Arya felt like she was in a different country on an exploration of a new society. It all seemed so illusory with a little bit of fantastical mixed in and she was caught up in it. She hadn't thought of Lars for a few hours for the first time in a week.

Arya approached me from the side and caught my eye with a smile. I had been wrapped up in the homecoming and the lessons Alimon imparted upon me that I had not checked in with her to see how she was doing with all of this.

"How are you doing, Arya?" I asked.

"I was about to ask you the same." Arya said. She slipped her hand under my arm and asked if we could go for a walk before seeing my mother. I admired how well she could read people.

"Probably a good idea. I need to clear my head before talking to her." I said as I escorted her down the road. Lolo stayed behind with Alimon discussing how he would arrange the evening gathering.

We didn't say a word as we walked a few hundred yards. It was nice to just walk in silence with no agenda, no secrets, no case on the mind at the moment. She made small movements and gestures to let me know she was there and she cared. A slight squeeze, a small tug to avoid a pothole in the street. Then Arya broke the silence.

"I've been thinking." She said.

"Do tell." I said as I gave her a slight hip bump. She smiled at that as she regained her cadence with me.

"I don't want any secrets between us, so I have a confession." She said with a serious face now.

"I'm ready if you are. But know this, I firmly believe that some truths should never be told."

"I think you are a great lover." She said quickly.

"I, uh, thank you? I think you are too." I started to say back.

"I'm not finished." She said. "I think you are a great lover, but...not God like." She said as she pushed me and started to laugh.

"What?! That's a truth never to be repeated again." I said with a smirk. "Your humor...it cuts deep."

"I'm surrounded by people who think you are a demi-god. I need to laugh to stay sane Lou."

"And at my expense..."

"Oh, come here and kiss me." She said as she made herself look very inviting, "and promise me you will try harder in bed."

I was about to kiss her and then burst into a laugh. She joined in.

"I really needed that. Thank you." I said as I kissed her.

She kissed me back and looked into my eyes as she said, "Any time."

I hadn't realized how far we walked, but we were only a few houses away from where Alimon directed me to find my mother. I asked Arya if she was ready to meet my mother.

"Normally, I would say this is a little early in a relationship to meet each other's parents, but considering the circumstances, I would be honored." she said smiling.

We entered the house and were taken to a back room where my mother was sitting and reading. She looked peaceful as she sat wrapped in a blanket, holding the book in the sunlight that peered through the small window. Arya stayed in the hallway as I walked in to greet my mother.

"Hello, Mom." I said as I approached.

She lit up with a smile as she stood for a hug. We embraced for a moment and then I asked Arya to come in. I introduced Arya and my Mom gave her a long hug.

"Arya, you must be very special to my son. Other than Lolotea, I believe you are the first women my son has introduced to me. It is so nice to meet you."

"Thank you. It is a pleasure meeting you as well." Arya said as she took a seat.

My mother wasted no time asking personal questions aimed at the two of us. After enduring the interrogation I was able to transition the conversation to her health and the reason I was out here.

"Lusio, I know what you want and I know what I want. There are things you don't understand or chose not to believe. I have an agreement with Simoqueis." she said unemotionally.

"How am I supposed to respond to that? What do you mean you have an agreement with death?" The frustration in my voice started to show.

"Simoqueis is not death. Lusio, I'm a touched one. Do you remember what that means?" she asked me apprehensively.

"Are you referring to the night the God's descend upon us mortals and chose ones they want to have children with and supposedly take the young children that are theirs from previous encounters? I don't see the connection with your kidney's failing?"

"Lusio, I was sixteen when I was awakened by Apoyan Tachu, Father Sky, son of the creator. He came to me in the night. I did not know it was him at the time. It took many years to figure it out. Years after seeing you grow and find your powers from the sun. However, I'm sure of it now as I was 20 years ago when you healed Motuka's sister."

"This is crazy. You came to the city and met dad."

"Your dad thought he could handle the truth and did well with it for many years, but he kept finding ways to be further and further away until he just didn't come home anymore." she said as tears welled up in her eyes.

This is not the way I saw this visit going. I would come home, convince my mother to let me heal her and be on my way to catch a killer. Instead, I have made my mother cry and the pueblo wants to celebrate my return. Oh, and everyone is convinced I'm the descendant of the Zuni Sky God.

I settled my mother down with a few reassuring hugs and kisses and told her I would respect her wishes, but I did not have to be happy about it. I kept that to myself though. Alimon and Lolo entered a few minutes later to check in on my mother. Alimon had been providing healing herbs and daily prayers for the last 2 months. As they caught up, I motioned Arya to follow me out.

"I need some coffee. You interested?" I asked as I slowly walked towards the kitchen. Arya joined me and sat at the small round table in the kitchen. I looked around for a coffee pot and the ingredients but came up empty.

Arya noticed my frustration and took over. She took the kettle off the stove, filled it with water and returned it on the stove. After lighting the burner, she went to the window where a long planter sat with grass growing in it. She plunked a handful of grass from the planter and cut them into two inch strips and added them to the kettle of water.

"In India, lemongrass tea is a soothing treat to those that worry, but also known for its powers to heal those fighting cancer. I noticed it when we walked in. The citrus smell gave it away." she said as she sat next to me.

There was so much I did not know about Arya, but I was comfortable around her and I had a feeling we would have the time to learn about each other. She seemed to be getting the crash course on my history as everyone around me seems to be fine with sharing my past.

One thing no one knew about me was bugging me these last couple of days. It seemed small, almost insignificant in comparison to what we have been dealing with lately, but I felt I had to get it off my chest.

"I have a confession to make." I said to Arya.

"This sounds serious. Should we wait 10 more minutes until the tea is ready?" She said as she turned and looked at me.

"When I landed this case, I was starting to get to know someone from my duplex. Her name is Lacey and we were supposed to have diner the other night." I told her.

"Were you two, uh..." She was looking down as she struggled to ask me the obvious question.

"No. We have talked a few times and had coffee once. I haven't had the chance to properly speak with her since meeting you. It's been a crazy week." I said.

"Well, this is kind of awkward. I'm not sure what to say at the moment." She said.

"I think I owe it to her to say I have met someone special, so she doesn't get the wrong impression when I return home." I explained.

"Was she the beautiful lady that was talking to you before you were shot? You two seemed...very comfortable with each other." Arya said, but not with jealousy or malice, more as a matter of fact.

"Well, the circumstances of our meeting each other kind of sped up the process. You know...the whole damsel in distress thing." I said with a shrug of the shoulders.

"This is now moving from awkward to interesting, do tell, sir."

"Ah, I knew this was a bad idea. Okay, some guys were being jerks to her and her roommate and I put a stop to it."

"Oh. The gorgeous girl has a roommate too. The plot thickens." Arya said as she perked up and tried putting on a serious face.

"See, this is not how this played out in my head when I thought it would be a good idea to not have any secrets between us."

"Calm down, Don Juan. Thank you for telling me. I appreciate the gesture and trusting me enough to share that. If you have not learned yet, I will poke fun at you every chance I get. Your twinkle toes comment was the ringing of the bell, so appreciate my comments as terms of endearment." she said as she smiled at me and stood up.

This woman is special, and I really like her style. She was pouring us tea as I looked her over and thought how strange this week had been and here she is, standing at my side during very odd times. "Kismet." I thought out loud.

"Did you say Kismet?" she said.

I did not realize how loud I said it.

"In Hindi, fate or destiny is pronounced 'kismet.' What made you say that?" Arya said as she set the cup of lemongrass tea in front of me.

Its lemon potent smell heightened my senses and widened my eye as if smelling salt was placed under my noise.

"I'll tell you later." I said almost out of embarrassment for speaking aloud.

"I know you will, because I'm a master interrogator." Arya said as she pinched my arm.

The lemongrass tea was a much better choice than coffee. It helped clear my head and I rejoined my mother and others.

We all enjoyed each other's company for a few hours and my mother appreciated the rest of the lemongrass tea Arya made.

It was Alimon that reminded me that in a few hours we would be driving up to Dowa Yalanne for a celebration of sorts. Although some of the pueblo still lived in the adobe structures up there on the plateau, we would need camping gear for the cold night. It is customary to start late and have the stars above, so being prepared for the weather changes and staying the night is common.

As we started to leave to go gather what we needed for the night, Alimon pulled Arya off to the side.

"The energy will be strong tonight. You will see much. Are you prepared for this?" It was a bit cryptic as most of his wise thoughts were.

"Lolotea has described it well, so I think I'm ready for the celebration." Arya said with confidence.

"It is not the celebration I talk about. It is your own gift that will be strong tonight. Our prayers put out energy and the Gods respond with theirs. This creates a powerful presence that can elevate Shaman's and others alike. Your visions will be strong tonight." He said as he walked away. Obviously, Lolo had been talking to Alimon.

CHAPTER 18

Mercy, hope, and humanity were stripped from Lacey after enduring a day of physical and psychological torture. She woke up choking on the drainage from her bloody nose. This was one of those moments where she found herself alone and struggling to get her bearings.

Her head was pounding all the time, which added to the confusion and difficulty to focus on her situation. The physical exhaustion she felt every time she woke up from a beating or being choked out had her thinking days had passed.

So many horrible thoughts crept into her head when he was not around. Her hands were numb from the heavy fertilizer bags that lay on her elbows and hands. If she survived, she thought of how her hands would look with no blood circulating to them. Would the doctors amputate them? It's been days. Is the discoloration on her upper arm from dirt, blood, and bruising or was it from gangrene setting in.

Lacy did not need a mirror to tell her what her capturer had done to rob her of any beauty she once possessed. At one point she could feel the areas where Lars had either bitten her, burned her or cut her. Strangely they all hurt the same after the act was done. However, the acts came in waves and the number of painful inflictions had increased to the point that they were everywhere on her body.

She had to look hideous. If she survived and was ever able to even think about another man in her life, what would he think of her grotesque scars and bite marks? If she lost her hands, how could she work? How silly of a thought at a time like this, or was it? If she could bear a child, would she even be able to lift it or hug it? Tears started to formulate but then gave up to dehydration. She was so thirsty.

The door opened and her heart stopped. A tall man walked in with the light to his back. He has wearing khaki pants and a dark green shirt. He froze just a few feet away from her and stared in disbelief.

"Jesus!" he said as he quickly looked around. He disappeared for what seemed like eternity and returned with an empty burlap sack. He walked over to her and laid it over her naked body.

"What the hell is going on here?" he said as he started to lift the bags of fertilizer off her hands and arms.

Lacy tried to speak but choked on her dry throat and spit up some blood that was draining again down the back of her throat.

Once her left arm was free, she tried moving it to her chest. It was a very awkward and uncoordinated movement as her arm was asleep and she could not feel anything.

"I will be right back. I need a knife or something to cut these ropes off your legs." the man said. He quickly removed the last bag from her other arm.

"No, please don't leave me." Lacey managed to whisper.

"It will just take a second. My phone and gear are in my truck just outside. I won't leave you." he said as he dashed out the door.

She lay there on the floor, looking at her hands, trying to grab at the burlap sack to adjust it on her chest. They were slightly discolored and not cooperating. The man rushed back in startling her.

"Sorry, I'm a bit freaked out by all this. I found a shirt for you." He placed the shirt on her chest for her to manage. As he cut the ropes from her legs he said, "I can cut the sack and make it fit like a skirt." He did his best not to look at her uncovered parts as he worked to remove the heavy bags of fertilizer that kept her legs elevated and secure.

Lacey was having a difficult time trying to put the shirt on, but thankfully it was extra-large giving her a fighting chance to slip into it. Once she got the shirt on the man leaned over her as she still lay on the floor. He said "excuse me" as he grabbed the bottom of the shirt and tugged it down past her hips to about the top of her thighs. Then he removed the sack and cut the bottom out.

He carefully slipped her legs through the top and worked it up over the shirt to her waist. The sack had a draw-string and he drew it just enough to keep it from falling off. There, she was covered.

She caught a glimpse of his face. He was an older man, clean shaven, and very sun worn from working outdoors. His face showed every bit of the worry and concern he was feeling. She must look like the nightmare she had been through.

"Did you call the police? Where are we?" Lacey asked between breathes.

"I think my phone fell between the seats. We can look for it once I get you in the truck. We are at West Point Lake, south part, Alabama side, in one of several park storage units for grounds keeping." he said as he started to help Lacey to her feet. Her legs did not want to cooperate. She winced in pain as he adjusted his hold on her. This made the man even more nervous that he was hurting her, so he put her down.

"No, please pick me up. Ignore any pain I'm in. Please get me out of here." She begged.

"I'm sorry. Here we go." He bent down and put her arm around his shoulder and his other around her back and waist. He lifted and she was standing.

Her ribs, waist and groin areas were in so much pain. She could not help but to cry in pain as her muscle tried to keep her upright. The man just kept saying he was sorry as he started to slowly guide her out the door to the truck.

When they breached the door to the storage unit she could see the lake and a small picnic area about two hundred yards away. His truck had Evansville Parks and Recreation on the side of it and she could immediately start to feel a calm come over her.

"Do you have a radio?" Lacey asked.

"I do, but it has been on the fritz lately needing repairs. My cell is in there somewhere. I just made a call on it before stopping here. I'm sure I will find it in a second. If not, we are only about 20 minutes from a fire station." He replied.

This information gave Lacey a feeling of positive anticipation, which was a nice change from monstrous acts of violence she had been put through repeatedly.

He opened the passenger door and helped her into the seat. Her legs were still lethargic and not holding her weight, so she couldn't step into the seat. He had to practically pick her up and place her in the truck. He closed the door and Lacey managed to adjust herself and started to work on the seatbelt. This man saved her life and she has not even asked his name yet. Where were her manners? She immediately forgave herself, admitting she was not in the best frame of mind right now.

As he walked around the front of the truck, she was compelled to lower the visor and look at herself in the mirror. Thankfully there was no mirror, as her reflection might have frightened her. She brought her hand to her cheek and was about to touch it to feel how badly it was swollen.

"Don't do that." the man said as he opened the driver side door. "I mean, you probably don't want to touch your cheek. It's a pretty bad gash and your hands don't look very clean and you might have fertilizer on them. It would really sting."

"Oh." Lacey said as her body slumped a little as if defeated. "I must look horrible."

"Don't worry, they will fix you up at the hospital. Do you need help with your seatbelt?" As he looked her over, she noticed how he was not looking at her face. He was talking in her direction trying not to react to how bad her face looked.

"I got it. Thanks. Wha...what is your name?" Lacey

asked.

"Rob." He said with a genuine smile as he started the truck. He lifted his right hand to the gear shift on the steering wheel shaft to put it in drive when his chest exploded sending flesh fragments and blood all over Lacey's shoulder and face.

Lacey heard the shot, but her senses almost completely muffled it out as she was shocked by the scene unfolding in the cab of the truck. Rob lurched up in his seat and then fell forward hitting the steering wheel and then slid over on his right side resting his head next to Lacey's lap. His eyes were wide open, but he was gone a second ago. Lacey closed her eyes in hopes that when she opened them again this would all be a bad dream.

Instincts kicked in though and Lacey opened the door as she opened her eyes. She saw a figure walking in front of the truck. She fell out to the ground and rolled underneath the truck.

It wasn't until she was fully underneath the truck that she realized she broke the fall to the ground with her face. She could see the blood pooling on the ground under her nose and taste the dirt and gravel in her mouth. The trucks engine suddenly turned off. Then his voice hit her like a thousand needles to her skin.

"Lacey?" Lars called out. She became paralyzed with fear. Her heart was beating so fast now that she started to feel lightheaded.

CHAPTER 19

Over three hundred years ago the Zuni sought refuge from the Spaniards 7,000 feet on top of Dowa Yalanne Mesa. Many different Zuni groups came together and built a complex social network and structure fortifying them from possible attacks from the Spaniards and other raiding parties. That period was a direct result for how closely knit the Zuni became and continue to be to this day.

The Zuni Pueblo looks at Dowa Yalanne as a spiritual and very historical place. Some structures and outer barrier walls have worn down from weather and natural neglect from lack of inhabitants. Others look as they did three hundred years ago.

The general public has never set eyes on the city and the Zuni have no thoughts of making it a pit stop for tourists. It helps that it is in the middle of nowhere and difficult to reach.

Surrounded by steep cliffs that rose over 2,000 feet from the rocky terrain below, there were only two likely routes that could be navigated by experts. We had just finishing traveling on one of those routes and it was not for the faint of heart; 45 minutes by truck to the base, followed by an hour trek by foot up steep trails, a few small stretches of vertical cracks with hand and foot holes, some ladders and a few breaks for rest and prayer for safe passage.

For obvious reasons, gatherers had to make the ascent before dark.

When we reached the adobe fortress, I was shocked to see hundreds of people ranging from infants to elders. They say no one has 'really' lived up here for hundreds of years, but that is clearly not true.

There were gardens, small lots of corn, soy, and other greens. There were large oak vats of water throughout the plazas and courtyards surrounding the small adobe homes thought to be ruins.

Rainwater would run off the angled roof tops to the corner were walls with gutter like grooves on top would guide the rainwater to the vats. One oak vat was a trunk of an oak tree carved out and burned with charcoal inside to seal it. Others were made of hand carved planks with signs of charcoaling inside, held together by an adobe base. It was an amazing sight. I could not believe that I had never made the trip up here before with my mother.

Lolo had Arya by the hand and was showing her around, giving her the history of how this place came to be. She had just finished describing what was once a great outer wall and then went into how the Zuni had started to dig a secret staircase that led to nowhere. It was said to have been an impressive collection of descending caverns connected by hand carved staircases. Most of the rocks displaced from making the stairs were used in the topside great outer wall for fortification. After years of mining it became too labor intensive. The outer wall was complete and raiders were finding it too difficult to ascend the plateau. Eventually the staircase to nowhere turned into a freshwater well.

Alimon took us to an adobe home near the plaza where we would set up our sleeping bags for the night. It wasn't much, but with four walls and a partial ceiling it beat making the tent. We dropped our gear and went to the courtyard adjacent to the plaza.

There, gathering around a huge bonfire, were well over 200 people and many more still coming out of the adobe structures.

The temperature was still dropping and nearly everyone was wrapped in a blanket as they found their spot to settle in. We joined them all and the ceremony began a little later.

When the shaman and Chief finished their ceremonial speeches and the low chanting and praying began, my head was flooded with adolescent memories. My mother brought me to the pueblo many times and I always healed a few people during each visit.

What amazed me was that the disorganized chanting would always sync up after a few minutes. I always tried to listen for a ring leader or conductor that they all stepped in line with, but could never figure out how they naturally found harmony and cadence.

People with inflictions made their way to the edge of the bonfire. There were so many ... 15 to 20 people of all ages. Lolo grabbed my hand and squeezed it as a sign of gratitude, reassurance and caution. She had never seen me heal more than 3-4 people in a night and knew how exhausted I would get.

What she didn't know was how advanced the healing had become and how I had learned to power up, for lack of a better term. Arya was not sure what would come next, so she leaned in and asked.

"What's going on, Lou?" Arya asked as I started to shift away from our warm spot under a blanket.

"I'm going to see what I can do for them. Are you going to be alright?" I asked as I stood up.

"Sure, I'm keeping an open mind and Lolo is here with me." she said with a smile. Lolo slide over next to Arya and took my place under the blanket.

Alimon appeared by my side and walked me over to a young man who appeared to have mangled his thumb and index finger. I put my right hand on the back of his neck and brought his head to my right shoulder. Holding his wrist steady with my left hand I focused on my energy on his pain. It only took a second for my chest, gut and hands to feel hot. I felt him jerk out of fear, but held him steady. He immediately relaxed when his pain left his hand. I opened my eyes and saw that his fingers were normal again and he was smiling through tears.

Alimon guided me to several more over the next 10 minutes; an eye infection in a little girl, a man with a broken jaw, and an elderly lady who lived on the plateau who had a very high fever. All went well and I was not feeling tired.

The chanting continued as Alimon took me to a woman. She sat near the fire with a smile, wrapped in several blankets. She looked about 40 years old and her husband sat with her obviously carrying all the stress of her ailment through his facial expressions.

Alimon whispered in my ear that she had poison in her blood. I knew what he meant. Many of the people caught desert fever from bacteria unearthed in desert dust storms. There wasn't much you could do for it unless hospitalized. Even then, the prognosis was determined on how fast it was diagnosed and treated. The bacteria attacks everything, including the brain.

I knelt down in front of her and placed both hands behind her neck. After a few seconds I could feel something different happening between us. An instant migraine came over me and my stomach spasmed violently. I tried to ignore it as the healing process completed, but the pain did not go away. Alimon could tell something was wrong and took me past the group to a dark corner. Arya and Lolo were on the other side of the bonfire and could not see where we were or where we went.

"Are you tired, Lusio?" Alimon asked.

I responded by vomiting up a concerning amount of black substances. Alimon's eyes were wide open now as he looked back and forth at me and the black puddle next to me. I was just as shocked as he was, but I immediately felt better.

"Is that normal?" Alimon asked as he helped me up.

"That's a first for me, but I feel much better now Alimon."

"Well, you do look a little better than before, but perhaps we should stop." He said.

"No, honestly I think I'm fine to help a few more. Please take me to who is next." I said as I turned back towards the group.

We worked our way around the bonfire healing another 10 people. Thankfully most of the remaining people had very minor injuries or ailments. Some would have healed on their own quickly, but I think people wanted to experience the healing to have their story. I'm not sure if that makes me impudent or not, but the thought crossed my mind, nevertheless.

I released myself of that thought as I approached the last person. She was twelve and she was only 15 feet from Arya and Lolo. She sat patiently for well over an hour. Half of her face and both hands were wrapped in bandages. Her mother removed the head bandaged exposing a severe burn that covered her cheek, nose, eye and forehead. A patch of hair was missing too.

At this point, I was actually feeling very exhausted. I was thinking we should have organized this from people that needed healing the most first to those that could possibly do without. I could not end this with failure or not feeling up to it.

This girl was severely damaged, and my heart went out to her. I looked over at Lolo and Arya and they were in tears. I could only imagine what they were thinking. I looked down at the girl only to find her looking down at her hands. She was also trying to hide her face. The wounds looked like they were about a week old, at best guess.

I took a seat next to her and put my arm around her. She was quiet and shy, mostly because she was in pain and embarrassed at how she looked. Being desired and making a family is very important. Her future as a productive and accepted member in the Zuni pueblo was uncertain. Thinking of this girl's future helped me find the needed strength to start the healing.

We gently embraced each other as the energy built up in my hands. After about 10 seconds my hands felt like they were on fire. At one point I wanted to scream out and it took every bit of my focus to not look at my hands and break the healing process. She was now crying, and I released her.

I was officially useless for the rest of the night. She raised her head and looked at me as tears ran down two perfect looking cheeks. Her mother unwrapped the girl's hands and they were fine as well. Their whole family embraced me for a few moments before Alimon took me back to Lolo and Arya.

The chanting was starting to break up as different groups started to celebrate. Lolo moved over allowing me to drop heavily between both of them. I just realized that my body felt like it had been through 12 rounds of boxing.

"Lusio, I'm very proud of you." Lolo said as she patted my shoulder.

I threw a smile Lolo's way and fell backwards taking Arya with me. Arya was smart enough to break her fall on me and brought the blanket with her. She was half giggling half crying as she pulled the blanket over us. Her face was buried in my chest and neck for a moment as she managed to reel in the tears.

Still buried under the blanket her crying stopped. "Arya, are you okay?" I asked.

She popped out from under the blanket that lay over us and looked at me with this puzzled face. "I am fine. I just witnessed a dozen miracles and will probably never talk about it, but I'm fine. That girls face, her skin…it changed right before my eyes."

"Yeah, that's probably a lot to take in. I know it is for me." I wiped away some tear trails from her face.

"What was that like, Lou? What does that do to you?"

"Honestly? That was stressful, painful, irritating, exhausting and a blessing. Not necessarily in that order and sometimes in combinations, mostly exhausting."

"Do you need anything?" She asked as she brought her face closer to mine.

I started to smile and she immediately withdrew a few inches. "Lou, your teeth have black stuff on them and your breath is something special."

"Sorry about that. I got sick after healing someone on the other side over there. She was really bad off. It was as if I took it from her and then my body expelled it. It was very unpleasant. I also felt the girl's burns as I healed her." She helped me up and we started to go back to our shelter to freshen up and get a bite to eat.

Lolo stayed back with Alimon and was deep in conversation. I'm not even sure she noticed us leaving.

After repeatedly brushing my teeth and eating some food, I was feeling better but still really tired. I told Arya what the night would be like out by the bonfire. She seemed interested but when I said I really needed to sleep, she insisted on going to bed with me. We laid out the sleeping bags and blankets and then cuddled up for the night. The stars were bright above us and with no line of sight of the bon fire we had our own observatory of constellations. I was fading off quickly, but Arya had other plans.

"Lou?"

"Yeah?"

"What did you mean earlier today when you said the word Kismet?"

"No fair catching a man when he is worn out." I groaned.

"It's okay if you don't want to say." Arya said setting the trap. I knew I would be better off sharing now.

"Well, I was reflecting on the week we have had and are still having. I got the overwhelming feeling we were meant to meet, no matter the circumstances. How quickly we connected and the unique qualities we hide from others is interesting, in a good way. I was trying to make sense of it and 'Kismet' came out." I explained. I had her attention now. She was up on her side looking right at me.

"You were thinking of us when you said Kismet?" She said.

"That's right. What do you think of that?" This was my attempt to turn the tables.

"I'm usually pretty reserved with my feelings, so I have to admit this is very quick for me. I feel the same way though, Lou. Although, after seeing some of the things I have seen this week, I'm surprised I did not shoot you or run away...or both." Arya was smiling at me.

"I think you came close a couple of times, shooting me that is." I laughed and she gave me a nod of affirmation and then she laughed too.

"What I saw in the hospital and then tonight is enough to freak out just about anyone. But here I lie with you feeling safe. The feeling is so strong tonight I don't think anything could pull me away." She snuggled closer and laid her head on my chest. Moments later we fell into a peaceful sleep.

I woke up in the middle of the night to dead silence. I was sleeping on my side and I could see Lolo about 5 feet away in her sleeping bag. As I rolled over I saw a bright figure in the shape of a man standing over Arya looking at her. I must have been dreaming.

The figure paid no attention to me as it started to reach down towards Arya's chest, hand stretched out, palm flat. My reaction was pure reflex. I reached out and grabbed the thing's wrist. It was obviously startled at my grip on its wrist and it jerked away from me. It took a step back and looked from its wrist to me very slowly. That's when I noticed its deep blue eyes examining me with curiosity.

It was about 7 feet tall and still standing on the other side of Arya. Neither of us made a sound, but I was standing now practically face to face with it, Arya still between us. We couldn't take our eyes off each other.

Just then another one walked around the corner into

our area and stopped about 5 feet from me. It was looking at the other one and tilted its head sideways. They spoke to each other, but I could not hear their words.

Then the one that just walked in appeared to move with such speed it turned into a long blur. A split second later it was inches from my face looking down at me. I shoved its chest to back it up and its eyes burned bright red as it shot into the sky.

The other one came at me fast, too fast. It sent me flying across the room past Lolo, slamming me into the adobe wall. My impact against the wall had Lolo and Arya waking up alarmed at the commotion. Before their eyes adjusted to the scene, the blue- eyed light figure joined its partner in the sky. It looked like a reverse lightning strike as it exited towards the sky.

My chest was in immense pain as I lay on the ground gasping for air. Lolo was the first to realize my position and noticed my struggle for air.

"Lusio, what's going on, what's wrong?" She called out as she tried to get out of her sleeping bag.

I just lay their besieged with chest pain. Arya was now up and coming over to me.

"Breathe, Lou! Put your arms up and breathe." She was kneeling beside me now as Arya joined her.

Finally, my lungs let in air and I started to control my breathing. They could see the panic and pain start to leave my face as I took in each breath.

I finally said, "Holly shit!"

CHAPTER 20

Lolo was determined not to let me go back to sleep. After explaining my ordeal to Lolo and Arya, Lolo went to get the Chief and Alimon. Arya sat in front of me with her arms around her knees looking bewildered, probably questioning my sanity.

How much more can this wonderful person endure before she starts questioning her own sanity? She watched me get shot, delivered me to the doctors, watched me heal myself in a day, cough up a bullet fragment, constantly getting teased by the energy between us, watches me heal a dozen people, and now has heard me talk of Sky People or Gods that basically had a confrontation with me.

My ribs were killing me and Arya noticed I was constantly shifting and grimacing with every other breath. She snapped out of her daze and helped me to me feet. She asked me to raise my arm so she could shimmy my shirts up high enough to see my ribs. It was painful but I managed to get the shirt up to my armpits, with her help. She paused for a couple of seconds staring at my ribs.

"Hold tight, Lou, I'm going to get something to wrap you with." she said as she went into her bag. She came back with a long scarf that was loosely knit and was stretchy. She tossed it onto her shoulder and took out her smart phone and took a picture of me.

"Really, this is the photo you want of me?" I could have thought of a dozen better opportunities to get a keepsake snap shot.

She smiled and put the phone back in her pocket. Then she carefully wrapped my mid-section with her scarf and helped lower my shirt. I felt slightly better, but not enough to hug her. I was so drained from my earlier activities that I could not heal myself until after I could absorb some morning sunlight.

Alimon and the Chief walked in a moment later, Lolo in tow. The Chief looked visibly angry with the Shaman and they were exchanges words as they came towards me.

Alimon made a gesture to the Chief and then spoke to me. "Lusio, Lolotea has advised us of what you think you experienced. The Chief would like to believe the blessing this land has received with two Sky Walkers gracing us with their presence. However, Sky Walkers do not reveal themselves to us, not even to the most powerful Shaman. We Shaman have a special connection with the Gods, we hear their wishes and heed their advice, but we never see them."

"Alimon, I saw what I saw. I'm sorry the Chief is upset. I'm not trying to upset the balance or bring question to beliefs." I said patiently and respectfully between breaths.

"Yes, yes, I understand." Alimon replied.

The Chief laid into Alimon again. Alimon was nodding and throwing in a few shrugs of the shoulders.

Lolo was with Arya and they were talking. I was just standing there thinking how badly I wanted to sleep and for the sun to hit my face in the morning.

"Lusio, please understand that the Chief has great respect for you, but he is worried how these stories will be interpreted. People can't see or touch Gods." Alimon explained.

"Look, I don't know what to say. Maybe I am a little different from others. I grabbed its arm and it shoved me across this room. That sure felt real. My ribs would agree." At this point I had had enough and I patted Alimon on the shoulder and nodded to the Chief as I walked over to my bedding.

Arya and Lolo went to Alimon and the Chief and were showing them Arya's phone. The Chief went silent and Alimon was now the one giving it to the Chief. I really didn't care at this point.

Slowly and carefully I managed to get myself to the ground. Now I just needed them all to be quiet. Alimon and the Chief left the area. Arya came and lay down next to me, but not before shooting a wink in my direction.

"What was that all about?" I asked.

"I showed them the picture of your ribs. It was quite compelling." She brought the phone to my face and showed me what looked like a large red imprint of a hand over my ribs and chest.

"It hurts worse than it looks." I said.

"You will be alright soon though, right?" She asked

"I should be fine after a cup of coffee in the morning sun." I said as we got comfortable.

Lolo was getting ready to go to sleep, but not before saying, "This is all going to be great material for my next book."

"Nice, Lolo. Make sure to use fictitious names, please, and I want some of those royalties." I could use the help with my retirement fund.

"Yeah, yeah" she said as she rolled over. I was pretty sure my demands were just ignored.

Arya was carefully cuddling up to me while whispering, "Just your typical camping trip."

Hours later, it was Arya's turn to be awoken. She was deep in sleep when a strong vision came to her in her dreams. It started with heavy rain in a parking lot. She could clearly see a man picking up a woman and taking her away in a dark colored truck.

The vision became a bit confusing when she saw the man dumping a truck into a lake. The truck was white with writing on the side. Then she was walking in a large shed and found herself staring into the eyes of a beautiful but bloodied lady who looked very much like the woman Lou was talking to outside his duplex days ago.

The woman was slowly walking backwards away from Arya and then gracefully lay down on her back. Bruises and cuts started to appear all over her and then she closed her eyes. A man appeared over her with a large buck knife. His back was turned to Arya as he knelt down and slowly stuck the knife in the woman's thigh. Her eyes opened as she screamed in pain.

The man whispered something in the woman's ear and then slowly turned around facing Arya. It was Lars. He stood up and walked right towards Arya. She froze in fear as the deranged psychopath walked right through her.

She woke up gasping for air and sweating. She looked around quickly to make sure the dream or vision was over and that she was back in reality. This one felt so real, and when Lars walked through her she felt deep anger, violent thoughts and pure evil tug at her soul.

Lou and Lolo were sound asleep, and she could barely tell that dawn was about to break. She turned on her phone and quickly made a text message to agent Jones describing all the detail she could possibly share with him and their analyst. She put in the subject line "Anonymous tip, please look into this ASAP!!!" She hit send, not knowing when they would be in range of a cell tower.

I woke up as soon as the sun hit my face. Perhaps my sleeping in was a thing of the past. I smelt something that resembled coffee but was still not motivated enough to move. I moved the blanket aside and lifted my shirt up to my chest, exposing it to the morning sun. Lolo sat up and looked at my exposed midsection.

"Yikes, that looks bad. How fast do you heal in the sun now, Lusio?"

"Let's find out." I just lay there focusing on the warmth of the rays in the cool morning air. The hairs on my arms starting to tingle and goose bumps appeared. I could feel the cartilage move between my ribs and then the pressure and pain were gone.

"That is incredible, Lusio! You are something else." Lolo said as she started to pack up her things.

"Yeah, I'm something else alright."

Arya walked over holding two cups of coffee.

"I hate to rush you all, but we need to go now." She said as she handed me the cup.

I drank a sip. "I agree. We need to find some real coffee. This will not do."

"Hey, I tried my best with what we had." She took a sip and then dumped it out.

"What's the hurry?" I asked

"I think I have a lead on Lars. We need to get on the next plane back to Atlanta. Let's pack up."

"Wha...how?"

"I had a vision in a dream last night." She said as she started to follow Lolo's routine of packing. Arya described as much detail as she could remember as she was packing. When she came to the part about who she thought the woman looked like, she paused before saying, "She looked just like Lacey."

Lolo was listening as she finished packing. "Who is Lacey?"

I looked at Arya, "Really? Are you sure? I mean you only saw her once for a brief moment."

I was trying not to come off sounding desperate for it not to be Lacey, as I didn't want Arya feeling threatened by my acquaintance. After examining my feelings for Arya these past couple of days, Lacey was now categorized in my head as a kind and interesting neighbor, a friend. Nothing more than that, right? I had to answer my own thoughts. That's right, just friends.

Arya looked at me for a few seconds examining my facial expressions as I played out the conversation in my head.

"Lou, I hate to say it, but I am pretty sure. Even though I only saw Lacey for a moment, I'm not likely going to forget what the women looked like that got very touchy and close to you hours after we had an intimate night together." She had this look on her face, with her head slightly cocked and a small smirk to one side of the cheek. It clearly read...watch what you say next, I'm two steps ahead of you.

"I would feel responsible for any harm that comes to her. I promised her there was nothing to worry about." That day raced through my mind as I thought about how things could have played out differently.

I could have put another unit or two on the residences that lived there in case Lars had plans to come back for others. Did he see me talking with her? Did he see the same signs of affection in that brief moment that Arya saw before taking a shot at me? How did I not see this coming? How could I be so careless?

"Lou, I know what you are doing. Stop it. There is no way you are responsible for the acts of a mad man. He could have been following her and there is no way you could have prevented that." She seemed to be done packing and had moved on to my stuff.

She was right. Our resources were limited and spread out. If she had a vision, then we needed to act quickly. I was instantly frustrated on how much distance we had put between ourselves and Lars. However, I wouldn't change my decision on coming out here to see my mother for possibly the last time.

Four hours later the three of us were on the road again. I had given my heartfelt goodbye to my mother, knowing it could very well be our last time together.

She was so happy to have seen me and to have met Arya. In her mind, I think she already had us married and was playing with our children. I wish I could have made that a reality for her. To some, seeing the family tree continue to grow is more than a wish or a desire, it's a life's work. My mom gave me so much love as a child. I only hope she felt the same love and appreciation from me over the years.

I started to feel selfish that I had been putting so many years into my career and not letting anyone too close to me. What if I could have been more trusting 5 years ago? Perhaps I would have married and had children for my mother to have met and played with.

Perhaps not, as fate can deal a blissful or pitiless hand for reasons not knowing. Where doors close or opportunities slip away, it seems there is a hidden purpose, and it is not always unveiled in a timely fashion.

If Arya turns out to be the one, why now? Why not a few years earlier? On the bright side, she met Arya and could tell that we really liked each other. That gave my mom hope for my happiness and future. That gave my mom peace.

Arya had already connected with agent Jones earlier to further explain her details. She had to embellish a bit on how she came to the information. I overheard Arya mentioning something about calling in and checking the tip hotline for reports that sounded reasonable to follow and came across one that sounded connected based on something she saw at the duplex. Believable enough, unless someone checks the tip hotline for the same details and discovers the tip is not real and Arya made it up. We both have to lie to conceal the good we do.

By early afternoon we were on a plane and headed back to Atlanta. Lolo promised to come out to Atlanta, after we caught the bad guy. She really liked Arya and I could tell the feeling was mutual. They were already planning a shopping trip together. In fact, I don't even recall Lolo mentioning visiting me in her trip to Atlanta.

"It's happening again, Lou." Arya said as she sat next to me on the plane.

"What, another vision?" I replied as I put down the in-flight magazine.

She leaned over to me, "No, your energy is really teasing me. I feel warm all over."

I looked over her shoulders in the direction of the lavatory, "You know, we could go..."

"Don't even go there." She said with smile. "I need to find a way to stay in control in these moments."

"Agreed. Concentrate on something that helps you clear your mind." I suggested.

Arya leaned back and closed her eyes. A few moments went by and she opened her eyes and gave herself a smile and nod of success.

"Did it work? What did you think about?" I asked.

She thought about it for a few seconds is if deciding if it were something she wanted to share. It turns out she was just looking for how to say it.

"My family, they are very traditional. My two older brothers did what pleased my father and returned to Mumbai to run a family silk and cloth business in Bhuleshwar Market. My mother had wishes for me to return and help as well with designing Sari's.

Science and then the FBI were not on the list. Although they constantly pressured me and burdened me with guilt, there was a moment..." she paused with this proud look on her face. "There was a moment at graduation from the academy that they both looked amazed and proud. When I think of my parents, I think of that moment. It lets me know that all is well."

We talked for almost two hours about random moments in time, hobbies, family, our careers, the case, but avoided talking about the past few days of supernatural events.

A few times we caught ourselves having moments of deep laughter that brought glares from nearby passengers who were reading or trying to sleep. We didn't seem to care. We needed an outlet and we got caught up in sharing funning stories from when we were on duty.

She had this laugh that started out as a smile. Then she would start to lean in with her eyes closed, still smiling, suddenly jerk back slightly taking in a deep breath and then let out a soft laugh. She would sometimes put a hand on her upper chest when laughing quietly, other times she would cover her mouth like a little girl trying to keep herself quiet.

Arya had a great sense of humor. She had no problem making fun of herself and did so many times to get a laugh out of me. However, the moment that had me laughing the hardest was her story about gun qualification at Quantico. She had a dream about being dressed in her leotards while at the shooting range. She mistook it as a vision and was so paranoid for weeks, double checking her outfit every time she left her room or entering a class.

About 45 minutes before we landed, we were focused on the case again. Getting to know each other better was a welcomed distraction from thinking about Lars and the possibility of my neighbor being tortured by him.

Agent Jones and other detectives were still trying to track her down at home or work, coming up with nothing before we departed from Albuquerque. I was really hoping to receive some good news when we landed. As soon as we touched down, we were both on our phones looking for updates.

CHAPTER 21

Roy was the first person to answer his phone and gave the update I was not looking for. Lacey's bosses had not heard from her and it was unlike her. She was working on some litigation for them and they were looking for an update.

The police had not seen her at the duplex and her roommate had not heard from her either. I had a sick feeling in my stomach.

Arya got off the phone with agent Jones who was with the Sheriff's men organizing a search of shelters, cabins and storage sheds on the lake front of West Point Lake. There was a missing person's report from the Parks and Recreational staff, which helped narrow down the search to about 5 miles of roads and lakefront.

The FBI analysts were able to cross reference Arya's "tip" on the truck, the words "West Point" and the water with the missing person's report and came up with the proximity of the Park employee's route.

As we were getting our bags from the carousel, I received a call from my Captain. He was checking in on me to see how I was feeling. He reminded me I was on leave until the doctors and psychologist cleared me for duty. We argued for a few minutes about me being fine and sitting this one out which was not an option. It ended with him pretty much saying "rules are rules, Lou."

I told Arya I was coming with her no matter what. She knew she was not going to stop me and figured it better to have me with her than out there on my own wondering what trouble I was getting into.

We stopped by my place to pick up a few things. Agent Jones had dropped off Arya's work gear and cloths. There were still two police officers in the parking lot and security guards walking the perimeter.

As we entered the house a surprise greeting awaited. Andy rushed to the front door barking. His tail was wagging so hard that his hind end almost won the race to us.

While Arya gave Andy some serious attention, I went and grabbed an overnight bag which I keep packed, and tucked my reserve gun in the side pocket. As I went to the kitchen, Arya and Andy were still greeting each other. I picked up Andy's day kit that had 3 water bottles, food, treats, vest and a few other necessities.

Arya saw her FBI duffle bag on the couch and picked it up as I was headed for the door. Andy saw his day kit in my hand and knew he was coming with us.

The Sheriff and FBI already had K9 units on site, but Andy could still be useful. While driving south Arya gave me more details on her recent conversation with agent Jones.

Evansville PD, local Sheriff's department and FBI had already built up their staging area in one of the parks recreational areas at West Point Lake. The roads in and out were blocked.

She admitted she was feeling an enormous amount of pressure and anxiety about sharing this vision as a tip. If things don't go well, this could be a career killer.

I was about to remind her that someone I knew could be dying or be dead for the second time this week, but she followed up her statement with, "I would never forgive myself if we didn't follow up on this vision." Arya had really put herself out there on this case a few times now.

She must have years of trepidation and nervous tension pulling at her, constantly fighting to make the right decision that kept her in the clear but able to help others. Most people would play it safe and ignore their inner thoughts, gut feeling, hunch or in her case, visions in fear of ridicule or repercussions. Not Arya, she defied her parents' wishes and took her gift to a job that could really use it, whether her coworkers knew it or not.

We had about an hour of daylight left and about 30 minutes left on our journey to the staging area. The trees on the side of the road were still heavy with foliage but starting to turn colors due to the cold nights.

"It's going to rain." I said as I looked up at the clouds.

"You're not afraid of a little rain, are you?" Arya replied.

"No, but it will not help the dogs any." Andy was the king of tracking, but rain could easily wash away scents or send a dog in the wrong direction. Maybe we would luck out and the lake area would get reprieve from the rinse. It was about time a little luck went our way on this case.

CHAPTER 22

Earlier, when Lars returned from eating breakfast at a busy truck stop 10 miles away, he was disappointment to find a visitor. He had parked his truck about a hundred yards away just beyond the sight of the shed. As he observed the man helping Lacey, he felt like a cat stalking the unsuspected mouse.

As Lars approached the shed through the tree line, he kept himself hidden behind tall evergreens or bushes along the way. The 12-gauge sawed off shotgun he was carrying was less than ideal for hitting anything less than 15 to 20 feet away, but he had no plans to shoot from that far away. He was now about 30 feet from the truck and could hear the two talking as the man began to help Lacey into the truck.

As the man opened the driver door, Lars stood up from behind the bush and started to walk calming towards the vehicle. He decided not to run, unless the truck started and the brake lights released, but they never did. He was already in the driver's blind spot and only a few feet away when he stopped to listen to the conversation.

Lacey said something about how horrible she looked. Lars smiled and started to think about each moment he had with lacey last night and how he put thought into her wounds. He was starting to enjoy the reminiscences, but was interrupted as the driver reached for the gear shift.

The moment had come to reclaim his prize. Lars was a master at stoking the fire that fed his ego. He really enjoyed the stalking of unsuspecting victims and how mindless pedestrians were to his actions and presence. It made him feel larger than life, like a King walking among his commoners who were afraid to look at him.

He was a very conflicted individual. Half the time he saw himself as the bullied kid who had no one on his side. Other times, he was the King of the land and everything was his for the taking. His years of resentment, fear, disappointment and ridicule came out in rage and acts of violence that over time became planned events to release his pain.

Lars took a large step towards the window and pulled the trigger on the short barrel shotgun. The spread of lead grew to over a foot wide in the short distance it traveled from the gun to the man's chest, instantly shredding him to pieces. The inside of the cab changed colors as the man fell over towards Lacey. Seconds later, she was out of the truck and crawling underneath it.

"Lacey?" Lars called out. He looked around to see if the burst from the shotgun had attracted any attention. Other than birds flying away, he could not see another soul in sight.

"Are you going to come out, or make me come get you??

Lacey just lay there crying.

Lars got in the truck and started it up. He slowly rolled it backwards, slightly indifferent if he ran over Lacey or not. He figured she would lay still and his hunch was right. After Lars drove backwards for about 12 feet, Lacey came into view. He put the truck in park and got out. Lacey looked up and her face was covered with blood and dirt. He wasn't looking to do any work today, but now he had some to do.

As he approached Lacey she was mumbling "no, no more, please."

"Let's go." He said as he lifted her using the fireman technique. She was on his shoulders seconds later as he walked up the path towards his truck. Moments later he had her in the back seat and bound again. With Lacey secured, he focused his attention on the Park and Recreations vehicle with the dead man in it.

Lars stood by the edge of the lake with his arms crossed soaking in the rays from the late morning sun. He stared at the water, watching big bubbles boil to the surface just 40 feet off-shore from where he ran the truck into the lake.

He knew it was not the safest area to enjoy his prize, but he had hoped the remote shed would not see any action any-time soon. After straightening up the shed a bit and throwing a few buckets of dirt on the floor to cover the blood, he started to walk up the path towards the truck where Lacey lay waiting.

Lars was about ten feet from the truck and he stopped walking. Something was not right. He stood there starring for a moment and then realized that the truck looked lopsided. He walked around to the passenger side and there it was...a flat tire. He just stood there for a few minutes thinking. "How silly was this?" He had no spare and he just dumped the other vehicle in the lake. After debating limited options in his head, Lars got in his truck and started to drive slowly down the path.

There were at least 50 miles of paved and dirt roads around the lake. Lars happened to be on a 5 mile stretch that was all dirt.

He patiently drove slowly to avoid tearing up the tire, but after the fourth mile it was hopeless. The tire was in shreds and he was having a very difficult time handling the ride. When he final hit pavement, he noticed a small lake house about 50 yards up in the woods. There was an over grown lawn that stretched from the back porch to the road.

Lars turned the wheel and cut through the lawn, taking the truck around front. The back tire was void of tread and cut into the lawn throwing turf and leaving a sloppy groove from the road to the side of the house.

The house looked empty, as most were this time of year. Many of the lake front properties were summer homes or time shares.

It only took Lars a few minutes to break a window and find his way in. The house was small, but very comfortable. It had one main room down stairs where the open kitchen flowed in the half dining room and family room. There was a sliding glass door that led out to the backyard and a scenic view of the lake. The stairs leading to the second floor were narrow and the two bedrooms upstairs were small, but he wasn't picky.

After bringing Lacey in and putting her on the couch, he made some rice and heated up some chili from a can he found in the pantry. Lacey was looking somewhat interested in the smell, so he promised her some food if she was good. He sat across from her and ate as he looked her over.

The oversized shirt and sack for a skirt were not at all what he had in mind for the evening. Her face and hair were covered in dirt and dried blood, but he still felt a renewed interest in her beauty and wanted to clean her up. By no means was he feeling sorry for her or even thinking of letting her go.

It was a struggle getting Lacey up the stairs since she was dehydrated and very lethargic, but Lars managed. He was driven by excitement, excitement of renewing his prize. He had never been interrupted from his ritual before and felt like he had to start over with Lacey.

If she only knew what the shower really represented, she would fight to her death not to step foot in it. However, all she could think about was drinking the water. She did not have any energy to fight him as he took off her clothes and placed her in the small 3x3 foot shower. She had to keep one hand on the rail to keep from falling as the cold water hit her face and chest.

After several minutes of rinsing and drinking she collapsed to the floor of the shower and closed her eyes. The reek of fertilizer and sweat was now removed and the warm water helped her quickly drifted off to sleep.

Lars stood over the sink using the owner's toothbrush

and then razor for a shave. He could see that Lacey was on the floor in the shower and seemed indifferent about it as he continued to groom himself.

When Lacey woke up, she was tucked away in bed. The sheets were damp, so she figured Lars deposited her here directly from the shower. She saw a plate of rice covered with chili sitting on the nightstand. Next to it was a glass of water and a spoon. As Lacey pulled herself up to a sitting position her legs were met with unforgiving resistance.

She pulled the covers back and discovered what looked like a bicycle lock around her right foot, securing her to the foot of the bed. There was a split second where she thought things were going to be different. That thought left quickly with the feel of metal around her ankle.

Lars walked in just as she finished her food and water. He had this awkward smile on his face as he walked over to her.

"What do you do for a living, Lacey?" He grabbed a small chair from the corner of the room and placed it down next to the bed.

She was naked and tried to pull the sheet up to her chest to cover herself. When that failed, she lay back down and slide down a bit to hide herself under the sheet.

"I like that. Have me use my imagination. I'll pretend like I have not seen everything there is to see, and you can play hard to get." he said as he leaned the chair back on its hind legs. She could hear the old wood cry out as he tested its limits.

"Why are you doing this to me?" She was looking for some connection, some way into his head to find any leverage or sense of bargaining. Without it, she would continue to feel helpless and the outcome was inevitable and bleak.

"Oh, honey, it would only disappoint you if I told you."

"Please, tell me." She begged. She needed something, anything.

Lars shifted his weight forward and brought the front legs of the chair down hard. "You want to know? Alright, I will tell you." He was standing now, looking down at her.

"You are not my first. You're not even my second, third or fourth. You are lucky number seven." The wild smile returned to his face as he spun around and walked around the bed.

Lacey already wished she had never asked. Her captor was a serial killer. Her stomach began to knot up and she was trying to control her breathing so as not to lose the meal she just ate.

"Your eyes are so beautiful. However, they can't hide what you already know about how this ends." He stopped and pulled out this large kitchen knife and started to tap it on the foot of the bed.

She really wanted him to stop talking now.

"I shot your cop boyfriend in the back the other day for sticking his nose in my business. I'm not sure if he survived it." Lars was looking for a reaction from Lacey, but fear was the only thing she was showing.

"You all asked the same question, but the answer has always been…'does there have to be a reason?' The real truth is, in their death…in your death…I find a reason to live. The longer it takes for you to die, the more alive I feel."

Lacey was drowning in dreadful thoughts. Her heart was beating so hard she was getting light headed.

Lars flipped the knife in his hand catching the blade and threw it at the wall above her head. It stuck in the drywall with ease. He reached down to the floor out of her sight and came up with a roll of duck tap and oven mittens. He crawled onto the bed and grabbed one of her wrists while placing his shin on her neck.

Moments later she had the oven mittens duck taped on her hands and he was removing the sheets from the bed. She started to sob as he sat on top of her pelvis and took the pillowcase off one of the pillows. He twisted it tight and jammed it in her mouth, wrapping it around the back of her head and then tying it in a knot.

"There, now we are ready to have some fun." He took off his shirt and started to lean in towards her face, but she put both hands up on his chest trying to slow his progress. She was too weak, but he stopped anyways inches from her nose. "You're right, something is missing." He got up and left the room.

Lacey could hear him walking around and then galloping down the stairs. She immediately tried to loosen the knot on the pillowcase acting as a gag. She fumbled with it through her mittens for the longest minute or two of her life.

Finally, she felt the gag loosen to the point where she could push it with her tongue past her teeth. Satisfied with this small victory, she chewed the gag back in place so it appeared to be doing its job. She could hear Lars coming back up the stairs now.

He entered the room with a small portable radio and plugged it in next to the night stand. After a few minutes he found a station that was playing something close to Rock-n-Roll and turned it up.

When he turned his attention back to Lacey, she had herself balled up in the fetal position afraid to even look at him. He stood there looking her over, thinking about how the others would try to hide by making themselves smaller or closing their eyes. He was absent of guilt and remorse. He just stood there thinking about what he wanted from her.

Lars was many things, evil things, but a mastermind was not one of them. He made plenty of errors along the way and certain parts of his rituals simply flaunted his ego and mistakes. He knew his appetite was out of control, but he had to finish what he started before he went underground. He stood there looking at Lacey's curves, wondering if he could walk away from the pleasure his victims gave him. How long could he go without this euphoric release?

Lars lit a cigarette and turned out the light. It was already dark outside, so the cherry on the end of his cigarette would make his face glow orange in the unlit room each time he inhaled its contents.

The moon was covered as a storm moved in the area. They couldn't hear the thunder yet, but every minute or so a flash of lightening would give the room a strobe light effect for a few seconds. Shadows would dance around on the walls and ceiling enhancing the evil ambiance Lars had created.

Lacey took advantage of the room being dark and pushed the gag out of her mouth and onto her chin. Still in the fetal position, Lars could not tell what she had done.

When he came onto the bed, she immediately felt the red-hot cherry from the cigarette burn into the middle of her back. Her back instantly arched and she brought her hand around fast to swipe at the source of the pain. Lars was anticipating the reaction and had pounced like a cat onto her now exposed body. Once again, she found herself underneath this horrid man and he seemed to be in control.

She hit him a few times but it seemed like the blows only punished her by draining her strength. Lars seemed to like the fighting and just slapped at her face and ribs as if they were play fighting. Then he quickly grabbed her wrist and pinned them above her head.

This was her chance to give him a little taste of his own medicine. Lars was now holding down both her hands with one of his as he watched himself rub her breast with the other. His face was inches from hers. She lifted her head and bit down on the top of his ear so hard she could feel the cartilage giving way to the pressure of her bite.

He screamed in pain, but she would not release. He tried to push himself away but they both could feel his ear ripping from his head. That was the same moment a train collided with her jaw. Lars struck her so hard that he dislocated and broke her jaw, but not without losing the top of his ear in the process. The impact from his punch made her teeth slice right through his upper ear sending a two- inch piece of ear and one of her teeth into the air.

Lars was still screaming over the music while he felt the

damage on the side of his head. He jumped up and slapped the radio to the floor and then kicked it across the room.

"Oh, you bitch! You bitch!" He was pacing back and forth, still feeling his ear and how much was missing and then stopped at the foot of the bed.

Lacey's jaw was stuck slightly open and askew. She could not move it and was afraid to touch it. When she finally noticed Lars had stopped pacing, she saw him bend down and come back up with the huge kitchen knife.

This was it. She was finally going to die and not have to put up with his shit anymore. She closed her eyes thinking peace would come in the form of a knife through the heart or the cutting of her throat. Either would be quick enough. No such luck for Lacey.

Lars walked over to the side of the bed with the knife and stuck it deep into Lacey's stomach. She let out a deep groan as her hands instantly appeared around the knife. Lars let go and left the knife buried in her belly.

He stepped back a few feet from the bed and put his hands on his head, "You stupid, stupid girl." Lars turned quickly and left the room slamming the door behind him.

Lacey was taking short shallow breathes in hopes that the less she moved the less it would hurt. It was not working but she couldn't stop breathing that way. Her oven mittens were on her stomach surrounding the inch of blade that was not buried in her.

The pain was so unbearable she wanted to scream, but her jaw would not allow it. All that would come out of her was a moan that trailed off. She could feel the blood running out of her wound and down her side. The sheets already felt wet underneath her, so she knew she was losing blood fast. She didn't know it, but the 12-inch blade ran through her leaving an exit wound that was also bleeding badly.

She could feel the chills coming. Trying to keep her body still during the chills was almost impossible and it only intensified the pain as she quivered from the loss of blood.

CHAPTER 23

We were about a mile out from the staging area at the lake when Arya opened her duffle bag and pulled out a 9mm H&K MP5SD3 submachine gun. She secured the shoulder strap, jammed a 30-round magazine into its underbelly and extended the stock.

Jones had hooked up with the FBI's Hostage Rescue Team earlier and checked out the 9mm submachine gun for Arya. It was a very accurate weapon within 650 feet and coming in just under 7 pounds was very easy to handle.

She then removed a .40 Glock 22 from the bag and an ankle holster. After strapping the ankle holster to her right ankle, she removed her off-duty Glock 27 from her hip and placed it in her ankle holster before pulling her slacks over it. The trained eye could easily tell the concealed weapon was tucked away near her foot, but that was irrelevant because she looked like she was ready for battle. Arya was holding her vest as we pulled up to the area.

"Lou, I don't know how involved they will let you be here. I only have one vest and I'm definitely not giving you a gun." I put the car in park, and she stepped out.

She quickly put the vest on and then slung the submachine gun over her shoulder. Agent Jones walked up with a plastic bag in his hand and exchanged words with Arya before handing it over to her. She lowered her head to find me still sitting in the car.

"You getting out?" She asked

I stepped out with Andy following me. We came around

to her side and she was already on one knee letting Andy sniff the contents in the bag.

"Agent Jones had Lacey's roommate hand off some of Lacey's cloths for tracking."

It really hit me then. Not the culpability, but the urgency to catch this bastard before one more person was harmed or murdered.

"Arya, I need to be involved. Help convince them I'm here strictly to give canine search support." I knew my captain had passed along a message, but once you were there, people tended to take the professional help they could get.

She nodded and walked off towards the cornucopia of law enforcement gathered under a covered picnic area.

I opened the trunk and took out my bullet proof vest. While adjusting the Velcro straps, Arya walked back over with Jones and a Deputy U.S. Marshal.

The Marshal introduced himself. "Tom Holliday, U.S.M.S." He was all geared up with his tactical vest, radio, and gun in a chest vest holster.

"Lou Abrams, Mableton PD, Detective." I said as we shook hands.

He looked at Andy and then back to me, "I'm sure glad you both are here. FBI HRT and PD have the South pretty well covered and started their canvas an hour ago. They have about 4 storage sheds and 30 homes to cover. That leaves the Sheriff's department and a few of us Marshals to cover the North. We have two park sheds and 10 homes that fit in the grid. We are short man power and dogs, so no time to waste."

"Glad to help." I said.

"I hear you took a bullet a few days ago and shouldn't even be here?" Holliday said as he looked me over and then looked at agent Jones as if confirming where the news came from.

"I'm fine, plus Andy doesn't respond to anyone else. He is the best I know at tracking. Show us our grid and send us out." I politely demanded.

"No time for politics, right? Let's go to the table and get our bearings." Holliday wasn't in charge, but he obviously had been involved in a few manhunts. People listened to those with experience in times like these and Holliday had the experience.

Unbeknownst to us, he had served as a D.U.S. Marshal for 15 years and had been either part of or led on close to 50 manhunts. Holliday had been involved in several different states U.S.M.S Fugitive Tasks Force, building a name for himself as a relentless, dependable, hardworking, no nonsense and highly successful law enforcement agent.

We were assigned to cover about five miles of dirt and paved road. Normally, this was not a great deal of area to cover, but the scattered roads, no street lights, tree canopy, rain that was now coming down, and the fact that the houses were all a few hundred yards apart made this tedious.

Holliday started to split us up and assign grids to cover. Arya asked for one of the grids with a Park storage shed in it. As teams were assigned a grid, they grabbed their gear and left immediately.

Holliday and Jones stayed behind with a couple of others to act as command central. There was chatter coming in on the radio with updates to put on the grids. The teams were making good time clearing houses in the south sectors. Holliday was also keeping in touch with seven Park Ranger boats patrolling the shores from a distance to ensure Lars didn't take a lake exit.

A couple of civilians were also involved in the water security, but only in the capacity of using their fishing boats and their depth finders to locate the possible Park and Recreations truck. Each boat had a couple of plain clothed deputies posing as fisherman as they trolled the shores. The sonar devices sent sound waves that bounced back off objects showing shape and depth.

Everything within a mile was already cleared, leaving

Arya, Andy and me to travel up the lakeshore drive a mile and a half to the first house. Arya was not at all surprised that I had a gun with me. As we walked up to the front door, the house looked occupied. On our map, someone had already highlighted homes that were believed to be lived in year-round versus the summer homes and timeshares that might be empty. This was one of the lived-in homes.

We both stood on opposite sides of the door frame as the door opened slowly. An elderly man stood there looking puzzled before asking what we needed. After a few questions and both parties showing I.D., he let us in for a moment to ensure no one was under duress.

After clearing the home, we stuck an 11x8 inch red notice on the door so that other law enforcement agents new this house was cleared and then radioed it in. On to the next one we went. We were about an hour into the evening and despite the rain we had quickly clear five homes. Two were vacant, but there were no signs of foot prints, car tracks or forced entry.

Arya pointed out that we were headed towards the storage shed in our grid. The rain let up to a drizzle as we approached the shed and parked about 40 feet away. Andy got another sniff of Lacey's clothes before jumping out and going to work. There had already been over an hour of steady rain, which could remove some tracks and scents from outdoors. Andy was busy sniffing around out front as we both approached the shed door.

We were both holding our guns out with our flashlights crossed under our gun hand. The door looked forced open and slightly ajar. I made a "psst" sound and Andy appeared by my side. Arya slowly opened the door and Andy went in alone. About ten seconds went by with complete silence before Andy reappeared at the door again. If he had barked, we would have rushed in. Silence meant the room was cleared and he would not alarm anyone of our presence. We went in and quickly found a light switch.

My stomach immediately clinched up as we found ourselves standing where a gruesome act obviously took place. There were signs of restraints and blood smears all over the center of the floor, poorly covered by dirt thrown over it.

Arya was examining a strip of bloody duct tape on the floor. Andy was stiff as he stood next to the area and gave a few half barks half whimpers. He was clearly upset as he identified with the smell, confirming it was where lacey lay hours or a day before.

As I pushed the horrific thoughts out of my head, the knots in my stomach seem to be growing. There was no avoiding the personal connection I had with Lacey as a victim, and I was really struggling with the thought of her in the hands of this monster.

Arya was staring at me, reading my reaction, as she radioed Holliday and Jones of what we found. She then advised them to start moving resources from the south to north of our location. Holliday responded back with confirmation and advised that a couple of boats and the depth finder were on their way as well. Before Arya could ask me how I was doing, I took Andy outside and put him back to work.

I started to pick up on some tracks just outside. One set of tire tracks was barely visible and led towards the lake before disappearing in puddles and loose gravel 30 feet from the lake. Another set of tracks indicated the back tire was low or flat as the tracks wiggled their way down the dirt road heading north.

Arya came out and the rain started to pick up again.

"Did you guys find anything out here?" She asked.

"Some tracks leading to the lake and another set heading north, possibly a flat tire." I replied.

"Well, we can either wait here protecting this scene until others arrive or head north wasting no time." It was a bit rhetorical as we both were already heading to the car to head north.

Once in the car, Arya was looking over the map and said,

"There are 7 houses in the next 3 miles, but they are all set pretty far in the woods and it doesn't seem like you would have access or even see them from this road. Let's call it in that we are skipping ahead to the lakeshore drive homes only. The first one is about 4 miles up."

"It's a slight gamble to skip ahead, but I'm with you that he probably would not go off road with a bad tire." I doubt Lars knew this area at all, so sticking to the road seemed logical and faster to find his current location.

Holliday came over the radio advising us we already have U.S. Marshals closing in on the houses we are skipping. They were coming from another set of outer roads. We were the leads on the Lakeshore road. Our driving was slowed due to the muddy conditions. When we finally hit the paved road, we almost missed the first house. It was perfectly timed lightening that gave the yard away and made the house barely noticeable in the dark rain.

I stopped the car and backed it up a bit to get a better view of the house. Arya was unafraid of the down pour and was already stepping out to take a closer look. I radioed Command Center of our location and that we were heading up to the house. An unfamiliar voice radioed back that backup was on the way. I hadn't asked for backup.

The radio voice came back again. "Be advised, suspect possibly in house. Owner is out of town. Neighbor called in suspicious truck out front. Wait for back up."

I turned off the car and lights and radioed back, "We are going in for a closer look" and then stepped out into the rain, but not after turning off the radio. I wasn't willing to wait or fight with a voice over the radio.

Arya was hunched over in the yard looking at the truck's tracks that led through the yard to the side of the house. I leaned over and passed along the information I just received. We drew our guns and followed the tree line towards the side of the house the truck went around. We were about 25 yards away when we noticed a very dim light on in a room upstairs and one on downstairs as well. When we were about 5 yards away, the downstairs went dark followed by the upstairs light a minute later. The house was now totally dark inside.

I whispered to Arya, "Do you think he knows we are out here?"

As she was answering me a huge flash of lightening lit up the yard and house. I couldn't hear her, but could tell she mouthed the work 'no' during the cracking of the thunder that accompanied the flash.

I continued to move forward around the side of the house with Andy at my side and Arya 5 feet behind. We were breaking sticks as we walked through the woods, but the noise from the rain and thunder drowned out any sound we made as we approached the front drive way. The truck was now visible and I brought Andy to the passenger side door facing the woods. I slowly opened it and let Andy jump in. He immediately sniffed around and whimpered confirming he was on Lacey's scent.

Arya was now crouched at my side hiding from the view of the front windows. "This is the truck he had her in. How do you want to breach the house?" I asked.

"Wait for the next series of lightening and then we make a B-line to the front door. If it's not chained, I can pick it." she said as she patted her vest to show she had a lock set with her. She then moved towards the back tailgate and prepared for the 20 yard dash. I was now behind her ready to go. It only took a minute for the next series of lightening and as soon as it finished, we started the run.

About halfway there, thunder sounding like a shotgun going off in my ear almost stopped me in mid stride. Seeing Arya continue to run kept me going and we both reached the front door stoop.

Arya was on the side of the door with the handle and I was on the opposite side. She knelt down and put her left hand on the door knob and slowly turned it until I heard a soft click followed by the door moving open about a fourth of an inch before Arya kept it steady. She looked at me and mouthed 'Are you ready?' I nodded and pointed my gun at the opening when she slowly opened the door.

CHAPTER 24

When you know an armed criminal or killer awaits you on the other side of a door, one of the most intense moments of your life can be simply entering a room and then clearing it. You must have superb self-control, self-awareness and a partner you trust and have trained with so you both can be on the same page. Your self-control will give you the edge when shooting in close quarters.

It is amazing how you can miss a target from 10-20 feet away when your nerves are getting the better of you. Knowing how your partner moves and what each of you are responsible to look for while entering a room is critical to avoid blind spots that could get you or your partner killed.

Only being the two of us, if we enter a room that has a closet and a bathroom door, the odds are immediately not in our favor. Two people have to keep an eye on each other, the door they just came in and the two doors in the room. It is what we call a "High Risk Situation". Hand signals and pace are another factor as well when the partners have not trained together.

Arya took off her FBI hat and set it on the welcome mat. We then stepped into the house and were greeted with darkness as the noise from the rain outside followed us in. If someone were in the living room or kitchen downstairs, they would have noticed our entrance. Immediately I was looking to Arya's left, sweeping the dark room for objects in the shape of a man standing or sitting. I almost squeezed off a round when a standing lamp came into my peripheral.

Arya stepped into the house scanning my right side and then locking her sights on the stairs 10 feet to the right of me. I gave Andy the hand gesture to go to the back of the house where the kitchen was laid out and looked around as we held our positions. Andy immediately stopped at the couch and gave it a few scratches letting me know he was still on Lacey's scent.

Seconds later we heard a door slam upstairs followed by a few heavy steps and another door closing. Andy finished looking around and without delay was back by my side awaiting his next command. Arya came over to me and in the darkness, I could see her big white eyes as she looked at me thinking about our next move. We both knew how dangerous it was going up the stairs completely exposed.

"You cover high and right...I cover low and left and keep Andy in front in attack mode." she whispered.

I nodded and then knelt down next to Andy. I had to think for a second and then gave him the command for taking lead and strike at will. Andy rarely had opportunities in the past couple of years to hear the word 'strike' which gave him the go ahead to attack anything. There wasn't much for light in the house, but as Andy cautiously ascended the narrow staircase, I could see the fur on his neck and shoulders standing straight up. He had clearly switched to kill mode and was leading us up the stairs slowly.

We reached the top and peaked around the corner seeing a short hallway and two closed doors. I knew we were at that point again that behind one of these doors was our armed assailant ready to take our lives without hesitation. We both stepped up to door number one and Andy was sniffing wildly at the bottom of the door.

I tapped him on the back and pointed to the other door. Andy went over and sniffed around and then went stiff. He must have heard something alarming as I could see his hair stick up again as he slowly backed up from the door but never taking his eyes off of it. He was ready to pounce if the door opened.

Arya was not looking behind her where Andy was, so I whispered, "Lars" as I pointed to the other door. We still had to clear this room first, so I put my hand on the doorknob and slowly opened it.

Arya was the first one in and I immediately heard a harsh whisper that sounded like 'No" spill out of her. I spun in right on her heels looking to our right. There was a door open to a bathroom that I rushed towards and quickly cleared. As I turned around, I could see Arya hovering over Lacey deciding what to do.

I went back to the door and peaked out to find Andy still staring at the other door. I closed our door and turned back towards Arya and Lacey. Arya was checking Lacey's pulse and that is when I saw the handle of the knife buried in Lacey's stomach. There was so much blood on her and the bed.

"She barely has a pulse and she is cold. She is almost gone, Lou." Arya said as she took the blanket from the floor and covered Lacey.

"Hold the back of her head and cover her mouth. I will pull the knife out and then heal her."

"I can't watch the door and hold her too, Lou"

"Okay...shit. Tighten her gag then." I felt terrible as I said it, but we could not afford a blind spot. Not even for a few seconds.

Arya looked at me and nodded before placing the gag back in Lacey's mouth and tightening the back of it. As soon as Arya had her gun drawn on the door again, I pulled the knife from Lacey's stomach. She immediately came to life as her hands went to her stomach. It looked like Lacey was trying to scream but then blood started to come out of her mouth. She was now choking.

"Hang in there, Lacey." I said as I removed the gag and cleared her airway. Placing a hand on her forehead and one on her stomach, I began to focus on her pain. Instantly the warmth shot up through my stomach to my hands.

Andy started to bark wildly, followed by a man's voice yelling "What the hell! Shit!"

Lars had obviously opened the door and was greeted with Andy attacking him. The barking now turned into growling as Andy had a hold of him now. Arya was now opening the door to step out and help Andy. I was trying to stay focused, but was interrupted with two gun shots from two different makes and then the other door slamming shut again.

Arya poked her head back in. "I'm fine. I think I hit him. Andy is now in the room with him."

"I'm still working on this. The gun shots distracted me." I knew she was thinking should she stay here and wait for me leaving Andy alone with no support, or does she go help Andy knowing more confrontation could interrupt me and cost Lacey her life.

"I have to go, Lou." I could see she struggled to say it, but I knew it was the right move. I nodded and turned back to Lacey.

"Be careful." I said as she opened the door. I quickly took my ear plugs out of my vest and put them in my ears. I knew it was careless, but I needed to focus for 30 seconds. I decided to focus my healing on her wounds to save time. I could try for her memory too, but I felt I had to back Arya up and time was not on our side. Save her life. Then, go kill Lars.

With the ear plugs in I started to hum loudly to make my own background noise in hopes to drown out what was going to happen in the other room. The healing started immediately and that's when I started to notice all the bite marks and cuts all over her body. I tried my best to push out the awful images and thoughts creeping into my head. The pain I started to feel in my stomach helped clear my mind.

I saw her stomach wound close and other cuts and bite marks start to disappear. I looked at Lacey's face and saw her eyes open wide and she started to slap at me widely. I didn't bother to fight with her as I jumped up off the bed. Just as I took out my ear plugs and started to head for the door, I heard three quick pops of a Glock go off.

"Get away from me!" Lacey screamed before falling into an uncontrollable sob. I reached the door and was immediately tackled to the ground.

◆ ◆ ◆

Arya had left the room and as she approached the other door, she could still hear Lars and Andy going at it. Trying the door and finding it was locked, she stepped back and gave it a solid kick next to the handle. The door came open and she saw Lars across the room picking up a sawed off shot gun, wheeling it around in her direction. Andy was attached to the back of Lars' upper thigh making it hard for him to stand steady, but he still squeezed off a round at Arya.

Arya saw the blast from Lars' gun as she discharged her gun and instantaneously felt the pellets pepper her left upper chest, shoulder and cheek. She spun around and hit a dresser knocking the breath out of her. As she tried to steady herself to finish off Lars, she heard three pops of a gun and clinched up falling to the floor.

Expecting to feel other rounds enter her body, she still only felt the burning pain from the shot gun wound. As she rolled over, she was greeted by agent Jones staring down at her.

"Are you okay?" He said as he quickly looked her over. Two U.S. Marshals ran past Jones towards Lars as Andy appeared next to Arya.

She was slow getting up and then felt lightheaded. Jones tucked an arm around her waist and helped her out of the room. As they left the room, Arya noticed an old musket pistol on the floor just outside the room.

"He was a minute away from shooting Lacey with that gun, Jones. We did the right thing by not waiting for back up." She justified her actions and Jones agreed as he helped her down the stairs and out of the house.

They were greeted by a sheriff's deputy. "Let me take a look. I'm a trained EMT and have some gear in my car. Come with me."

Arya was now coming down from her adrenaline high and was really feeling the pain take over in her shoulder. The rain had let up and she just wanted to lie down. Jones kept her upright until they made it to the deputy's car.

"Sit her up in the backseat and I will go around and dress her wound." He said as he ran around the car and entered the backseat from the other side.

Jones helped Arya take off her vest and then sat her in the backseat. The deputy quickly cut the collar, shoulder and sleeve off to see what he was dealing with. Arya had about 8 small holes in her shoulder and upper chest and one in her left cheek. The one in the cheek bleed a little but had now swollen so much it was hard for her to talk. The Deputy was particularly concerned with three of the shoulder holes that continued to bleed.

"This is going to hurt like hell, but I have to put pressure here until the medics arrive." He peeled a sealed bandage from its wrapper and pressed it to her shoulder.

She tried not to scream, so the awful throbbing forced her to cry as she focused on not passing out. Jones held her hand and said, "It's okay, Arya. It's okay."

She looked past Jones and starred at the blue and red light show that danced on the front of the house. She could hear more vehicles pulling up and wondered how Lou and Lacey were doing.

Jones broke her attention away from the light show by shouting, "Over here. Gunshot wound to the shoulder." Two paramedics pushed their way in and before Arya could protest her being moved from the spot she now deemed comfortable, they had her in the ambulance and hooking up to an I.V. The deputy was at her side the whole time applying pressure.

Jones was told to wait outside because they were told by a Marshal to make room for a second victim.

"Sorry about that, Lou." I was on my back with Holliday already getting up and extending a hand. He lifted me up and then put a finger to his ear. He then told me, "Lars is dead."

"What about Arya?" As soon as I asked, I saw agent Jones helping Arya walk down the hall.

Holliday was already over the bed calming Lacey down and I quickly joined him.

"Lacey, it's me, Lou. You are okay. We got him. He's dead." She looked really pale and the contrast of her blood on the bed, sheets and her body made her look like she was on death's door step. Still, she was alive.

Lacey remained curled up trying to cover herself as she slowly started to get control of her emotions and take in the seen.

She finally locked eyes with me and said, "Thank you."

Holliday already had his vest off and was unbuttoning his shirt. He quickly took it off and laid it next to Lacey as I took the oven mittens off of her hands. We both turned and made a wall as she slowly put the shirt on. Holliday was on his radio asking for bolt cutters while more deputies roamed the halls towards the room Lars lay silently in.

Lacey had the shirt on and the blanket was back over her keeping her warm and covered as she still had no pants. As a deputy entered with bolt cutters, I started to look through drawers for something she could wear. Thankfully, I found a pair of sweats and a pair of shorts. I opted for the sweats. As I went back to the bed, they had removed the lock from her ankle. I showed her the sweats and helped her by putting both feet through and hoisting them up to her middle thighs before letting her take over.

She was shivering and pale. Holliday went into action. He was about my height, but built like a football player.

"I'm going to pick you up sweetie and carry you downstairs." he said. She nodded as he slid an arm under her upper back and another just below her butt. With ease he lifted her to his chest, and she wrapped her arms around his shoulder and back.

She was looking at me like she was trying to figure out what had just happened. I knew a million thoughts were going through her head. I just hoped she could keep them to herself until we could talk alone.

Holliday carried her down the stairs and out to the awaiting ambulance. She was very tired and could barely keep her eyes open. As the paramedic helped Holliday put her on the gurney and into the back of the bus, I notice Arya was already inside receiving medical attention. As I tried to climb in, the paramedic told me there would be no room.

Arya heard my voice and raised her arm giving me a small 'hello' wave and then thumbs up. I couldn't see how bad the wound was, but the deputy had his hand on her shoulder while the other paramedic was injecting something into her I.V. The other paramedic quickly put an I.V. into Lacey and covered her with two blankets before climbing into the driver seat.

"Holliday, my car is way over there. Can you take Jones and me where they are going?" I asked as the paramedic inside closed the doors on us.

"Sure thing, come on." He led the way to his cruiser and as we climbed in Andy came out of nowhere leaping into the back seat with me. Holliday gave a slight laugh and said, "I hear your dog was a bit of a stud tonight. He chewed off half of the suspect's leg."

"Sounds like Andy." I said as I thought about Arya.

"I'm glad the son of a bitch felt some serious pain before Jones lit him up." Holliday said as he pulled out and started to follow the ambulance.

I looked at Jones and then stuck out my hand. He smiled and shook it.

"It all happened so fast." Jones said. "As we entered, we heard gun shots upstairs. I was the first up the stairs and saw Arya kicking in the door. A second later they both fired at each other. I saw her take a hit to the shoulder and as I entered, Lars was still standing. I didn't even think as I put three in his chest."

"Textbook on your part, Jones." Holliday said.

"Come to find out, Arya shot him right in the chest too." Jones added.

CHAPTER 25

At the hospital, Arya was immediately taken to surgery and Lacey was being examined by a team in the E.R. Jones and I went with Arya as far as they would let us.

Before taking her in, she squeezed my hand and said with a smile, "I know you want to help, just be there when I wake up."

She was right. I wanted to take over. As they took her in, I caught Jones looking at me with curiosity.

"Is something going on between you two?" he asked as we started walking back to the waiting room.

"We have quickly built a solid bond in our partnership. Hypothetically though, would it be a problem if it led to something more?" It wasn't my place to tell her partner anything, but I was curious what he thought of the scenario.

"I've known Arya for a couple of years. She is a great agent, but never seemed to have a personal life. I would encourage it. The Bureau only prohibits partners outside work from being partners at work. You two wouldn't have that problem."

We arrived at the waiting room and Holliday joined us soon after. "The doctors are baffled with Lacey's conditions."

"What do you mean?" asked Jones.

"They had to give her 4 units of blood, but haven't figured out how she lost it. She doesn't have a scratch on her, but has definitely been traumatized. She has barely said a word." Holliday advised us.

"She was coughing up a lot of blood when I got there." I

added.

"I'm sure they will figure it out. The important thing is, she is alive." Jones said as he took out his phone and called his Director to give him another update. After speaking for several minutes, he tapped my leg to get my attention and was holding the phone out to me. "Here you go, FBI Director Cooley wants a word with you."

I took the phone, "Director. This is Detective Lou Abrams."

"Let me be blunt, did you get my agent shot?" Director Cooley asked in a harsh voice.

"No sir. We were faced with a tough situation." I responded with confidence and not defensiveness.

He cut in, "I'm sure you were. Why didn't you have her back?"

"Pardon me sir, but you were not there. If you can stop taking cheap shots for a second, I would be happy to fill you in." I still had a calm and steady voice, but was done with his line of questioning. I wasn't going to get bullied over the phone by someone other than my Captain, which I'm sure was going to happen soon enough.

"Alright, lets here it then." The Director said.

I had Holliday and Jones attention now too. More so for speaking to the FBI Director the way I did, but also to hear what went down. I walked him through it in detail. He didn't say a word until I was done.

"Detective, I don't think I would have done anything differently. I want to apologize for how I treated you. Arya spoke highly of you and I wanted to see how you handled yourself." He said.

"And..." I wanted to see if I could coerce more out of him.

"And...you obviously don't take shit from others. Would you talk that way to me if I were your boss?" The Director asked.

"I don't know, perhaps my Captain could answer that for

you." I shot back.

"He did answer that for me already." he said and we both went silent for a few seconds.

I thought to myself that he was coming on very direct about this move to the FBI.

"Detective, I'm not a headhunter, so I'm not going to waste your time or mine. I'm holding paperwork with your name on it for joining the FBI class at Quantico this year. Its starts in a month and I need your answer next week to fast track this. It's 19 weeks long, bearing in mind you pass all the prerequisites." He paused for a second and I imagined him leaning back in his leather chair taking a sip of a hot toddy before calling it a night. "We have a few neighbors and friends we would like to talk to, complete the background and then the polygraph."

"Sounds like you are betting on a Yes." I said.

"I would bet on my agents every time. If they think you have what it takes and believe you may be interested in a career change, then it's time not wasted. Three days, Abram. Now go get me some good news on Arya please. You now have my number. Good evening."

With that, the phone went dead. I handed it back to Jones who said, "What was that all about?"

"I'll tell you later. I'm going to go check on Lacey." I was hoping she would be doing okay and be willing to talk to me.

Once I arrived at the E.R., I asked the nurse's station for a status update. She informed me that Lacey was doing fine and had been given a room for overnight observation, allowing doctors to run a few more test to ensure they were not missing anything serious that led to her blood loss. I took the elevator up to her floor and checked in with the nurses to let them know I'm not just an officer but a friend of hers as well. It was getting late, but they allowed me a visit. I walked into her room and she was on her side facing the door.

"May I come in, Lacey?" I asked.

She nodded as she sat herself upright still holding the big pillow that she was cuddling with seconds ago.

I pointed to the chair about 5 feet from the bed and then the bed. She pointed to the bed, so I sat by her feet.

"How are you doing?" There was so much I wanted to say, but I had to put her first. She didn't say anything for a minute so I followed up with, "I know you haven't been talking, but you can to me."

"I'm not doing so good. I can't close my eyes without seeing him or feeling him. I'm in Hell." Her eyes were watering up and I noticed her hands and lips were trembling.

"I'm so sorry, Lacey." I tried to reach for her hand and she slowly moved it down into her lap out of reach.

"You don't have anything to fear, I'm one of the good ones. However, I imagine you have questions. I know I would." I said in a soft voice as I scooted back a half foot on the bed.

"I...I...I don't even know what is real or what really happened to me. The memories are vivid and horrific. But the pain, the cuts, bruises, and bi...bite marks are all gone." She lowered her voice to a whisper, "I had a knife in my stomach and bled out. I know that happened, because I watched the blood leave me and an hour ago I watched the doctors put more blood back in me."

"You're not going crazy. Unfortunately, that all happened to you." I explained

"Then how...how did you make it all go away? What are you?" she asked

"I'm normal in every way, except for an extraordinary gift of healing that I cannot explain." I said.

Tears came out of her eyes and ran down her cheeks, but she made no movements.

"I discovered it when I was around 12 years old. It freaked me out. I've been hiding it ever since." I admitted.

She finally wiped her tears away and said, "I knew something was different about you. I felt warm all over both times we were close and then that same feeling came over me when you had your hands on my stomach. How is this possible?"

"Sorry Lacey, I have been spending years hiding it and not explaining it, so I'm not very good at it. I just hope you can accept this as one of those good but unexplainable things." I suggested.

"That's why I haven't been talking, because I wouldn't know what to say that sounded believable. I don't want to be the victim they send to the psych ward." She was still whispering, but was showing signs of leaning towards me.

Perhaps the trust was slowly seeping back in or I really felt she could handle it. I decided to offer more help. "Lacey, if you feel like you want the memories of the kidnapping to be gone permanently, I can offer my ability to take them away." It sounded strange as I said it and it came across even more bizarre the way she heard it.

"You want to brain wash me?" Her voice picked up a little, but was still a whisper.

"No, not exactly. Let me explain." I told her about Tammy and her memory. Only the appalling memories washed away. She still remembered being taken and being rescued, but nothing in between.

Lacey leaned all the way back and closed her eyes for several minutes. When she opened them, more tears poured down her cheeks.

"I literally can't even close my eyes without him invading me. If you do this, will it hurt? What if you take all my memories away? Is there no fixing what you break?" She was clearly nervous and apprehensive.

"It will not hurt. You may feel that warmth between us. It will only take seconds. One of the joys of this gift is that I get to experience the ailments I remove or reverse. As soon as I feel the pain is when it stops." I gave her a few seconds to take in what I just said and then added, "I'm that same guy that pulled you out of the pool. I'm only here to help. Trust me."

"I'm scared, but I'm ready for this nightmare to be over.

What do I need to do?" She asked.

"Nothing really, just let me give you a quick hug, then we will say our goodnights and I'll let you get a peaceful night's rest." I said with a smile to reassure her.

"Okay." She leaned forward with her arms out and I scooted closer.

As soon as I hugged her, I casually moved one hand from her back to her head. The warmth shot up through my chest and then my hands felt it. She tried to pull away and then the pain hit my head and stomach. She went limp in my arms and I lay her down.

"What is going on in here!" the nurse said as she walked in with a fast pace. "Her vitals are all over the place. Is she okay?"

I stepped back from the bed and said, "I was just giving her a hug goodnight."

Lacey opened her eyes and looked at me with a huge smile. It reminded me of the smile she gave me when walking up to me at the coffee shop. At that moment, I knew she was going to be okay.

As soon as Arya went through the doors to the operating- room they hooked her up to the monitors and injected her I.V. with a general anesthesia to put her asleep. She quickly drifted off and the surgery only took an hour and a half. Right before she woke up, she had a vision. She watched herself standing in front of Director Cooley's desk conversing and then she placed her credentials and gun on his desk and started to walk out. When she opened her eyes, she saw Lou sitting in a chair next to her. It did not last long though as she drifted right back to sleep.

When she opened her eyes again Lou was sleeping next to her in the hospital bed. She smiled and then the pain hit

I woke up to Arya groaning. The surgery went very well, but she was going to be feeling very stiff and sore for a while or at least until I got her out of the hospital.

"Try not to move your head too much, Arya. Your surgery went fine, but you are going to be very sore until I can get you home." I said as I sat up for her to see me easier.

"I can't tell you how much I'm looking forward to that." she said and reached up and patted me on my chest. "I'm really tired, Lou. Thank you for being here." She was already drifting back to sleep, so I did the same.

Jones came in around 7:00 A.M. with coffee, but I was already up looking out the window taking in the morning sun.

"How's our girl doing?" He asked as he extended a cup to me.

I happily took the coffee, "Thanks. She is sore but fine. The doctor says she can go home tomorrow if all continues to go well. However, it would have to be under supervision to ensure she did nothing to aggravate the wound or internal stitches."

"I volunteer you and Andy. I haven't seen my kids in a week, so this is my 'goodbye' or 'until next time'." Jones said as he extended his hand. "It's been a pleasure working with you, Detective."

"Likewise, Special Agent Jones." As I shook his hand, I saw Arya lift hers up.

"Say 'Hi' to Gloria for me and stop by sometime next week. Keep me in the loop on things." Arya said.

"Typical. Even when you're shot, you still want to work. Take care you two. I'll bring Gloria by when I visit you. She will want to see that you are doing okay." With that, Jones left the room.

After another uneventful evening the hospital released

Arya and she agreed to let me drive her back to Atlanta to the comfort of her home. Andy tagged along at the request of Arya. On the ride over, Arya reluctantly asked me not to heal her as she would have a hard time explaining no signs of scars or injuring at her next FBI physical. I didn't say anything about it on the way to her apartment, but I knew she would soon figure out why I was so quiet about the topic.

She lived in a small two-story duplex that had a comfortable size living room and kitchen downstairs and a nice size bedroom upstairs. The furniture looked new and gave the appearance of a contemporary style with a nice touch of India throughout the room.

A couple of colorful Kantha blankets well positioned on the long couch brought wondering eyes back to the center of the room. The blankets consisted of richly colored patterns of patchwork from old sari cloth stitched together giving them a vintage quilt look. They were pieces of art that brought warmth to the room.

Later that evening, Quantico was on my mind. I helped Arya get ready for bed and tucked her in for the night before excusing myself downstairs to think about my career. She was done influencing me and left me to decide. The FBI already started their background check, but more would be questioned. How far would they go? Was there anything to find? Being healed, Lacey and Tammy did not fit Lars' pattern of sadistic abuse and that could raise questioning. Could I keep my gift under control or concealed to the FBI as a field agent?

There was so much to think about, but one thing was for sure. I wanted to keep working with Arya. Or was it that I just wanted to be with Arya? Did I have to work for the FBI to have Arya in my life? The answer was no, but I really enjoyed her partnership and the fact that she knew my secret made my days a bit less stressful.

Close to an hour into my internal debate, Arya came down the stairs and stood in front of me wearing just the extra-large FBI shirt that passed for a nightgown I helped her put on earlier.

"If you were to hold me, kiss me or make love to me a couple of weeks from now, would you be able to not heal my scars?" She asked as she moved her bangs out of her face and over the top of her head.

"I'm pretty sure if one of us thinks about it, it will happen before we can stop it." I reluctantly admitted.

"That's what I thought. No wonder you were so quiet earlier." She said leaning forward, putting her right hand on my shoulder as she climbed onto my lap straddling me.

"Arya. I really like where we are going, but I would not forgive myself for putting your career at risk. We should wait and talk about this, right?" I asked with sincerity and concern as she pushed her nose against mine.

She managed to whisper "no" just as she began to kiss me. She winced as she shifted her weight on my lap, but that would be the last time her shoulder would give her any problems.

I guess we would figure it all out tomorrow.

CHAPTER 26

FBI Director Cooley would have his hands full today, but at the moment he was right on schedule in his morning routine. After completing his 5:00AM morning workout and picking up his favorite cup of coffee, he would head into the office to make his rounds. One of the first things he did as he walked into the building and headed to the security check point, was look for Riley Cooper. Riley was the department Lead Analyst and if something looked priority, he would be standing in the center of the FBI seal in the foyer just past security waiting for the Director.

As Director Cooley entered the FBI building, he saw Cooper waiting for him with a file in hand. Some days the file would be a summarized debrief that the Director needed to read before his first meeting. Other times it would be case details or analytics field agents wanted to act on. None would warrant the disconcert Cooper wore on his face as he extended the file out to the Director to retrieve.

"What's this Coop?"

"I can't talk about it here, best you read it on the elevator, sir." he replied to his Director

The Director was half way done reading the summary as they entered the elevator. He flipped through the rest quickly and then closed the file.

"Who has seen this?" the Director asked in a calm voice.

"I worked on this one myself. Just the two of us, sir." Cooper answered.

"Very well. Keep it that way until I look into it myself

and find a reasonable explanation for this. Thanks, Coop." As they exited the elevator, each went their separate ways.

As the Director approached his office, he stopped at his assistant's desk and asked her to schedule an appointment in the afternoon with Arya.

"Clear my schedule to make time for her. It's been a week since she was released from the hospital. Let her know I have an urgent matter that I need her to review with me. Don't take no for an answer." he instructed as he entered his office.

When Director Cooley sat down at his desk, he removed a coffee infused cigar from the mahogany box that sat on the left corner. He had no plans to light it. He just ran it slowly under his nose taking in the aroma. It was something he did to gather his thoughts.

As he placed it back in the box as gently as he removed it, he slowly reopened the folder Coop gave him minutes earlier. Nothing gets by that kid. Out of thousands of pages of data filed weekly, he finds anomalies like an ocean treasure hunter relentlessly searching the sea for lost wreckage, scrutinizing every object on the ocean, floor looking for anything that looks out of place.

This entry looked as normal as any entry made by a field agent. The facts where stated, the lead was followed, the intelligence proved to be valuable, and following the lead produced results. What made this so strange was that Cooper saw something out of place that no one else would have seen. There was no true origin of this intelligence. It was as if the tip came from thin air.

There had to be an explanation. Arya was a great agent, proven loyal and trustworthy and soon to be decorated as a hero. He knew he owed her the benefit of doubt, and had to listen to her explanation before taking this any further. Agents missed detail in their reports all the time, but simple cross checking with others cleared it up.

Arya's report was missing the actual call that supposedly came in with the tip. Jones' report referenced a call from Arya while he was at the cabin. A call that led them back to Detective Abrams neighbors, where they found another one of Lar's victims. No other report had any detail to back up the mystery call, or origin of where Arya received the information linking the watch to Anita Banks. So where did the tip on the watch come from? How did Agent Shah know to ask about the watch and quickly link it to the Detective's neighbor?

Later that afternoon Arya showed up to the Director's office in a suit with her arm in a sling. The Director did not know it was all for show, as her arm and cheek were healed a week ago. She wore a band aid on her cheek and a little makeup that made it look yellow and brown as if a bruise was in its final stages. The door was open to his office, but she knocked on it anyways.

"Arya, come in. How are you feeling?" He asked as he stood up and came around the desk to greet her. He pointed to a chair in front of his desk as he went past her to close his door.

"I'm feeling pretty good, Director. Those doctors are top notch." she said as she sat down.

"Good. Glad to hear it. I can't have one of my best field agents out for too long. We have work waiting for you." he said smiling as he sat back down on the other side of the desk.

"Thank you, sir for the concern and the confidence in my return to duty." Arya replied

"Arya, you have been on my team for a couple of years now and you know I'm a straight shooter. I'm going to get right to the point on why I called you in today." the Director said unemotionally.

"I respect that about you, sir." she interjected.

"Well, hold the niceties until after you hear what I have to say." He was so calm with his delivery of such an unsettling statement that Arya could not help shifting slightly in her seat in anticipation for what would come next.

"Arya, Special Agent Jones has no idea we are talking.

His report of a conversation involving you and a lead on a watch in the cabin clearly states that your call lead them to the next victim." The Director paused to see if he was going to get a reaction from Arya, but she played it cool. She didn't budge and her breathing looking calm.

"However, my analyst has no record of where you could have logically discovered this intel to draw upon those conclusions. Odd right?" Now he was baiting her purposefully.

Without skipping a beat Arya replied "I have full confidence your analyst is great at his job, so the explanation must come from me."

Director Cooley sat up a little straighter as he prepared to receive Arya's explanation.

"I'm clairvoyant, sir and I had a vision that connected these facts together. I passed them off as legitimate tips so that Detective Abrams and Special Agent Jones would follow them post haste." Her reply was smooth, almost rehearsed and Director Cooley just sat there mulling it over expressionless.

Arya felt like she should say something else to fill the quiet room, but better judgment prevailed and she sat in the stare off with her superior. She knew this was the end of her career, so she chose to go out with honesty and dignity.

"That is such an interesting response, Special Agent. I almost don't know what to say to that explanation." He slowly turned his chair ninety degrees to the right and began to look out the window, as if the answer was somewhere outside hidden in the tree tops.

Arya just waited for the inevitable.

A full minute passed, which seemed like eternity before Director Cooley started his response.

"There is only one course of action you leave me to take." he said as he started to turn his chair back to Arya.

She figured she would save them both time and started to stand up. She wanted to go out on her terms dammit.

"Pardon me, sir. I hate that I put you and the department in this position. Therefore, I would like to go on the record as formally resigning my commission with the FBI effective immediately." She started to place her shield and then the badge on the table before realizing she would never get to work with Lou again. Arya really enjoyed their connection in the field. Although nothing was really set, she was hoping that they could find a way to work together again.

What will her family think? They may not have fully approved the career choice, but they were proud of how she owned it and made herself successful. They also admired her positive contribution to society and the fact that she risked her life for what she believed in. Maybe they would be relieved. Maybe they would feel dishonored by her noncommittal reasons for no longer being with the FBI after boasting such a promising career path. She was about to wander further down this rabbit hole of thoughts, but was interrupted by Director Cooley.

"You think I'm going to let you off that easily?" he said as he reached across the table pushing the credentials and badge back towards her.

"I, I don't understand, sir. This is the logical course to protect your career and others. You would risk that just to punish me?"

"Who said anything about punishing you? I have invested a great deal of time in you Special Agent Shah."

"I'm really confused. So, you're not firing me, and you're not administering disciplinary action. You do realize I feel horrible about keeping this from not just you, but almost everyone in my life? This ability is a heavy burden and I don't need you or anyone else making me feel worse than I already do." She was starting to show emotion and she hated that this situation was starting to get the best of her.

"Almost everyone?" the Director asked.

"Excuse me?" Arya didn't understand the short inquiry.

"You said, almost everyone in your life does not know about you being clairvoyant. "Who knows?" he pointedly asked.

"I think this is when I respectively stop talking and go back on leave until you decide what to do with me, sir." She started to collect her items from the desk as she planned her getaway.

Director Cooley said one word as she started to walk out, "Dover."

"Dover, sir?"

"You know, leave DC, drive by Annapolis, head over to Dover." He said.

"Yes, I know where Dover is. What are you saying?"

"Take your belongings, go home. When you are ready to return to work in a month or two, I'm sending you to Dover. There are some people there I think you need to meet. Once you return, I will have your next assignment lined up."

Arya was in disbelief on how the Director had taken her confession and how he was already planning her next assignment. She left the office somewhat bewildered how to act or where to go next.

An hour later she found herself at home alone, wanting to call Lou. Lou had returned to work the day before and advised his Captain of his plans to join the FBI. She was excited about his choice, but already feeling a deep ache starting to build up inside her chest. This last week was filled with intimate moments and long conversations that really brought them very close. They had even talked about a weekend getaway to Hilton Head in a few weeks.

As she sat on the couch, she wandered off into thought. She had very few relations that went longer than 6 months to a year and none of them came close to the bond and love she was feeling for Lou in such a short time. She thought it was crazy to fall this hard for someone in just a couple of weeks. She knew she was in no condition to return to work and would use her full leave time before returning. Yes, she was healed. However, her mind was clouded with her new love interest, and focusing on her job was not going to happen until Lou left and they had some time apart for her to clear her head.

CHAPTER 27

The first couple of weeks were harsh on those that came unprepared for the physicality of the training. They don't play around at Quantico. The instructors kept us busy from 8:00AM to 5:30PM daily. There was studying and extra training outside of these hours as well. It was not until the third week that I had some time to leave on the weekend to see Arya and Andy. Before leaving for Quantico, I had given up my duplex home as it seemed tainted and it seemed like time to start a new. For the time being, Andy was with Arya.

We had been staying in touch via phone a few times a week. It was nice to hear each other's voice and talk about how much Andy did not miss me while in her care. Arya always had a good laugh over that topic.

It was Friday afternoon, and I was about to leave to catch a shuttle to Atlanta to spend the weekend with her. It was fulfilling to have a girlfriend where secrets were not plaguing the natural progression in the course of a potential long term relationship. There was nothing weighing me down, preventing me from commitment. This might be a scary thought for some, but I was ready to find that special someone that could help me find normality and give unconditional love. My phone rang.

"Lou, its Arya. Oh, you're going to hate me for this." She reluctantly admitted.

"This is starting to sound like you will owe me one." I exhaled as I looked at my 5pm ticket to Atlanta with slight disenchantment.

She explained that Director Cooley was sending her to Dover for a week and wanted her there yesterday. She had to drop everything and fly there tonight. All she knew at this time was that it had something to do with her next assignment. I could tell she was not sharing everything, but over the phone was not the right time to get into it.

We had a nice conversation and made tentative plans to see each other during the week once she was settled in and knew what her schedule would look like. Quantico to Dover is a manageable two and a half hour, drive when traffic cooperates. Maybe there would be a little rendezvous this week.

After we said our goodbyes, I dropped my go bag in the closet and put the ticket back in the drawer for another weekend. I was a little antsy and wanted to get out for a while, so I partnered up with a few classmates and headed into town for a drink and a good meal.

We hit Main Street and stopped at a local pub. The crowd was a random collection of local government aids and law enforcement winding down after the work week. As we ordered a drink at the bar and waited for a table, I noticed a man in a cowboy hat at a table with his back to me. He stuck out like a sore thumb.

I was about to continue scanning the room, but I noticed his hand raise up shoulder height and made a motion as if waving me over with two fingers. I ignored the gesture at first, but he did it again.

I excused myself from my classmates and started to walk over to the table. There were two suits barely paying me any attention sitting opposite the cowboy. As I started to come around the table bringing the man's face into view, U.S. Marshal Tom Holliday sat there with a huge grin on his face.

"I clocked you through the window, which doubles as a great mirror." he pointed out as he laughed and pulled a chair out at the table.

"Marshal, you are far from home. It's nice to see a familiar face though." I shook his hand and sat down.

I would quickly find out just how connected Tom Holliday was in law enforcement. He introduced me to Ron Sharpe who has 20 years in the Secret Service and Glynn Coppicino who has a colorful background of law enforcement agencies in his resume, but currently an agent in the Department of Homeland Security.

Holliday shared that they all went through FLETC together many years ago and stayed close. Sharpe was Special Agent in Charge of the DC field office, well connected, and rumor at the table was he could soon be the Deputy Director of the US Secret Service. Coppicino, on the other hand, was somewhat of a savant in profiling and highly regarded and sought after in all law enforcement agencies.

Holliday shared he was in town to conduct a multi-agency seminar on Monday at Quantico and then heading to Dover on Tuesday. I could feel their eyes shift from Holliday to me as if waiting for my reaction. I gave none. Intuition kicked in and mentioning Arya's itinerary did not seem appropriate.

"So, will this seminar be one that new recruits attend or just for department heads?" I asked in hopes to take the attention off of myself.

Holliday smiled and gave a small head nod as if appreciating what I had just done.

"We have the main auditorium. I'm sure everyone will attend. So, Lou, how is Quantico treating you?" Holliday asked.

"Thankfully, I can shoot and I'm in good shape, allowing all my extra time to be spent on studying versus recovery and practice." I replied.

Coppicino chimed in, "It never gets old seeing people show up to FLETC or Quantico ill prepared for the physical aspect."

"How did you get the FBI to waive their age limit restriction to let you in, Lou?" Holliday fired off with a straight face before laughing a few seconds later.

"I'll have you know that I legitimately beat the age limit by days, no waiver required." I jokingly explained as I noticed the approving nods and smiles coming from Coppicino and Sharpe.

Holliday laughed. He then invited me to stay for dinner while they talked shop.

I politely declined as I did not want to leave my classmates behind. I could also tell that they had things to chat about that I didn't need to hear. I made sure to exchange numbers with Holliday before excusing myself from the group.

I don't think I could have stayed with them for dinner without asking about Dover. This was no coincidence that both Arya and Holliday were in town going to the same place. Whatever it was, it could wait until I met up with Arya. If she was able to loop me in, she would.

It was Saturday and I had just returned to my room coming from studying with a few classmates. I checked my cell phone to find a message from Arya that she would not be able to meet up this week. Dover. It was on my mind and I had to do something to get it out. I decided and pulled some information on Dover.

Built in 1941, converted to an Army Military Base and later converted to an Air Force base. Many squadrons and units have been stationed and passed through. The base also receives our fallen soldiers and cares for them in every way from cleaning personal affects to be returned to family to repatriating the soldier.

I'm not sure what I was looking for, but I figured I would know when I see it. I found detail on housing and building structures outlining how cheap they were originally built and the base had to do a major renovation decades later. There was housing, BOQ's, bunkers, ordinance bunkers, runways, two control towers, the original and the newer one, and typical buildings for offices and events. On paper, it looked like any other base. I studied pictures and basic layout to see if anything looked out of place. Nothing.

I was about to quit the search when Lauren O'Quinn knocked on the open doorframe of my room, came in and sat down across from me with a heavy sigh. She was top of her class at MIT and destroying all of us in the cyber classes at Quantico. Honestly, she was top of almost every class.

"What seems to be bothering you, Lauren?" I reluctantly asked.

She was hesitant at first but held fast to why she was here. "I need help." She replied.

"What could you possibly need help in? You are mastering everything, even the physical training."

"Well, that is where you are wrong. You have not been in my Martial Arts class. I cannot find my balance and have been failing the lessons. I need help outside of class. Would you be willing to spend the time with me?" she asked. There was a sense of desperation in her voice.

"I can and I will on one or two conditions." I said.

"Great! What are the conditions?"

"One, help me be at least proficient in the Intelligence Courses. These books on data mining and analytics might as well be in Russian to me." I stated.

"Sure. I created a really cool APP that I can put on your phone that will help. It links to a mini mainframe I built from throw away drives from an MIT dumpster in which my very own program interacts with a Quad interface linked in to my laptop, smart phone, tablet and Bluetooth recorder." She rattled off.

"What? That will help me how?"

"This program breaks down technical jargon and computer analytical terms into layman terms. It's in testing now. Well, you would be my test pilot."

"So, if your program translates things incorrectly to me, I would basically fail versus barely pass the course, which is where I think I sit today?"

"Well, yes. However, I'm fully confident this will help.

What is your second condition?" Lauren asked.

"I'm not sure I'm on board with your solution to my first..."

"Moving on. What is the second?" She insisted as she ignored my fear of her solution to my first condition.

"I have a side project I'm working on. There are meetings taking place at Dover the next couple of weeks between multiple law enforcement agencies, FBI being one of them. I want to know more about this."

"That sounds a little over our pay grade, but I will dig around and see what I can find without drawing attention or being arrested." She gave me a look like this was asking too much.

She came around the table and opened her laptop. Minutes later I was given an overview of her algorithm in action. I read a page from our online cyber-crime course. Her recorder sent the audio through her processors and on the screen displayed a popup with an explanation of what I just read in terms a child could understand.

"This is amazing. You could sell this and be rich." I suggested.

"I don't do it for the money. I mean, I have sold a few programs, but mainly I do it for fun." She explained.

After talking for a bit, it turns out that Lauren O'Quinn, at the ripe old age of 22, has made her fortune already on patented software, such as anti-malware programs, the "How to of Corporate Analytics", and two spyware programs that caught the FBI's attention. When the FBI came to recruit Lauren, she immediately said yes.

Lauren instantly wanted to be part of the FBI's Cyber Crimes Division. She detested that people were violated all the time by hackers, stalkers, predators, organized crime, and even corporations.

She knew she had to be in shape before arriving at Quantico, so she ran and trained for months. However, some of the training was intimidating. She had never fired a gun or ever thought of fighting someone. The FBI now trains for close quarter combat and Lauren's confidence is going down after each training session.

The next morning, I met Lauren in the gym at 6:00AM for some basic Judo takedowns and self-defense moves. We were both wearing our standard FBI sweats. She already had the mats out and the gym was ours. Lauren was about 5'7 with a runner's physique. She had her short blond hair in a half pony tail and I could see sweat on her face.

"Were you running before you came here?" I asked.

"I love morning runs. The day is out of sync for me if I don't get a run in first." She replied as she used her sleeve to wipe a bead of sweat running down her temple.

"I know how you feel. Andy and I run every morning if we can." The comment made me miss that dog. I started to wonder who would be taking care of him when Arya was in Dover.

"Is Andy your roommate here?" Lauren asked.

"My dog. Police dog." I replied as I started to walk towards her. "You know, must fatalities in law enforcement happen up close." I was only a few feet from her now. She stood her ground trying to look serious but was putting too much effort into her persona and not enough into her stance.

I took a quick step, landing my foot on top of hers as I barely pushed her shoulders. She was helplessly falling backwards with her foot still trapped under mind. Had I not released her foot, she would have likely damaged her ankle or knee trying to compensate for the fall.

"What the hell!" she shouted as she picked herself up. I placed a kick to her head that stopped inches in front of her face. Her eyes were wide open and she froze.

I helped her up and accepted a few choice comments she threw my way before I joined in.

"Look, this is your problem and I need to show you a different way to solve it. But first, let's establish where your line is." I said

"My line?" She asked.

We spent an hour going over establishing one's area, and if compromised, be prepared for anything. We reviewed the importance of balance and positioning one's self when others are around. I taught her a one leg and two leg takedown, as well as the hip takedown. She was clearly worn out, but kept her focus and wanted to practice close combat handgun and knife techniques. Before we knew it, two hours passed and we were both worn out.

We agreed to get cleaned up and meet for breakfast to discuss Dover a bit more. At the cafeteria we both did not talk much as we ate a large breakfast. The morning workout obviously created some hearty appetites. As we got some coffee, the real conversations began.

Lauren wanted to impress me after just one day of research. She took out a pen and wrote all over a couple of napkins illustrating the layout of Dover Air Force Base. Some structures were not labeled, others were not found on public record, including two underground bunkers.

She explained that she pulled blueprints from a contractor database that outlined updates for electrical wiring throughout the base 15 years ago. Someone did not know what they were uploading at the time, and that is the only thread Lauren needed to find what she was looking for. It just had to be electronically filed and she apparently could find it.

We trained again in the late afternoon. She seemed to be a fast learner. I frequently boosted her confidence with reassuring remarks and like her algorithm, I broke the moves down to 3 or 4 simple steps.

I frequently talked about balance, weight, position and leverage over and over through the moves until one time she stopped me and had this look on her face. She said she could see the moves clearly now in her mind. They made sense. The sequences, the steps, everything just made sense now.

"It helps to remove fear and just react. React to what

you have been trained to do." I said.

She is intelligent, well built, young, stronger than she looks, and has the wherewithal to allow her instincts to kick in. She seems to have mastered the takedowns and is feeling more comfortable with the hand to hand combat.

We still had an hour until dinner, so I showed her how to apply four different arm bars. These quickly became her favorite things to do. She was really impressed with how little effort could incapacitate an individual.

I was also making breakthroughs of my own. That evening, I reread three chapters of our cyber-crimes material using Lauren's recorder and software. Things were starting to make more sense and I was starting to feel like I had a handle on what was going on in class. I, too, was teachable and understanding the lingo, knowing what the references meant and how to research cases systematically on the internet using FBI programs was not going to be the death of me after all.

The next morning, I got up early for a run. I needed some time to think about why I was so fascinated with Dover and if I should just leave it alone or press the issue. Was it an issue?

CHAPTER 28

I received a call from Arya explaining everything, which defused my half-baked little plan to get into Dover and explore for answers. That idea had high potential for disaster. It was not the brightest plan and when I shared it with Arya, she took it as endearing while declaring it very thick minded.

The weeks started to fly by. I was not able to connect with Arya for dinner or a weekend together, as the FBI had assigned her to a new task force that had her traveling and working multiple cases at a time. In a semi cryptic message, she basically advised me that Director Cooley knew of her special skills and was betting on her to drive results on a forward moving task force to head off high profile unknown subjects. The hope was that Arya could sense or get visions that would give them creditable leads. However, she was having a hard time receiving clear visions in my absence.

Arya expressed how wonderful it would be to have me on the team. I could hear a bit of worry in her tone as she explained her frustration with honing her visions. It's not like I haven't imagined joining the team and working with her. The show stopper in my mind was my fear of acceptance. The fear of others mistreating what is misunderstood. The dreams that haunted me becoming reality weighed on my mind.

As a result of much studying and training together, Lauren and I had become pretty close over the weeks. We acted like siblings during training, kicking each other's ass. She had become so good at Judo that she was winning matches against me half the time. I think she was training 5 hours a day, boarder line obsessed with martial arts now. She gave me a black eye a few days ago. It was a sparring accident, and she felt horrible about it for all of one day.

Without even noticing, we worked our way to the head of the class. We thought we deserved a break.

I asked Arya if she would mind me taking Lauren to Atlanta to spend time with Andy. Andy was staying with Roy while Arya traveled.

Lauren was an only child like me and her parents were in Hawaii. Traveling to see them was not possible on a weekend. She did not have any friends except for me and as much as we had been helping and pushing each other at Quantico, it did not feel right leaving her behind while I took leave.

Arya had heard all about Lauren and was surprisingly open to the idea. She said, "You both deserve some time away from there, and Andy will keep you both busy." She was in Kentucky tracking a serial rapist and expressed how she wished she was there waiting for us. We were both missing each other.

When I told Lauren that she was coming with me to Atlanta for the weekend, you would have thought a sixteen year old just got her new dream car. It was week 12 of 19 and this would be the first trip out of town for either of us.

We grabbed a shuttle to Atlanta Friday evening where to our surprise Roy and his son Jack, who had Andy on a leash, where waiting for us outside security. Andy was excited to see me. However, as soon as I introduced Lauren to Roy and Jack, that was Andy's queue to quickly befriend the attractive young lady.

The dog has a sickness, and he could not help himself as he was already rubbing Lauren's legs with his head. Lauren showed her appreciation by rubbing Andy's head and neck, instantly making her his current favorite for the moment.

Even though Roy and I were close, I had not seen Jack in well over two years. He is Roy's oldest son at 26 and works in Fraud & Security for a National Bank.

On the way to Roy's for dinner, Lauren and Jack were talking it up in the backseat. He seemed fascinated by her career choice as an MIT graduate and she seemed to be genuinely interested in what he did for the bank.

Once arriving at Roy's house, Andy started to pay me some attention. Lauren and Jack were sticking close to each other chatting it up, so Andy decided I would do for company.

By the time we finished dinner at Roy's, Lauren and Jack already made plans to meet up the next evening. They were not sure yet what they were going to do, but that did not stop Lauren from asking me several times if I would mind her going out the next night with Jack. She didn't want to seem ungrateful for the invite by running off with someone else. I assured her that I was fine and having a good time with Jack would probably be good for her.

It was nice catching up with Roy and his family over a nice home cooked meal. Throughout the night, unsolicited, Roy constantly assured me that the department is doing fine without me and running at a nice leisurely pace that constantly frustrates the Captain. We had a good time busting each other's chops during and after dinner. It had been a long day though, so Lauren and I went on our way to Arya's to crash for the evening.

"Lou, thank you for inviting me here this weekend. You and Roy are too funny. I have not laughed that hard in a long time. And those ribs! They were so good." She said.

"You're welcome. Roy was telling me that Jack made those ribs with his special rub. It looks like you two were hitting it off." I poked.

"He is sweet. It is nice to talk to someone who is knowledgeable in the areas of my expertise. Was this all to set me up with someone?" She asked.

"I'm not that clever." However, it made me think for a second if Arya and Roy conspired.

When we entered Arya's apartment, everything looked

the same with the exception of a picture on mantel of her and me with Andy. It made me smile.

Lauren looked around and gave the place a few compliments. It was getting late, so I showed her to Arya's room. She was insistent on taking the couch, but I won the battle and claimed the downstairs couch.

Andy was looking for food, so I led him into the kitchen where I found a couple of bowls for food and water and set him up in the corner. I stood, leaning forward, with my hands on the kitchen island watching Andy devour his food when two hands came from behind me and slowly ran up my ribs and around to my chest.

"Wait a minute" I said as I removed her hands from my chest and turned around to tell Lauren that this was not my intent for having her here. She was a beautiful woman, but I thought we had a mutual understanding that it was friendly and professional. I did not want to jeopardize our friendship or my relationship with Arya.

"I don't think I can wait another minute, Lou." Her smiling face, she was softly biting her lower lip, the way her eyes were lit up, Arya never look more beautiful and inviting.

"Wholly shit, where did you come from?" This was so unexpected, but very welcomed.

"I had Roy plan the dinner to give me time to fly in and surprise you." She was still smiling and now had a little bounce in her.

"This is a very nice surprise. For a second there, I thought you were Lauren. That would had been very disappointing, because we work well together and I would have felt really guilty if I sent the wrong message to her." I explained as I gave her a hug and then a kiss.

There was a slight, but noticeably deliberate cough coming from the kitchen doorway. Lauren had come down stairs to get a glass of water and was trying to let us know she was about to interrupt our reunion.

"Hi. I'm sorry to interrupt. I was coming in for a glass of

water. I'm Lauren. You must be Arya. Lou and Roy have told me so much about you." Lauren walked over extending her hand.

Arya released me and shook Lauren's hand, "Nice to finally meet you, Lauren."

"I'm really thankful you both invited me here. I needed some normalcy and relaxation." Lauren said as she started to look around for a glass.

Arya pointed to the cabinet by the sink, "You are very welcome. I'm beat, so I'm going to help get you situated down here, Lauren, and then hit the sack."

Lauren smiled at me, "I told you I should take the couch." She filed her glass and put it next to the couch, before running up the stairs to gathering her things from Arya's room.

"She is beautiful, Lou. You never mentioned how beautiful she was, did you?" Arya said with her hands on her hips.

"That never presented itself in conversation and has no bearing on the friendship we have together. She is not as beautiful as you though." I shot a smile her way and she smiled back.

Lauren came skipping down the stairs, "Okay you two love birds, get on up there and give each other a real hello. I will be fine down here. Arya, I would love to have some morning coffee with you after my run. How does that sound?"

"Sounds nice, thank you, Lauren. Have a good night." Arya replied as she led me up the stairs. We caught up that evening and then got a great night's rest together.

Waking up with Arya's leg over mine, arm over my chest and head on my shoulder was the recipe for a perfect start to the day. I could have stayed there with her all morning. A few minutes later she woke up and planted a good morning kiss on me before hitting the shower and then joining Lauren down stairs for coffee. After I showered, I joined them downstairs and found them enjoying themselves in conversation. Thankfully, they were not talking about me. It seems Lauren was getting a feel for what the field work is like through Arya's stories.

I said my good mornings to them and sat down to just listen in. Arya was describing her recent case work and was picking Lauren's brain on how to triangulate leads through the sporadic information she had gathered.

Lauren already had her laptop out and was playing around on it. Arya was sharing location detail from memory regarding the Kentucky serial rapist. Lauren brought up a map of the area which consisted of Elizabethtown, just south of Fort Knox, and then further south, Glasgow and Bowling Green. Mammoth Cave National Park and Interstate 65 where the two things that were noticeable to Lauren. Bowling Green and Mammoth Cave National park are two very touristy places.

"I hate to even say it, but have you looked at the possibility this could be a military man from Fort Knox, a Park Ranger or an imposter of either? The reports from the victims all state they were abducted in early evening and dumped on the 65 early in the morning, none catching a glimpse of the attacker." Lauren said to keep the brainstorming going.

"What if the attacker was in uniform? People have a propensity to trust those in uniform and not pay them much attention." I added.

"Arya said the victims did not see the attackers. However, is it possible to re-interview the victims but narrow the questioning from verbal to touch? Have them close their eyes and feel swabs of cloth. In the pile, have swabs from Army uniforms and Park Ranger uniforms. See if that brings to light any connections." Lauren devised.

"That is an interesting take on how to make the connection, if there is a connection. I will definitely set that up. Thank you. Then comes the seemingly impossible, which is to find the predator. You have a formula for that?" Arya asked half joking.

"Actually, if I had credentials and FBI access to certain

databases, I could write a program that could give you a list of subjects based on driving patterns, cell phone tower pings, work and home addresses, grocery and gas stops, and recreation; not to mention if there was any past behavior on record to cross reference, or security cams to cross reference from surrounding stores and traffic cams." she added.

"That would be amazing! I'm going to speak with my Director about giving you special access. I just need to figure out how to coordinate it with your training so you don't miss anything you can't catch up on." Arya sat back and started thinking as she sipped her coffee.

Jack proved to be very interested in Lauren as he called her around noon with plans for the night all worked out. Lauren was very excited for the opportunity to be social and Arya jumped in to share her closet for some suitable dresses for the day. They seemed to be finding each other's company enjoyable. Although Arya was a few inches taller than Lauren, they were able to find a few outfits that fit very well.

While changing into one of the dresses in the closet, she admitted to Arya that she had not been on a date in over a year. She was surprised by Jack's forwardness last night to ask her out, and couldn't help but wonder if the others put him up to it. When Lauren came out in the dress, Arya new the dress found a new owner.

"Come look at yourself in the mirror. You are absolutely stunning and we haven't even done make up or hair yet. From what Roy and Lou tell me, Jack is a hardworking, honest guy with his head screwed on straight. I think he is the one surprised that you said yes, because you are a catch." Arya said as Lauren smiled into the mirror.

"Thank you, Arya. I have had my nose in books or in front of the computer for so long that I don't even know what people do on dates. Damn, I'm almost 23 years old and I have no idea what I'm doing." She laughed at herself and then hugged Arya. "I'm normally more together than this, I promise. Thank you so much for helping me, for this weekend, for..." She trailed off wondering what else to say.

"You are welcome. Now let's get hair and makeup done before Jack gets here."

When Jack showed up to take Lauren out on the town, Lauren came downstairs wearing a sleeveless green silk blouse with a slightly low neckline and a black skirt that flowed to her knees, but showed off her curves. Jack had seen her last night in a polo shirt, jeans, tennis shoes and a ponytail, but her transformation today had him dumbstruck. She was wearing heals, showing off her athletic legs and her hair was flowing just past her shoulders. We all saw him mouth the word "wow" as Lauren walked up to him smiling.

"You look gorgeous, Lauren." Jack said as he looked her over and then locked on to Lauren's smile.

"Thank you, Jack. Will this do for our plans today?" she asked innocently. She was on the verge of shaking with excitement.

"It most definitely will." He replied as he stuck his arm out for her to take.

As they started to head out, I said, "Jack, have her back by curfew."

He stopped and asked, "What time is curfew?"

I looked at Arya and then Lauren before the three of us started to laugh. He quickly realized he took the bait and laughed too.

"Oh, wait!" Arya said as she ran into the kitchen. She came back out and handed a spare key to Lauren. "Have fun you too, be safe."

The apartment was ours for the evening and we spent more time catching up. At one point we were on the couch and she straddled my lap to give me a hug. She stayed there and asked me to help her come up with some visions.

"How does this work, Arya?" I asked.

"Just hold me, clear your mind and warm me up a bit." She explained.

"Warm you up, huh?"

"Umm Hmm." She whispered in my ear.

We sat there for a few minutes embracing each other as I tried to keep my mind clear and focused on sending energy through my hands. She moved my right hand off her hip and up her back where my left hand was resting. She then seemed more relaxed and laid her forehead on my shoulder. She trembled a few times and seconds later she jolted upright and seemed out of breath.

"What is it?" I asked

"That was strange. How long have I been sitting here?" She asked.

"You only rested your head on my shoulder for a few seconds."

"Wow, I had a very clear vision that seemed like it was 10 -15 minutes long." Arya said. She went on to describe walking through an old slaughter house. There were chains hanging from rails and rusty iniquitous looking machines probably used for processing and packaging. She could smell something awful in the air.

After walking around for a while, she saw a girl standing towards the back of the large barn. She seemed pleasant but out of place for such a gruesome setting. As she walked over to her the girl slowly started to fade away. When she arrived at the very spot where the girl had been standing, before totally disappearing, Arya was overcome by the visceral fear that this place was a house of horrors. Then, she snapped out of it.

"Well, that is something. Creepy for sure, but something. I hope it is related to your case and it helps you."

"Well, I was thinking about my case the whole time, so I hope it was. Okay, so no hands on the hips when we are trying to summon a vision. That was very distracting. All that energy was going in the wrong direction." she said as she held my hands. "Speaking of energy, how do you control it when you and Lauren are rolling around during martial arts?"

I thought I heard a little jealousy in her tone and question. She knew I was faithful and would not do anything to hurt her or jeopardize what we have. However, she is human and Lauren is a very attractive woman. I was surprised a bit that I had not given more thought to how attractive Lauren was, until now. Perhaps now that I'm in my thirties, I have much more respect for relationships and connections. When I was in my twenties, I probably would have had thoughts about Lauren.

It takes discipline to not act on the thoughts, but it takes maturity and respect to look past the beauty and connect with someone to really get to know them. Lauren was very mature for her age and she made that connection with me easily. She came straight at me with business and did not use her looks to persuade me into doing anything. Most people her age would have flirted, even if the other person was not their type.

"It helps that I think of her like I think of Lolo. Getting punched in the face and groin a few times also keeps my focus on the moves and protecting myself. Honestly, I haven't given it much thought. It's not like when I'm around you. My energy seems to flare the closer I get to you." I said as I put both hands on her hips and sent a little energy her way. She tightened her thighs instantly and her mouth flew open.

"Lou!" She put a hand over her mouth and one on her chest as if trying to quiet herself as she gasped for air. The surge was a bit more than I expected. That was unfair and selfish of me, but she was driving me crazy too.

We had to make a trip to the bedroom where we mutually enjoyed each other's touches as I tried my best to keep the energy to a minimum. We exhausted ourselves and fell into a light sleep afterwards.

When we woke up around 8:00 PM, Arya pulled a pad of paper and pencil out of the nightstand. As she jotted down some notes, I ordered some food.

Arya went into work mode and was on the phone talking with her team when the food arrived. She was typing away on her computer and running through some of the ideas Lauren had proposed. She didn't miss a beat as she took food from me and ate while she worked.

The conversations and phone calls lasted for about an hour. She even had a brief call with Director Cooley about giving Lauren special access. She did not get the immediate support she was hoping for, but he did say he would look into how that could even be a possibility and get back with her tomorrow. After taking a small break to clean up the mess that surrounded her, she turned to me and took my hand.

"Do you want to be on my task force?" She asked

"I think you know that I would love to work with you again. Do you see an opening coming up in a couple of months?" I was curious where this was coming from.

"I think there could be under the right circumstances." she furtively suggested.

"What's going on, Arya?"

"I want you to consider talking with Director Cooley tomorrow. He has been very understanding with me and my gift and I think, no, I know he would be very open to our partnership if he had a reason to partner us." she hinted.

"Wait a minute, are you suggesting I demonstrate my abilities to the Director to convince him we are or should be a team? I know you had serious reservation about sharing your abilities and that was with a track record of authorities like the FBI and others working with clairvoyant people. I, on the other hand, could be seen as a freak or a specimen if they decide to want to find out how it all works. I think you had a couple hundred of years of clairvoyant people put through the ringer before acceptance outweighed fearful actions of burning people at the stake." I rattled off without thinking about it.

She just sat there holding my hand in silence. I was about to say something, but she squeezed my hand and said, "It was a lot to ask, I know. I just thought it would be the only way to work together and we work so well together. Is that selfish? It sounds selfish doesn't it?" She asked looking guilty for even bringing it up.

She was good. Now I was starting to feel guilty for being defensive. "On some level, it probably is, but I know it is for the right reasons. I'm sorry I reacted the way I did Arya. As you can clearly see, I'm not 100% sold on others accepting me for me. I guess I need to trust more people, but I don't know Cooley." I explained.

"No, you don't know Cooley. But I do know him and I know him very well. You know me and trust me, so I guess I would be asking you to trust me on this, Lou. It's a big one, I know." Arya said.

"This is a bit unexpected. Is there any significance with this happening tomorrow, Arya?"

"There is. You are in town. I am speaking with him again tomorrow. And as you might know, there is a great deal of politics involved at Director level and above for assigning duty requests to certain graduates. High profiled ones like you and Lauren will draw much attention and jockeying for rights to divisions. Most graduates go where they are needed. Some have connections, combined with their class ranking, can get what they want." She explained.

The conversation continued well into the night. Arya was very diplomatic and reassuring through it all. I went in and out of partial agreement all night, which surprisingly did not frustrate Arya. She was the Saint of persistence and compassion. However, I was not convinced this was the only way.

CHAPTER 29

She was smiling ear to ear as they walked into Palatrino's, an upscale three level lounge bar with rooftop garden and private cabanas. The entrance was a stone archway with ivy running up and along the bricks. There were two beautiful leather upholstered antique equestrian benches on either side of the inner entry way. A woman was sitting on the one to the left as her date spoke to the hostess. Without realizing it, Lauren started to hold her breathe as she watched the gentlemen get turned away. Apparently, the hostess explained that reservations had to be made weeks in advance. The woman went from looking elegant to appalled and undignified as she berated her boyfriend on the way out.

Before Jack stepped forward, he leaned into Lauren and showed her a twenty-dollar bill he was palming.

"This should do the trick." he said with confidence as he stepped up to the hostess.

Lauren tried to grab his arm to stop him from embarrassing himself, but it was too late. He was already talking to the hostess and surprisingly she was smiling. He handed her the money and she starting to laugh. Lauren decided it was enough and she started to walk towards her date to see if she could manage to say something witty to pull him away and salvage the evening. She really did not care where they went, she was just happy to be out.

"Jack, can we go somewhere else? I just want to relax and have a little fun tonight." she said quietly as she gently tugged on his arm.

The hostess was not done with him though. "I can't believe you came here and gave me this."

"Well, to be honest, I was hoping my date and I could get an all access pass for the evening. I think you call them a tri-pass?" Jack asked.

"A tri-pass? I'm going to go talk to security now." she said plainly as she left her podium.

"Okay, seriously, Jack, let's go. I have not been out in ages and I don't want to start the evening with security throwing us out because you offended the hostess." Lauren pleaded.

"If you want to go, we can go. I thought you might like to be treated like a lady after two months of kicking ass with the guys at Quantico." he said with what she thought was the most adorable smile. He was acting a little smug though and she was starting to see through his act.

The hostess returned with a security officer in tow. "Okay, here is the deal. These keys are for members only and special promotions. Please don't lose these, Jack." She handed over two gold swipe cards that had Palatrino's VIP written on them.

The security guard shook Jack's hand, "Good to see you again, Jack. The system works great. You wouldn't believe the information we gather on customers and how it helps our business."

"Actually..." Jack started to say.

"Of course, you would." The guard finished Jack's sentence for him and laughed. Then he gave a two-finger salute from the corner of his eyebrow to Lauren and said, "Ma'am". as he walked away, he shouted over his shoulder, "Have a good time you two."

Lauren was catching up fast and her shoulders were starting to relax a bit. Jack turned to her and handed her a VIP card. When she turned it over it had TRIPLE PASS written on the back with three shiny diamonds under the words.

The hostess explained the layout, but also added that part of the mystic was to find the "extra" rooms and see what they had to offer. She also added that all the hidden rooms change every two months, except for the Lion's Den and for good reasons. She didn't say why, she just winked when she said it.

"I worked for Dytec a few years ago and installed these card readers everywhere in this place. The layout is amazing. The members have access to about 60 percent more areas than the rest of the public. These hidden rooms are big, but I've never seen them finished." he explained.

"You had me worried there for a minute. I can't wait to get a drink and start to explore a bit." Lauren responded with a grin as she put her arm through his and followed him into the retreat.

Jack was not kidding when he mentioned the place was amazing. There were card readers everywhere, if you were looking for them. Jack already knew that red readers were for staff only. Black card readers would take you to hidden studies, private lounge areas, elevators that access the roof-top private cabana and gardens area. They both tried to play it cool, but each time they swiped their card they were even more astonished by the lavish designs. After finding 4 rooms, they both finally settled down on the second level in the main lounge area where most people gathered for drinks and en-trees.

The lights were low in the lounge and as they sat next to each other on a leather coach, sipping their drinks, they cas-ually people watched as they traded college stories.

Jack was ambitious and sure of himself, but not in an arrogant way. He was a good story teller and had her laughing on multiple occasions. As Jack was looking for the waitress across the room, he turned his attention back to Lauren and caught her smiling at him.

"You have a beautiful smile Lauren." Jack said as he took her hand and started to play with her fingers.

She was about to say something, but Jack leaned in for a kiss. She tried to stop smiling and forced her lips to relax to accept his kiss. He hovered just an inch away patiently as she found a way to loosen up and engaged with him. It had been so long since she had kissed a man, Lauren softly played with his lips with hers for a few seconds, enjoying the electricity and then backed away to catch her breath.

"I think I'm ready to go exploring again. Are you up for it?" Jack asked.

She was still trying to catch her breath and was about to answer him, but instead pulled him in for another kiss. This one lasted much longer as she remembered to breathe through her nose, not to mention she had a good hold on the back of Jack's head. He did not resist one bit. In fact, his hand lay gently on her cheek shielding most of their activity from others as he continued to kiss her back.

Satisfied, Lauren released Jack and slowly stood up. Her knees were a little wobbly but she made it look graceful as she straightened her skirt out. "I'm ready now." she said with a big smile as she extended her hand to him.

As they came to the landing at the top of the third story stairs, Jack pointed out a swipe on the wall behind some decorative curtains. As they entered it turned into a long hallway going to their right. There was a square hole shoulder height allowing passers a chance to look through a two-way mirror out into the third-floor lounge area.

Lauren stopped for a moment and looked out into the lounge and saw a few people slow dancing in the middle of the floor while others were socializing in small groups. She was about to start walking again when someone stepped right in front of the mirror. She let out a short scream from being startled, but the person on the other side did not hear her and kept messing with the contact lens in her eye before moving on seconds later.

"I suppose I should get use to that if I'm going to be an FBI agent." Lauren said to Jack as he pulled her away from the mirror and lead them further down the hall. They went around a corner and opened a large hand-crafted oak door. Inside was the Lion's Den. There was a grand fireplace to the left, a large lion skin and head on the floor about 5 feet from the fireplace. Couches and chairs surrounded the fur and fireplace in a large semicircle. Beyond the couches was a large oak table and chairs tucked under it. A self-services bar was in the corner.

"So, this is the Lion's Den. It's kind of intimidating." Lauren said as she pointed to the lion on the floor. Jack walked over to the bar.

"This bar is fully stocked. You want anything?" Jack asked as he ducked down to examine the choices closer.

"Is there a bottle of water back there?" she asked. Jack popped back up seconds later with two waters and walked over to hand one to Lauren.

"What do you think those are for?" Jack asked as he walked to the fireplace and pointed at five thumb-size rocks on the wall next to the mantle.

He pushed one in and the lights dimmed. Lauren chuckled and walked over. She pushed the second one in and the fire turned on.

"It's not cold enough for a fire. It's romantic though." She said as she pushed the rock again and the flames died out. Jack pushed the third rock in and a plasma TV started to come out of the ceiling above the fireplace. They sent it back up immediately.

The fourth button and fifth buttons did not do anything. They both looked at each other with slight disappointment. Then Jack pushed both rocks at the same time.

A noticeable click sound came from the wall to their left, beyond the fireplace. They walked over to it and notice a three-foot section ajar. Lauren pushed on the wall and it moved open with ease. A light automatically came on in the room they discovered. They both stood there starring for a moment.

"Did you plan this?" Lauren asked quietly as she turned to Jack.

The room was designed like a private dining room. There was a wall of wine to the left, a couch to the right, a private bathroom by the couch and a linen dresser next to the doorway they were still standing in.

"I had no idea about this, Lauren."

"It's just so..." She paused for a second.

"Out of place?" Jack asked.

"Yes. How strange. Who would use it? What if you were using it and someone walked in? That would be very awkward." she said.

They stepped in and the door closed behind them. Jack drew Lauren's attention to a lock system on the door that prevented the door from opening to outsiders when occupied. He jokingly slowly started to turn the latch to lock them in, just to see Lauren's reaction.

She was smiling, as she slowly shook her head no. He stopped and returned it to the resting position it was in seconds ago and shrugged his shoulders as he smiled back at Lauren.

She laughed and it came out loud, much louder than she wanted. It was probably because it was a nervous laugh.

The night could not have gone any better and although she would love nothing more than to fall onto the couch with the handsome Jack Cable, she thought it best to postpone their rendezvous. She knew he was kidding around, but nevertheless she valued the act too much to have it be in a random place. She wanted him to respect her and her him.

They wound up on the roof top later on and to their delight a three-piece jazz band was playing. Jack invited Lauren out to a little dance floor. The last time she danced was at prom. To her enjoyment he took the lead and they slow danced to a few songs. The harmonious notes marinated the air around her putting her into a surreal trance as Jack guided her around the small platform. She found herself kissing him again just as the music stopped.

"I can't believe I have to go back to Quantico tomorrow

afternoon." she said as they walked to a small table in the corner. The breeze on the rooftop cooled them off as they settled into a couple of cushioned wicker chairs.

"I still can't believe you are at Quantico and going to be an FBI agent." He did not mean to be off-putting with his comment. It was an innocent statement.

"I will take that as a compliment, I think." She wanted to give him the benefit of doubt, but the reality of it was she sometimes thought the same thing.

The past couple of months were intense and she wondered at times how she had changed. She never held a gun before and now she was a marksman and could not only defend herself, but she knew how to kill or incapacitate a person with her bare hands.

She had dreams of building programs that made a difference in society, programs that people with needs could use to better their lives. Now, she was thinking like a hunter, programming to hunt people. Yes, at times she wondered where all this would lead. However, right now, she just wanted to enjoy the weekend.

"I'm sorry. It's just that...well, growing up around law enforcement, I have never met one so beautiful and smart." He actually blushed as he made his confession.

"That was definitely a compliment." Lauren laughed as she said it.

Jacked looked at his watch and suggested they grab a bit to eat before heading home. Lauren wanted something easy like a pulled pork sandwich or fish and chips. Jack knew just the place. They both agreed that Palatrino's was a hit as they returned the VIP cards to the hostess on their way out.

They ended up at a small family owned and run sandwich shop around the corner. It had a nice front patio with rustic chairs and tables where they sat outside eating, talking and people watching again.

It was just after 11:00PM, and although they were really

enjoying each other's company, they knew the night was coming to an end. Jack got up and went back inside to get two coffees to go. Lauren waited patiently and kept watching the different waves of groups walk the streets. They all seemed to be having a good time, enjoying the clubs and restaurants in the immediate area.

Jack came out of the shop and called Lauren's name as he held up two coffees showing his achievement. She smiled at him as she got up and started walking over.

As she slung her purse over her shoulder, she heard a popping noise followed by her purse falling to ground. Her shoulder felt like it was on fire. Before she had a chance to assess the situation, she noticed the coffee in Jack's left hand explode into a mist and then the glass door to his right shattered. At this point screams erupted as a few patrons on the patio started diving to the floor. As Jack started falling backwards more popping sounds filled the air.

She lunged towards Jack and landed at his feet. Chaos stirred around them for several seconds as more gunfire could be heard. She looked up and saw Jack's hands shacking as he tried to cover his own wound. She managed to crawl up to his chest and could now see that he was shot in the lower left rib area.

Lauren looked around to see if more shooting should be anticipated but found that the street had thinned out. A few people were running around. She noticed several people lying on the ground on the sidewalk in front of the patio. Several people around her were on the ground as well, already talking to 911 operators and consoling each other.

"Jack, can you hear me? You are going to be okay. Just stay still while I keep pressure on your wound. You were shot, but you are going to be okay. Okay?" She was shaken from the explosive impulsive violent act, but her voice held together and was calm as she spoke to him.

He just nodded and laid his head back on the cement. He was clearly struggling to breathe. She started applying pressure with both hands and became even more nervous when she saw the amount of blood pooling next to Jack. She kept pressure with her left hand as she searched for an exit wound with her right hand. Her left arm went limp, causing her to fall right into Jack's chest. He let out a loud groan as she pulled herself off of him.

"Shit, I'm sorry, Jack." She went back to applying pressure, when the surge of pain struck her left shoulder again. Lauren looked at her left shoulder and realized she was shot too. The panic really started to set in now.

Just then the shop owner came out with some towels and knelt down next to Jack. He took over covering Jack with towels and then applying pressure. Lauren sat back against a chair and pulled her purse over to her with her left leg. Taking her phone out, she dialed Lou's number and did her best to hold it together, not cry or pass out as the phone rang.

CHAPTER 30

We agreed that the conversation was not over and that we would try to pick it up in the morning. As we started to get ready for bed my phone rang. I saw that it was Lauren.

"Looks like someone is calling to tell us not to wait up for her." I laughed as I answered the phone.

"Lou! Lou! Something terrible has happened. Jack and I were in West Midtown and I think we got caught up in some gang crossfire. I've been shot in the shoulder and Jack was hit in the chest. He looks pretty bad. The ambulances are just now getting here. I don't know where they are going to take us yet. Please tell his dad and find us. I'm sorry, I'm... I..."

"Calm down. It's okay. They will most likely take you to Emory. I will make the calls and we will see you soon. How are you holding up?"

"I'm about to pass out. My arm was hurting, now I can't feel anything."

"Tell the paramedics that, Lauren. That is really important. You will be okay. Try to keep the phone on. Arya will be on the line."

At this point Arya was jumping into her FBI sweats and grabbing the phone from me. I could hear her keeping Lauren calm as I quickly got dressed and grabbed Arya's go bag and phone. In two minutes, we were already out the door and driving. When we hit the highway, I saw Arya hang up.

"They are going to Emory, Lou. I'm going to call Roy now."

It was a short conversation with Roy. One that I knew

Roy hadn't digested fully as he probably went into cop mode. I was flying when Arya asked me to slow down a bit, something about getting there in one piece.

"Shit, Arya, they have to be okay. You know? I don't have much family."

"I know, Lou. They will be okay."

"What if they're not? How do I get to them to make a difference? This is crazy!"

"Just focus on driving right now. We will figure all that out when we get there, okay?"

Thirty minutes later we pulled into the E.R. parking lot and ran into the waiting room. Arya took over. She flashed her FBI badge at the admittance nurse and explained one of her own was just brought in. The nurse looked confused.

"We are notified if law enforcement is brought in and no one has mentioned anything."

"I don't care what people failed to find out, I'm telling you Lauren O'Quinn is here and she is FBI. Tell me where Lauren O'Quinn and Jack Cable are please."

"Okay, hold on a second." The nurse said. Just then, the E.R. doors opened and two more victims were rolled in. There was a paramedic straddling one on the gurney, pumping his chest as the other medic rolled them in. Doctors and nurses quickly surrounded them as they made their way to an open room. The other victim came in with less commotion as he had already passed.

Arya saw the admittance nurse start to walk down the hall and followed her.

"Lou!" she shouted as she pointed to a curtain. She stood looking in for only a few seconds and then kept walking with the nurse.

I ran over and saw a few doctors working on Lauren's shoulder. She was lying on her right side, eyes closed. They had cut away the once beautiful blouse Arya had given her and had a surgical cloth covering half her chest. Instruments and latex fingers were digging around in the exit wound just above her armpit and entrance wound on her back. She was hooked up to machines, intubated, and from what I could tell her vitals looked decent under the circumstances.

Arya shouted at me again. She was standing in the hallway when the gurney came rolling out from behind two double doors. Jack was on it and they were taking him to surgery. Arya met me halfway as I came over.

"They say he has a collapsed lung and damage to a kidney. He is going to surgery. How is Lauren doing?"

"She is out. She looks stable, but they are still working on her."

I went back to where they were working on Lauren and asked one of the nurses to make sure the doctors knew she had lost feeling in her arm prior to the medics arriving. Apparently, Lauren had advised them already. Good girl. She was a fighter. She didn't know she was when we first met, but I helped her find it within her. The nurse directed me to wait down the hall.

The night only got worse when Roy and his wife showed up. Jack was in surgery for three hours and it was a long three hours. I had no answers for Roy, other than what Lauren shared over the phone. Arya did a great job keeping Roy's wife calm.

It took a while, but Arya got permission for us to go visit Lauren in the ICU around 4:00AM. The lack of sleep and the absence of the adrenaline from earlier was now causing me to have irrational thoughts. I was feeling a great amount of guilt for Lauren's situation.

Had I not brought her with me, she would be at Quantico, in perfect health, with a bright future in the FBI. Now, she lay in the ICU, with questionable use of her left arm. In her current condition, she would have to leave Quantico, drop out. Sure, they would likely give her another chance to go through the entire training. Would she have odds stacked against her though? Would her arm cause her to fail physical training?

As Arya and I stood over Lauren in her room, I could not suppress the thought to help Lauren. I was standing at her bedside with my hand slowly drifting towards her shoulder.

"You take that road, I will back you, Lou. Just know that she keeps the memories and you explain everything. Too many people know what happened tonight."

I stood there with my hand hovering over Lauren's shoulder. Was I ready for another conversation similar to the one I had with Arya and Lacey? I did not want the guilt of her career being railroaded because of this weekend. She looked innocent as she lay there. I knew I had to do something, but I wasn't prepared for bringing another person in on my secret.

Arya was asking me to reveal my gift to her director to work with her and help her visions. None of this would make sense to Arya if I healed Lauren, revealing my gift, but did not trust Arya enough to speak to her director. I made my decision and I hoped it was the right one.

"I will speak to Director Cooley today, Arya, but on my terms. If he is going to bring me in to your unit, it will have to be a package deal. Lauren is part of the deal. I have to heal her, which means she will know about me. If she takes it as well as you did, then perhaps there is hope." I explained the guilt I would carry if she had to leave Quantico.

"I get it, Lou. I would be lucky to have her on my team. If you think you can trust Lauren with your secret, I can make it all work with Cooley. I'm sure of it."

"Well, this is turning out to be anything but a relaxing weekend away from Quantico."

"I will go keep the nurses occupied while you talk to Lauren." She turned me towards her and gave me a kiss and a hug before walking out.

I reached over and squeezed Lauren's left hand to get her attention. She was sleeping and not responding. I reached over her and took her right hand in mine and squeezed it as I said her name. She slowly opened her eyes and then started to look around. I could see fear start to build in her face as she started putting it all together.

"Where is Jack? How is he?"

"Jack came out of surgery fine and we are told he is expected to make a full recovery. His parents are with him."

"Good." She started to fade off again, but I tightened my hold on her hand. The morphine was not helping me keep her attention. Her body wanted to rest.

"Lauren, I need to talk to you for a moment."

"Can it wait? I'm tired."

"No, I'm afraid not. Stay with me."

"Am I okay? What's wrong?"

"Your shoulder is pretty bad. Bad enough to have you leave Quantico if I don't help you."

"I was doing so good. I don't want to go through it all again."

"I'm not sure you could go through it all again if your shoulder does not fully recover. Which is why I want to help you."

"That's twice you said you could help me. What do you mean Lou?"

"This may sound really odd, but I'm kind of like a medicine man. I can heal people. It doesn't sound possible, but I can make your shoulder like new so you don't have to leave Quantico."

"I'm on morphine, aren't I?"

"Yes, but this is real. Other than Arya and my immediate family on the reservation, no one knows about my gift."

"Are you going to perform a sacrifice or something? I don't have the stomach for that." She made a face like she was going to get sick and then smiled.

"Nothing like that. I would simply lay my hand on your shoulder and heal you. It would have to be our secret. Your career and my life would depend on it being our secret. Do you understand?"

"I never pegged you for crazy, Lou. You took the polygraph just like I did to get into Quantico, right?"

"Yes, I did. I'm not crazy." I thought she was going to buzz the nurse and have me removed.

"Give it your best shot, Looney Lou." She giggled a little.

"Not like this Lauren. I need you to take me seriously. I need to know you understand this is really going to happen."

She started to wave her hand as if to quiet me. I sat back in my chair to give her some space.

Arya walked in the room and went to Lauren's side. She looked over her shoulder at me for a sign and I just shook my head slightly from side to side.

"Hi, Lauren, how are you feeling?"

"Arya, I was having the best date ever. We kissed."

"Really? How was it?"

I toned them out for a moment and let them catch up. Perhaps this was Arya's way of connecting to get through to Lauren. I felt like the nurses were going to kick us out any second and my moment of opportunity would pass. Sure enough, a nurse came in seconds later and escorted us away.

Arya looked back at Lauren and said, "Remember what we talked about. Get some rest."

We met up with Roy and the family around 6:00AM for breakfast in the hospital cafeteria. They all looked worn out, but shared their relief as they had just received some good news from the doctor. Jack's surgery went exceptionally well. He woke up about forty minutes ago and talked for a few minutes with the doctors and nurses and then with his parents. They were thankful for the state Jack was in, as it could have been much worse. Roy knew how crazy a bullet can act in the chest cavity. He has seen many victims shredded on the inside as the bullet bounces around off of ribs or even the spine.

We were all very tired and decided to go home and get some rest. Visiting hours were open later and we decided to meet up in the afternoon. Roy was handling the situation very well, considering his oldest son was in the ICU after a date with my classmate. His wife showed equal empathy for Lauren as they mentioned they would stop by later to check in on her.

They were delighted that Jack had a date with such a promising young lady. They explained that his last two dates over the last year were huge busts and he kept throwing himself deeper into his work. I gave them both a quick hug and we went our separate ways.

CHAPTER 31

We returned to Arya's apartment and immediately went to bed. After about five hours of sleep we were both up and planning the day. Arya informed me that she had asked Lauren to believe me and to keep an open mind when we returned.

"Arya, call Cooley and put your idea in play. When you think you have his attention, let me speak to him."

"Lou, this isn't a phone conversation. We should meet with him in person."

"I understand that and we will, on my terms though."

Arya made the call. As she explained the nature of the call, I could tell the Director was losing his patience with Arya. She was finally able to finish explaining why she wanted Lauren and me on the team and then fell silent for a moment.

"Yes, Director, he is standing right here. Ask him yourself if either of us is crazy." She handed me the phone and said, "It's not going well. Phone call was a bad idea."

I took the phone and didn't even give the Director the courtesy of a hello as I knew I had to be aggressive.

"Sir, respectfully, I'm not going to bullshit with you over the phone. You want the best unit in the FBI state side, meet us at Emory in an hour under the name Lauren O'Quinn. You have one chance to see what Arya and I are capable of together, and then I'm on a plane to Quantico."

"Let me tell you how..." He started to say, but I hung up on him as he was still barking.

"What the hell, Lou? That is not the way to get Cooley

to respect this situation and put his neck out on the line to pull this team together." She was upset and sat down on the coach. "Shit, what have I done?"

"We will be fine, I hope. Perhaps now, he will show up to see for himself or show up to finish the conversation he was having with me as I hung up. Either way, I think he will meet me on my terms. One act with Lauren's consent will hopefully create a great team. My stomach can't think of the alternatives." I said as I sat down next to her.

The alternatives were plentiful and painful to think about. Director Cooley could easily arrest me for practicing medicine without a license. That probably wouldn't hold up in court, but I don't think I would be brought to court. If this did not go our way, we will have ruined our lives. We did not have much time to think about all of that right now, because we had to get to the hospital and speak with Lauren again before the FBI showed up.

We were both silent on the drive to the hospital. It wasn't until we were parking that Arya took my hand, keeping me from getting out of the car, and then broke the silence.

"I love you, Lou." she said with a slight sigh of relief in her voice and shoulders. It was the first time one of us had said it to each other.

My heart began an erratic rhythm. I turned towards her to give her my attention and she said it again. Only this time the flood gate of emotions opened from within her. It was as if she couldn't hold these words in any longer. Whether it was the uncertainty of how the next 30 minutes would unfold, not knowing if she would ever have the chance to say them to me again, or if it was just how overwhelming the weekend had become, her confession would not wait.

"I am madly in love with you. It hurts sometimes, physically hurts to not be around you. When I think of you, it's hard to stop. I get lost in thinking of your humor, your modesty, your company, the way I feel when you are around, your touch. I would be content living in a grass hut on an island with just you and Andy." I could see her eyes glassing over, but her voice was steady and passionate.

"I love you too, Arya." I said as I wiped away a tear that started to run down her cheek. "I think this is the first time either of us has said I love you to the other. I'm a little jealous you beat me to the punch."

She gave a little laugh as she leaned over and buried her head in my shoulder. She smelled good. She always smelled good.

I was never big on perfumes, but she always had this faintest hint of lavender oil that mixed so well with her natural scent or pheromones. Whatever it was, I missed it all the time. I was hooked on her too.

I went on to express what I loved about her and how she made me feel. She had an adorable smile painted on her face and her wide eyes owned me as if pulling more and more compliments from me.

When she released me from her spell, I asked her, "Do you think we are confessing our love for each other now, because we are afraid what might happen over the next 20 minutes?"

"Maybe, but I also think I am telling you now because I love you more than my career. You know me well enough to know how big of a deal that is. I'm willing to walk away from it all right now to have you in my life. I don't want to lose you because I wanted you closer to me, to my job, my team." she admitted.

"Arya, as much as I appreciate you saying that, I would not let you walk away from the FBI. Don't feel like you talked me into something. From my point of view, you have been very passive on your approach to pass ideas to me. I really enjoy working with you. Let's go do this and see how the cards fall. I'm betting on your judgment of Cooley."

With that, we gave each other a confident nod and left the car. We found our way to Lauren's new room in recovery. They had moved her from the ICU hours before. A nurse was just leaving the room as we walked in and interrupted Lauren eating a light lunch. She smiled at the sight of us and waved us in with her right hand, spoon still in it.

She was still hooked up to monitors. Her gown was only over her right shoulder, leaving her left side and chest fully accessible to the nurses and doctors. She had layers of bandages covering her shoulder as well as her left breast. I could see the betadine solution stains on her exposed neck, arm and upper chest where the bandage stopped.

"I know, I've looked better." she said as she stuffed another spoon full of something green in her mouth.

Arya spoke first. "You look great, considering. Would you like me to brush your hair?"

I hadn't even noticed that her hair was slightly a mess, but the gesture from Arya was a home run. Lauren thanked her profusely and mentioned that she could not look like a monster for her visitors. She even asked Arya for a little touch up on the face.

I was starting to get nervous that we would run out of time to talk to her, but then Arya spoke up as she took some base application from her purse and showed it to Lauren.

"Will this do? I grabbed it from your overnight kit." Arya asked. Lauren looked so thankful as she nodded with a mouth full of what might pass as a sausage patty.

"Do you remember what we spoke about earlier, Lauren?"

"Honestly, I don't remember much of anything after the ambulance ride. I do remember seeing you and Lou earlier."

"Well, we talked to you about leaving Quantico or speeding up your healing process. Does that sound familiar?"

Lauren paused for a minute as if collecting her thoughts or deciding if the brown object she was eating was truly edible. I decided to jump in.

"Do you remember me mentioning that I have a special gift of healing people? I'm like a medicine man on my reservation. I asked you if you would have an open mind to allow me to lay hands on your shoulder and heal it."

"Okay, I thought I was dreaming that. We seriously had that conversation?"

"Yes, we really did."

Arya then added, "And he really did heal my gunshot wound." We both could see that she had all her faculties back and was starting to grow a little concerned over this conversation.

"Look Lauren, I think I have earned your trust and friendship. I don't take that lightly and I don't want to ruin either. I am asking you to trust me though. It's painless. It requires nothing for you to do, and it only takes a minute. I'm not going to do anything to jeopardize your health or what the doctors have done."

Lauren started to laugh, "Sorry. That sounded a lot like an infomercial. Now list the side effects."

Just then, Director Cooley and two other field agents walked in.

I couldn't help myself as I said to Lauren, "No need to list them, they just arrived."

The two agents stood by the door as Cooley walked over to Arya and pulled her aside. He positioned himself so he could stare at me as he talked to her. As suspected, Cooley did not look very happy. I knew I only had another minute to talk to Lauren.

"Lauren, do you believe me?"

"Well, I trust you. But you have me a little concerned right now and that might be an understatement." She said as she pointed to all the suits in the room.

"Fair enough. It's like this, Arya's job is on the line, along with your career and mine. Your nerve may or may not heal completely and that may impact your next attempt at Quantico."

"I don't want to go through Q twice, Lou,"

"I know that. Just like I know you don't want to be kept to a desk. I want to remove those possibilities and allow you to finish Q with me and join Arya's team. What do you say?"

Before she could answer Cooley stepped in.

"Detective Abrams, you should be more careful how you speak to people. They may misinterpret your intent and react." He seemed all too calm now as he walked over and stood next to the other two agents. Director Cooley was an intimidating and big man.

"Okay, Abrams, you made it very clear this is your show."

"They wait outside." I said.

"They are not going anywhere"

I walked over to the Director, "They wait outside for your protection and plausible deniability."

He just stood there and stared at me. I think he started to realize that if something out of the norm were to happen, deniability might be good. He finally turned to the other two agents and asked them to wait outside.

When he turned back to me, I said, "If you speak a word of this to anyone, I'll have you tied up in tribal litigation until you retire or resign." I calmly added as I turned my attention to Lauren.

"You have my time and my attention. How about you show me a little respect, too?" Cooley said to me as he stepped forward.

I felt Arya pat my lower back a couple of times. I knew she was trying to tell me to cool my jets.

"You're right, my apologies. Let's start with introductions." After all, this was our first face to face. Tension in the room started to decrease after introducing Lauren formally to the Director. Cooley admitted to her that he had never met a candidate, only graduates. They both got a laugh out of that. He had had been briefed on her stats and accomplishments on the way to the hospital by Quantico's Training Division lead.

"Miss O'Quinn, I'm sorry about your unfortunate injuring. I was briefed on my way over and I must say you probably would have been head of your class if it weren't for this event."

The Director could not have known how powerful and perfectly timed those comments were.

Lauren looked over at me and I could see that reality had slapped her hard in the face. The picture I was trying to paint for her was completed by Cooley. I could see her eyes watering up as she waved me over with her right hand. Cooley stepped out of the way and allowed me to lean over her.

"Okay, I'm officially freaking out, Lou. I just got a glimpse at the next 12-18 months and I'm not happy."

"It will be okay"

"Can someone tell me what is going on here?" Cooley demanded.

"I'm asking Lauren if she would like to be healed, in order to avoid dropping out and having to go through Quantico all over again next year. We are all on edge, as this is a bit mystic to...well, to anyone off the Zuni reservation."

"Holy shit, really? This is why you brought me down here on a Sunday, to get this girl's hopes up?"

Arya started to unbutton her blouse, "Director, you know I was shot on the shoulder and neck. There were dozens of witnesses. A few days later Lou healed me and I don't even have the scars to prove I was shot." She had her blouse down to her elbow on her left side exposing the entire area for Cooley and Lauren to see.

"Impossible. That was only a few months ago. Where are the scars?" Cooley said as he examined her more closely.

"This will only take a few more minutes of your time sir." I said to Cooley as I looked at Lauren for a response.

Lauren looked stunned, but she regained her focus and gave me a nod.

"I'm going to carefully cut away the bandage so we can see her wound. Then I'm going to heal her. Then, Arya will politely ask you one more time to pull some strings to keep the three of us together when working under your division." I carefully cut away the bandage with a pair of bandage scissors that were on the table by the door.

Lauren was just as curious as Director Cooley to what her injury looked like. As I removed the final wrap, there was a patch over her exit would.

"Abrams, I don't think you should remove that. You could expose her to an infection." Cooley said.

Lauren responded for me. "It's okay, Director. I'm willing to take that risk."

I slowly peeled off the patch as Lauren made some grimacing faces. We all looked at the damage together.

"What is that?" Lauren asked as if grossed out by the object coming out of her skin just below her exit wound.

"It's a drainage tube." I said.

Her shoulder was many different colors from the damaged blood vessels. The hole was stitched up, but she had a drainage tub tucked into a slit below her wound to release any fluid build-up.

"My hand might feel warm and then hot. But seconds later, you will feel a hundred percent. You ready?"

"God, I hope so." She said as she started to grit her teeth and close her eyes.

I kept my hands hovering just above her wound as I started to focus my energy. I could feel it building up within me and then the warmth flowed from my stomach through my chest and down my arms to my hands. Just then I gently made connection with Lauren's skin and felt her spasm from the heat and the pain of me touching her wound.

It looked like she was going to scream as her eyes and mouth popped wide open. She held it in and started to embrace the warmth that replaced the pain. Just when I thought we were getting close to the end, I slightly moved my left hand to the tube and slowly started to pull it out. I could feel Cooley starting to pull me away, but I held my ground as Arya told him to stop. Seconds later I backed away from Lauren and was holding her drainage tub in my hand.

The room was silent. Lauren was poking her skin where the exit wound was a moment ago. Then she sat up holding her gown to her chest and started to move her left arm at will. She couldn't hold back the laughter and tears. The Director just stood there stoic. Outside the door a commotion had begun that broke the Director from his trance on Lauren. He quick went to the door and opened it. There were two nurses outside trying to get past the FBI agents.

"Nurses, everything is fine in here. Your patient is fine. You will see her in a few minutes. Thank you for your patience." With his closing comment, he closed the door and turned to me.

"Explain this."

I walked over to the corner and started to share some of the details and stories to help draw a picture of how I have come to learn about my gift and how to use it.

Cooley just kept nodding as I spoke to him. Meanwhile, Arya had taken the scissors and was shredding the bed sheets, cutting quickly. Without even interrupting us she managed to remove my shirt and gave it to Lauren to wear. Luckily, I had a T-shirt on underneath my polo shirt. About 3 minutes had past and Lauren was dressed in a white skirt Arya made from bed sheets. It could pass as store bought. With my polo untucked over it, she looked like a visitor.

"As you can guess, I have much to process after witnessing this today. I can tell you this much though, you both are going to be a day late to Quantico, because I'm going to want to talk to you both in depth tomorrow. I will make the arrangements with Quantico and call you three tomorrow."

"I'm putting my life and career in your hands and trusting you to keep this classified." I said as I offered my hand to him. He took it and gave a firm handshake.

"You can trust me." He said as he opened the door and invited the nurses in.

They both squawked at the site of the bed being empty and then identified Lauren standing next to Arya. They looked shocked.

Director Cooley's voice took over the room. "Ladies,

Miss O'Quinn is now in the custody of the FBI. These two gentlemen will stay behind and fill out any forms you think need filling out. Good day."

With that he motioned all of us to leave and we did. The other two agents took control and boxed the nurses in so they could not follow. We were in the elevator and out of the hospital moments later. Heading towards the parking lot, Cooley said a few words to Arya and then went a different direction. When we arrived at Arya's car Lauren stopped me and wrapped her arms around me, squeezing me as she rested her cheek on shoulder.

"Thank you, Lou. I don't understand how you did it, but thank you." She started to cry as she pulled away. Then she pulled me in and planted a kiss on my cheek. She turned to Arya smiling and mouthed the word 'sorry' as she climbed into the back seat. Arya just laughed and got into the driver's seat as I sat myself in the front seat next to her.

Lauren was talking and grilling me the whole way home. It wasn't until we pulled in to Arya's apartment complex that Lauren asked an honest but tough question.

"Why don't you heal Jack? He is your friend's son."

"It's more complicated than that Lauren. I most likely would have, if I felt I had to. However, he is expected to make a full recovery, while you were a gamble with your nerve damage. Plus, if you agree, we were hoping this was a good way to create a tight team that could work freely without secrets being kept from each other."

"Speaking of secrets..." Arya added. "I'm clairvoyant. My family does not even know this. With present company excluded, the Director has known for only a few months. My visions are very clear when around Lou, which is why we want to be on the same team."

"I'm starting to feel like a third wheel in this team. Why me?" Lauren asked.

I explained that her technical and analytical talents were valuable and extraordinary. We would be lucky to have her on the team. I also added that she had grown on me and she challenges me to be a better agent.

Maybe it was the competitive nature driven by her youth or just how smart she was. Either way, she keeps me on my toes. Also, she has an open mind to what I have to offer to help her build her law enforcement skills. If she wanted to be in the field, she needed people that not only believed in her, but had her back too. She seemed overwhelmed by the explanation and invite. As we entered the apartment, Andy was quick to greet everyone.

Lauren sat down on the couch and Andy lay down next to her.

"Is this normal?" she said as she rubbed her arms slowly trying to lay the tiny hairs down. "I'm tingly all over and I feel like I have rested for days."

Arya looked at me with a hint of jealousy or concern before excusing herself to the kitchen. I know she would like to think no one feels the way I make her feel. She must know this is not the same, this is just a side effect of the energy.

I have come to realize this year that my energy can be used for more than healing. I always had a feeling that the energy had a cause and effect between people beyond the healing. I hadn't fully realized that my inherited traits might be altering the body's chemistry, specifically people's testosterone.

Apoyan Tachu, "Father Sky" or "Sun Father" has many powers. When Sky people or Gods come down to select mates, the women are frightened in the middle of the night when awaken by the overwhelming presence of the God, but quickly calm and become willing participant in the mating ritual due to the energy passed on to them through touch. It has been described as if a 10-year relationship is formed in seconds and the women become and remain devoted the rest of their lives.

The Gods always return for their Star Children years later. Leaving them behind could upset the balance, as they could have powers that the Gods possess.

I have a feeling that I'm causing unbalance in the world every time I use my powers. Ever since returning from New Mexico a few months back, I can't help but to think I will be receiving a visit from the Sky people. They recognized that I was different and that not only could I see them, I could touch them. They may want to reset the balance. I'm not sure what that would mean for me.

I may have been too cavalier about the effects of the energy on others. As Lauren sat there rubbing her arms and smiling, I realized her afterglow could spell trouble. Perhaps Arya had a legitimate reason to feel threatened by how I made Lauren feel. I needed to assess the damage.

"It's hard to know how much energy to pass on in the moment. As you can imagine, this is not an exact science. However, that feeling should pass in a little while. Everything else okay?"

Lauren looked me over and hesitated for a moment. "I'm fine. I need to talk to Arya about something though, excuse me."

After a few minutes in the kitchen together they came out and told me they would be gone for a while to research Arya's case at the field office. After changing clothes, they left minutes later. I was left behind to work on rescheduling our flights for Monday night. I had a feeling though that everything was not alright and that research was not the only thing those two were going to talk about.

CHAPTER 32

On the ride to the field office, Lauren was staring out the window with her arms crossed. She had told Arya in the kitchen that she had to get out and do something. Researching Arya's case seemed like the most productive thing to do. Arya, however, knew there was more to it than that.

"You want to talk about what's bugging you, Lauren?" Arya asked.

"This is all very overwhelming. I was shot last night. Before I even have time to process the fact that I was shot, had major surgery, and was starting to think of a career change, Lou healed me. Lou healed me!" She repeated as if it was so ridiculous it needed to be repeated.

"It is a lot to process. When Lou was shot in the back a few months ago, he almost died. I was uneasy for a day or two when I saw him heal is own wound a day later." Arya explained.

"I have a pretty open mind to the unusual, but this takes the cake. It's not just the healing though that has me on edge." Lauren said.

Arya had a hunch what was coming next. She was not sure how she would feel if Lauren was overwhelmed by the energy from Lou and became attracted to him. She had questioned herself before if their relationship was based on honest feelings or manufactured ones from the energy. She had decided that the feelings were real months ago and never thought of it sense.

"I think Lou healing me brought me closer to him. For

a few minutes in your apartment, I thought I was becoming more attracted to him, but then I remembered...he is not my type. No offense intended."

"No offense taken." Arya said with a smile.

"It's strange, but maybe these strong feelings for him are a result of him healing me. I know, that doesn't make any sense, but I can't explain it otherwise."

"Are you thinking it may be too awkward to be around him or to be a part of the team?"

"No, no, nothing like that. It's like...seriously, I know that I'm not attracted to him. However, a bond, a strong bond is there that seems to pull me towards him. Like a bond you would have with a protector or your father. I know it's weird and like I said, hard to explain."

"I think you have explained it well. It is supernatural, so it is hard to explain." Arya was tempted to share more, like the night in New Mexico and what Lou went through, but stopped herself. That was not hers to share and really wasn't necessary for what Lauren was going through.

They pulled in to 2635 Century Parkway NE where the FBI field office was located and parked out front. There were not many vehicles out front, but a fair share of cars could probably be found in the parking garage on a typical Sunday. The work never stops.

After going through security and checking Lauren in, they went up in the elevator and found their way to Arya's cubicle. Lauren couldn't help but notice the picture of Arya, Lou and Andy on the desk next to the keyboard.

"You two make a very cute couple. He worries about you."

"Really, what makes you say that?"

"Oh, you know, typical guy stuff like staring off at nothing at lunch or planning a black ops mission to Dover to rescue you from covert meetings." Lauren said with a slight giggle in her voice.

"Yes, he told me about that. This is all new to him. A

grown man stumbling his way through love, well, with some grace. In the past, he had stopped himself from getting too close with others due to his secret."

"So, you broke the code eh? Good for you."

"Something like that." Arya said with a smile.

She pulled up a few files and reviewed them with Lauren before heading down stairs to the high-profile analysis bull pen. There, Lauren was introduced to a couple of data jocks.

Ricky and Shawn preferred the nick name 'data jocks' as part of an inside joke on Director Cooley, who himself was an admirable athlete in his day. Cooley, of course, understood the joke, but let it stick out of respect for the commendable work these two did day in and day out.

"Ricky and Shawn, this is Lauren O'Quinn from Quantico. She has about two months left until she graduates and hopefully will join our team."

They both popped up quickly extending their hands to Lauren very eagerly. She laughed and shook their hands while telling them she was very interested in their set up.

Shawn spoke first. "No really, why are you two down here?" It was obvious that Shawn and Ricky were surprised by their attractive visitor, but they felt like the joke was about to be on them.

Lauren pulled up a chair and wedged it in between the two data jocks. They moved over a little giving her room and then she broke into program talk that lost Arya on the third word.

Lauren went on and on and as she spoke, Ricky and Shawn tried to answer questions that Arya did not even hear Lauren ask. Every few sentences Ricky or Shawn would say "Yes" or "exactly" or "Wait, what?"

Shawn spoke again when Lauren took a breath from her questions and program review of what she wanted to do for Arya's investigation. "You just blew my mind, girl! Where the hell did you come from? The programming theories you are referencing are not even published or proven."

"I know, it's not coming out for another few months. My publisher wanted to wait until I graduated from Quantico." Lauren said.

Arya just laughed.

Ricky looked confused.

Shawn looked star struck for a second. "Holy shit. You're L. O'Quinn from M.I.T. Oh, wow. Wow." with that, Ricky caught on and the computer lingo started up again, but this time Ricky and Shawn were questioning Lauren.

Her programming theories and software were on the "Watch and Learn List" the FBI kept. Programmers and Analysts had to learn, dissect, use and track the use of these questionable programmers to understand and prevent illegal activity. Lauren got a kick out of it. Ricky and Shawn were in their 40's and acting like teenagers. This went on for 20 minutes before Arya interrupted.

The next two hours were dedicated to using Lauren's theories to enhance all cross-referencing programs of state, federal and private data to triangulate leads for Arya. Ricky and Shawn earned their nicknames as they needed little coaching from Lauren. They followed her lead and ran with it after a while.

All of the wall monitors were at their control displaying files, DMV records, employment files, credit card purchases, photos, traffic and street camera footage, satellite images, social network profiles, online pictures tagged with location and date, maps, computer code and much more. Images flashing at the speed of light, not really meant to be looked at.

One section displayed matches they would consider questionable due to the theory that there were no coincidences. Arya was amazed at the amount of footage and data they had compiled that had relevance to her case. The programs running were amazing. They were designed to essentially build a specific database of profiles for the case.

Whether it was a single photo pulled from social media or a still frame from a traffic cam capturing pedestrians and drivers, each was profiled and constantly cross- referenced giving timelines, travel patterns, habitual shopping, work routines and more. It was all too much to take in, which is why Lauren's programs took it a step further.

About an hour ago, Arya handed over her notes that she had written the other day. Notes from her vision with Lou and a dream she had. She explained it as notes from witnesses. Normally they would have asked for names and dates, but they were so engaged with Lauren's technique and input that they overlooked the technicality of protocol for case file references.

They had it narrowed down to five suspects living in a 50-mile radius of the raps. As Lauren suspected, there was a park ranger, two Army enlisted men, a factory worker, and a grocery store employee that fit the profile due to either police records some had or documented questionable behavior found in personnel files coupled with evidence placing them in the area around the times of the crimes.

There were 10 other people on the list with no criminal or questionable behavior in their background check, but were in the areas during each of the crimes. Normally they question the people with past history first, placing the top five with backgrounds as priority. This was a huge break and could lead to saving them weeks, perhaps months of research, and hopefully prevent further crimes. Now comes the hard part of tracking them down and questioning them.

Arya left Lauren with Ricky and Shawn while she made calls to her team to arrange for local support to begin locating suspects and questioning them. She knew Monday morning would be spent with the Director, so she planned her flight to rejoin her field team for late afternoon. If her team worked quickly, she could be doing interviews tomorrow evening.

When dealing with an unidentified subject, Arya always carried butterflies in her stomach. There is no worse feeling of not knowing the name of the person you are tracking or trying to find. Now, with the list of possible subjects, she was feeling more in control and hopeful to put a stop to these horrible acts of violence and vile behavior.

As they wrapped up their research and started to head out, Arya now had a portfolio filled with pictures, profiles and much more on her 15 subjects. Not to mention the link to this personalized database of material she could access on her laptop.

Lauren was giving Shawn and Ricky high fives and fist bumps as recognition for a job well down. They were eating it up. Arya was amazed how smart this beautiful young lady was. She had the full package for a great career. She was intelligent, creative, a good head for business, quick on her feet with problem solving, graceful, good looking, ability to bond quickly with people, and trustworthy. Oh, and soon enough or likely already trained to kill.

As they left together and started to drive back to Arya's place, Lauren seemed to be in a much better mood and no longer feeling the effects of Lou's energy. Hopefully that would hold true once reentering the apartment and being around him during dinner. She called ahead letting Lou know they were on their way and would bring some food home with them. They were all going to need a good meal and rest for the day they have ahead of them.

CHAPTER 33

Monday morning, at Lauren's request, we all went to the hospital to visit Jack. Roy would be at work, but there was a risk of running into his wife while visiting Jack. With a little bit of luck on our side we were able to arrive before any other visitors were allowed. Lauren was able to see that Jack was doing fine and got her delayed goodnight kiss from him. Just after they kissed, he said, "If you enjoyed our first date, wait to see what I have in store for our second date."

"I can't wait." she said laughing and then gave him a careful light hug.

He asked how she was doing. He and his parents had thought she was injured in the event as well.

Lauren had obviously given this more thought than both Arya and I had given it.

She explained she was lightheaded from hitting her head. That and the fact she was covered with his blood, she was rushed off and people thought she was seriously injured.

Jack was happy to see her healthy before saying their goodbyes for now.

We arrived together at the FBI field office and went up to meet with Director Cooley. Arya made a comment about never going to the Director's office in three years and this is her fourth or fifth time in the past few month. All seemed normal, meaning that no one was staring, no extra security lurking or any overall feeling that we were walking into a situation that was not going to go well. The Director's door was open and he waved us all in. Arya closed the door behind her as we all gathered around his desk. There were only two chairs in front of the desk, so I motioned the ladies to take them as I stood in between them.

"This may come as a shock to you all, but after witnessing Lauren's miraculous recovery and then getting very little sleep last night, I am not going to over think this unique situation we find ourselves in. I'd rather just build a winning team that gets me results." He picked up a folder and placed it in front of Lauren.

"What's this?" Lauren asked.

"That is your account of this weekend. It matches what I have already sent to the Assistant Director of the Quantico Training Division and buys you a day away from training. You will also find an IP release form for any program you have done and will do while receiving paychecks from the government."

"I'm not signing this."

"You will if you want a future with us."

"Change the date from being retro and specifically outline all previously started programming being exempt from Intellectual Property clause with the FBI. Then you can email it to my lawyer for review before I sign it."

"What the hell is going on here? Do you understand how this works?"

"Actually, I do. I'm not trying to be difficult. However, I have IP rights for pre-existing programming and non-related Government work. My Lawyer already arranged it prior to arriving at Quantico. This should not be necessary."

"Jesus. Alright, we will deal with this later." He put another folder on the table. "Here is yours, Abrams."

"This should be interesting." I said as I opened the file. It basically outlined my weekend and cover story. Apparently, Lauren and I had spent the last few days consulting with Arya's team. There was no mention of the healing or anything about my abilities, as expected.

The Director went on to advise us that he would keep

tabs on our progress at Quantico these next two months. He would use that time to position some favors and put Arya's plan into place for creating the team.

I would have never imagined anyone, let alone an FBI Field Office Director, being this laid back about my abilities. He seemed impassive about Arya's clairvoyance and my healing abilities. I knew he had bigger plans for us, but he was not showing those cards. From everything Arya has told me about the Director, he is one of the good ones and could be trusted.

"Abrams and O'Quinn, I need you to be available for weekend work with Arya. We have to wrap up a couple of cases. I heard about your tech skills this morning from the data jocks. They are not easy to impress and they seemed very excited about the possibility of you joining the Atlanta Field Office."

Although it meant very little down time between the Academy and case work in the field, we did not have any objections helping Arya catch her monsters. The Director had another folder filled with paperwork and release forms to make the arrangements legitimate. The only thing left to do now was to pack our bags and get back to Quantico. Missing a day would mean catching up. We both did not want to lose our standings in our class.

On the shuttle back to DC, Lauren took her chances and sat next to me. She felt like sharing the conversation she and Arya had the day before about me. To my surprise she was coping well with my powers.

I learned some valuable insight from her about the cause and effect of my healing. It was very interesting to hear her describe the pulling affect I had on her the day of the healing. She explained how she was confused about being attracted to me, when she knew she hadn't been before. More so, her strong feelings for Jack were covered up by the intense pull I had on her, which is why she had to leave for a while to see if her head would clear.

"So, no lasting effects, no problems sitting next to me?"

"None. After spending a few hours at the office yesterday, it seemed to have done the trick. The feelings subsided and Jack was back in my thoughts."

"That is great news. I would have felt horrible if I had caused issues between any of us. I've lived with this for around 20 years, but I'm still trying to figure a few things out. Side effects never really came up as an area of concern until recently." I explained.

I couldn't help remembering that I took people's memories away, for the better though, and now I'm learning I can have them feel attracted towards me.

"No, we are good, Lou. I told Arya that you are like a father figure to me. I really mean that." And she did. Her self-confidence was at an all-time high. She was becoming really good at martial arts, she was networking, building relationships, possibly starting a relationship, and just handled the Director like a pro. I was looking forward to working with Lauren in a team aspect. When you trust the people you work with, and know they are capable and have your back, the team dynamic has potential to achieve much higher success rates. Not to mention keeping each other safe.

CHAPTER 34

The flight from Atlanta to Louisville, Kentucky was a short one, but the storm lingering in the area made it a very unpleasant descent. After having her stomach return to its proper position, she found her way through the terminal to the rental cars and was soon headed southwest on the Dixie Highway towards Fort Knox.

The Ohio River was off to her right for a while until the highway took her due south. A few miles before Fort Knox, the rain was becoming relentless, causing her to pull into a rest stop. The wiper blades could not keep up the down pour, making it very difficult to park the car safely.

She really wanted to make it back to her team at the hotel in Elizabethtown before night fall. However, it was getting late and the rain delay was beating out the clock on the setting sun. She still had about 30 miles to go.

Not totally defeated, she decided to make the best of her pit stop and ran through the rain, quickly covering the short distance between her car and the door to the convenient store. She pushed her way through the door, but it was too late, she was soaking wet.

"It's really coming down out there, huh?" The man behind the counter said.

Arya gave him a polite smile and head nod as she wiped the water from her face. As she headed toward the back where she would likely find the restroom, she took note of the customers. Mainly out of habit, she clocked two Army soldiers approaching the counter with a few items, a middle-aged woman looking at the coffee machine with disappointment, and the truck driver of the rig she avoided as she pulled in. After freshening up, she headed towards the store area to find a Frappuccino in the refrigerated aisle.

◆ ◆ ◆

With the weather being what it was, he had some time to kill. After pulling into the gas station to wait for a break in the rain, he saw a tall brunette run into the convenient store. Dominated by his obsession, he was compelled to leave the vehicle and get a closer look.

Upon entering the store, he was disappointed by her absence. He didn't mind the effort of pursuit, in fact he never minded. Most times he would get a glimpse of a girl or women and follow her just to get a second look. It was a game of sorts. He would challenge himself by guessing if she was beautiful by his standards. The problem was, his standards were ever changing making his little game demanding. Unfortunately, there was nothing innocent about this game.

As he lurked by a postcard stand for a minute, his patience paid off as she came walking out from the back area. A smile formed on his face, because he guessed right, she was beautiful. She seemed a bit out of sorts as she stood in front of the refrigerated drinks.

Where the small back hallway opened to the store, there was a bulletin board with flyers on it. One caught Arya's eye as she was passing. It was a missing person picture of a female College student. She had a nice smile, but that is not what Arya was focused on. The girl went missing the day before Arya left for Atlanta. That puts her missing for 5 days now.

If this was her same predator, the pattern had changed. She took her phone out and called one of her team members in Elizabethtown. She was upset that she did not have the details on this girl yet. Her team explained that there was a delay in the notification of her missing due to friends and family thinking she was on a hiking trip.

The serial rapist the team was trying to track down only kept the girls for two days. Keeping them longer could be an unfortunate sign of escalation to prolonged torture or murder. She put the phone away and headed around the corner to the cold drinks section.

As she grabbed the handle to open the glass door, the lights went out and she felt the space around her close in. Her grip on the door handle could not be any tighter as the vision started to take shape in front of her.

Now it was pitch dark, silent as the store and customers no longer existed in this realm she was stepping into. Like recent visions, since being with Lou, she had tunnel vision as the scene in a distance started to move closer to her.

Seconds later, she was watching a man in dark pants and a grey shirt walking a woman to a white pickup truck. She looked young, wearing shorts, hiking shoes, and a backpack, but was clearly struggling to keep her balance. The man was casually holding her up, guiding her to the passenger door. It was not dramatic looking and would not have been enough to cause others in the area to come to her aid.

As the truck started to pull away, she caught a glimpse of a gas pump, but no signage. The scene faded away, but not before a new one came into focus.

The truck was now in the woods and pulling up to a house. The man was clearly carrying the woman, as she was incapable of walking anymore. Arya blinked and was now watching an awful scene unfold in the man's bedroom.

The woman was lying blindfolded completely naked on

a bed, tape around her wrist, and struggling to avoid the man having his way with her.

The vision stopped as quickly as it came over her. Arya was still holding the handle on the glass door but found herself looking around nervously to see if anyone was staring at her.

As she panned over to the counter, it seemed the customers had cleared out. There was a knot in her stomach from the vision she had just watched.

When she turned to look down the aisle, she was startled to see a large figure wearing a poncho, water dripping off it. The man's face was partially hidden by the shade of the hood pulled over his head and he looked ominous just standing there, ten feet away, facing her motionlessness.

It usually takes much more to startle Arya, but after seeing such a disturbing vision, she felt a little vulnerable. She slowly removed her hand from the door and started moving it towards her hip holster. Just then the man took a step forward and removed his hood. She saw a rough but handsome looking middle aged man appear from under the hood. He was trying for a smile, but was coming across a little worried.

"Ma'am, are you okay?"

"Yes, why?" Arya said with a hint of defensiveness in her voice. Her stance had slightly shifted, hiding the fact that her hand was now resting on the handle of her pistol.

"I'm sorry, I was doing everything I could to give you some distance and not startle you. You have been standing there in a daze for about 30-45 seconds. I was not sure if you were okay or not."

"I'm fine. Almost a minute, really?" Arya asked.

The man took a few more steps forward and Arya could now see the Department of Agriculture Forest Service insignia on the left sleeve of the poncho. She starting lowering her hand off her pistol without drawing attention to it and moved her coat to further conceal the pistol.

"You look like you saw a ghost next to the frozen coffee and energy drinks."

"I was having a moment, that's for sure. Do you work at Mammoth Caves?"

"No, I would be lost in there. Can you believe those caves have over 400 miles of connecting caverns? That's not for me. I spend most of my time in Hoosier National Forest. I'm Carl." He said as he extended his hand.

"Arya." She said as she shook his hand.

"Well, Arya, I hope you have better luck getting to your destination. Most of my routes are flooded."

"I'm almost there, just a few more minutes if the rain lightens up. Good luck, Carl, I have to be on my way." Arya grabbed her Frappuccino and went to go pay the clerk.

"Good luck to you as well. Drive safe, Arya." he said as he started to look through the cold soft drinks that were next to where Arya was standing.

Arya was tempted to chat it up with Carl about the area south of Fort Knox, but it seemed he would not have had much to say since his district was further west. Plus, she could not shake that dreadful feeling from the vision, and the knot in her stomach still had a grip on her. She just wasn't in the mood to talk.

She stepped outside to find that the rain had only slightly let up, so she jogged to the car and got in. As long as the rain did not come down hard again, she should be able to continue her drive south.

After being on the road for ten minutes, the rain was still coming down and the sun had disappeared. Arya had just pasted the exit to Fort Knox and knew that she would soon be coming up on Elizabethtown. There were not many cars out in the storm, which probably meant that they all left early from work to avoid low water crossings becoming dangerous.

She was traveling in the left lane as it had less standing water and made it easier for her to control the car in the rain. She noticed a vehicle behind her closing the distances and decided to move into the right lane to give way to its passing. As she looked at her speedometer, she estimated that the car was probably going a few miles over the speed limit, as she was traveling about 10 miles under the posted limited.

Just as the car was about to pass on the left, it breached her lane and made contact with her real left bumper. Arya had no idea what was going on as her rear end kicked out to the right. She immediately over compensated, sending the car straight for the guardrail.

Any efforts she tried now were pointless as she started to hydroplane. A second later her car slammed into the highway guardrail at 45 miles an hour. The airbag instantly deployed smacking her in the face, followed by a horrific sound of metal tearing and bending.

The wood posts on the guardrails made loud snapping noises followed by silence. She was tricked into thinking the horror was over for a second or two, not knowing the car went airborne over the rail.

The vehicle was on its way over the embankment, traveling just a few feet off the ground the whole way down. The engine had already gone silent from the first impact. Fifteen feet below the road at the bottom of the embankment three feet of running water was rushing from all the rain that had come downhill from the surrounding area and highway.

Arya knew a split second before the second impact that something bad was about to happen again, because she could feel her stomach floating to her chest. It was that same feeling when the roller coaster takes its first plunge.

The car slammed into the bottom of the hill, right front tire first. The water and soft ground parted like the Red Sea for a split second before momentum carried the vehicle back up into the air and then roughly laying it to rest on the driver's side door.

Arya was knocked out for a minute, but the rushing water coming through the broken front windshield woke her up in a panic. She fumbled with her seatbelt for a few seconds before realizing she was severely disorientated from the thrashing she just endured. The fact that the car was resting on its side was not helping either.

When she finally released the seat buckle, she found herself totally submerged in water. Her left shoulder was not cooperating, which made it even more difficult to lift herself up above the incoming water. With her rear against the headrest, she braced herself and kicked at the front windshield. It felt like someone jammed a hot needle up her heel into her calf muscle.

The window was not moving and her feet were sore from the crash. Her next move was to climb up and through the passenger door, which would have been a great idea if it were not jammed shut from the guardrail damage.

She opened her glove box and took out her asp. After breaking the window, she had a tough time climbing out, but managed it. As she sat on top of the passenger window frame, she looked around to get her bearings.

She became instantly relieved when she noticed the outline of a figure standing at the top of the hill. She couldn't help noticing how familiar the silhouette looked of a person wearing a poncho. Any other day in the rain, this would seem normal. But the knot returned in her gut telling her this person was not here to help her. Think of the worst-case scenario, but hope for the best. That is what they teach you.

With the car on its side, Arya eased herself down the roof of the car into the water, putting the car between her and the man on the hill.

The man disappeared for a few a minute before she noticed break lights and reverse lights coming from up the highway from where she went through the guardrail. As it came into full view, it parked right in front of the mangled opening in the rail, protecting it from view of passing by drivers.

The truck was white with a decal on the passenger door that looked like a tree. As the headlights went out, the hazard lights came on. This put Arya on high alert. She immediately started to assess her injuries and what she had on her person.

Her feet and ankles were in pain and so was her left shoulder and head. She ran her hand all over her head to see if there were any gashes she had to worry about. Other than a golfball size bump above her left ear, she seems somewhat intact.

The cold water was running up to her waist and she could feel the current trying to take her away. Arya was still holding the asp and felt her gun still on her waist. She had a clip in and one extra on the belt, but her pockets were empty. No phone to call for help.

The man reappeared with a flashlight in one hand as he climbed over the rail and started to walk sideways down the hill. Arya could make out a metal hook shaped object in the other hand now that he was half the distance to her.

"Are you okay?" The man called out.

The Poncho, the voice, the white truck, it was all adding up in her head very quickly. What are the odds that Carl, the man she just met, ran her off the road? What are the odds he is the serial rapist and she was his intended prey?

"I know you are on the other side of the car. Come around so I can help you up. I have a secured line to help us back up."

Arya had to make a decision. She was in no condition to handle a struggle. She was not going to play along putting herself in jeopardy.

She could not just shoot him, as she was not provoked and didn't know for sure he was the suspect and did not want to lose any chance of finding the missing girl. She decided to put herself in a position of strength and go from there. Arya came around the front of the car very aware that every footstep was a test to her willpower. The current was strong and her legs were killing her. She feared just how bad they were damaged from the wreck.

"There you are. Help has arrived." Carl said with open arms and a smile. He was only ten feet away and slightly above her on the hill. "Arya, is that you?" he said with a surprised voice.

Arya could now see that the hook was attached to a cable that ran up the hill to the front of the truck. It was probably attached to a winch.

"Help me? I don't believe in coincidence, Carl. Why do I have this disturbing feeling that paint from my car is on your front right bumper and that this was no accident?" Arya said as she kept her distance.

Carl's smile started to slowly fade away as he realized Arya was not going to be the gullible damsel in distress he was hoping for. He normally went for slightly younger women, but Arya seemed distracted in the store and a little vulnerable with her wet hair look. She was a very attractive woman and when he decided to start following her, he was hoping that she lived a bit closer. It was not until he had been driving for 15 minutes on the highway that he started to grow impatient with the thoughts of driving further and further south.

So, he made a rash decision to knock her off the road. He was hoping for a mild accident that left her dazed and scared. To avoid witnesses, he had planned to keep driving to the next exit and turning around to circle back and approach her from behind to avoid any suspicion of his involvement. However, when he saw her go through the guard rail, he pulled over and waited to see if any other cars bothered to stop and help. Lucky for him it was dark and the rain provided cover of the accident. No one was close enough to see the action.

Thinking that he had just pulled off the perfect accident, he was a bit perturbed that she blamed him and did not give him any appreciation for his efforts to save her.

"Don't be like that. I happened to have seen the accident on my way to a friend's house. I'm here to help. You don't have to make this awkward." he said as he started towards her.

Arya pulled her gun out and pointed at Carl's chest. "Neither do you. I'm Special Agent Arya Shah with the FBI."

"Oh? FBI, wow! Well, I don't think you will need that for this rescue?" he said as he shined the light on her pistol.

"I think I might. I think you have been involved in some

questionable acts Carl and I plan to take you in for questioning." She said as she noticed him giving some slack to the cable allowing the hook to slowly lower.

"You are crazy. Look, if you want my help, put the gun down and let me help you. Otherwise, I'm out of here."

Arya was not about to let him leave. Unfortunately, she felt like the situation was about to go from bad to awful in a few seconds if she couldn't convince him to peacefully turn himself over for questioning.

She was confident she would at least get him for running her off the road. So, she decided to lie, "We have been on to you for days, Carl. You have nowhere to go."

He stood there staring at her as if trying to read her mind. "Really? Why?"

"You know why. For the same reason I'm in this ditch and you are here to save me. Don't play dumb, it's above you." Arya said to try to play on his ego or take the bait.

"The last time I checked, law enforcement does not run away from suspects. So why did you drive away?" Not giving Arya a chance to respond, Carl took the bait. "No, no, I think I hit the lottery with you. I think this is fate that we met this way. What are the odds?"

"You are delusional. Now drop the hook before I putt a bullet in your arm."

"Arya, you're cold, you're hurt and you are shaking so much you will likely miss or take off my head. Put the gun away and let me take care of you."

She was having a hard time seeing now as the rain was coming right at her face. Arya couldn't decide what her biggest dilemma was at the moment. Climbing the hill would be impossible with the pain and injuries in her legs. Standing was becoming very painful. Shooting Carl was problematic as he has no gun and could still have the missing the girl. Waiting for help could lead to her losing her edge and succumbing to her injuries or Carl making a quick move to take her down.

Carl decided for her as he turned his back to Arya and

started to climb back up the hill.

"Stop! Don't make me shoot you!" she yelled.

"Sorry, babe, I don't think you will shoot an unarmed person in the back. You have nothing and this scene is getting old. Until we meet again."

"Do you still have her?!"

Carl paused his ascent. "Have who?"

"The missing girl. The hiker from the gas station." She added as she tried not to sound desperate.

Carl looked over his shoulder with indifference, but as he turned back to start climbing again, she saw a smile start to form.

She became enraged and lost control for a moment as she fired three rounds at the cable just above his head. He instinctively went into a semi crouched position as the bullets tossed up the earth in front of him. Although she missed the cable, she seemed to have rattled him enough to stop his journey.

"What, are you crazy?!" he yelled at her.

"I told you, you're not going anywhere."

"And I told you, you are not going to shoot me in the back." He started to climb again.

Arya took aim and gently squeezed the trigger sending a bullet into Carl.

CHAPTER 35

He spun around and grabbed for his leg, resulting in him losing his grip on the cable sending him sliding down the hill into the running water just behind the car. Arya holstered her gun and started to maneuver around the car to get a visual on Carl. Each step sent hot needles up her legs.

As she got close to the rear bumper, she had her asp out and was ready to strike. It would not be needed though as she saw Carl floating head first on his back down the make shift stream. He had this awful look of anger on his face as he continued to float further away.

She ran her hand over her lower back and felt the handcuffs in their rightful place. Without thinking further, Arya eased herself back into the running water and started to float after Carl.

He was now about 30 feet in front of her. Arya kept the asp in her hand as she let the current start to take her away feet first. Nothing about this seemed smart, but she was not about to let Carl get away. To think they were both on even ground now due to the injuries they had suffered could be a fatal miscalculation.

Fear of where the makeshift river would take them, Arya started to plan her exit. When the time came, she would have to jam the asp into the bank of grass to serve as a break to slow her down and eventually stop her to allow her to get out.

She could now see Carl grasping at the grass struggling to stop. His failed attempt only slowed him down allowing Arya to gain another 10 feet on him.

Just then, Arya noticed Carl approaching rough water. Before he knew what was going on, his back seemed to have hit something solid in the rough water, stopping him cold. With his back pinned against the object, water started to rush against his chest rising over his shoulders and head. His arms were frantically moving about, trying to stop the water and then a second later he was sucked under instantly disappearing.

Arya quickly realized the danger she was floating into could be a drainage tunnel and hurriedly started to use the asp as a break to stop her from becoming the tunnel's next victim.

Using her right hand, she dug the asp into the side of the grassy bank. It was cutting through the grass slowing her down, but the rough water was getting very close now. Arya twisted her body to grab onto the asp with both hands and dug in even deeper. She immediately felt her left shoulder pop out of its socket causing excruciating pain. She fought with the pain for several seconds, wanting to let go of the asp, but knowing that would only lead to her being be sucked under the water to her possible death.

She finally came to a stop about 5 feet before the rough water. The current felt stronger here, but she managed to get her feet under her leaning sideways into the current.

It took her a couple of exhausting minutes to crawl her way up the 45-degree grassy ditch. She was now on the side of the water opposite the highway. She found herself on flat land looking up the 20-foot grassy embankment to the highway. To her right she could see that the drainage tunnel ran under a road that went under the highway. As she walked over to the road, she noticed a set of train tracks. She knew those would lead her to Fort Knox if she followed them for about a mile.

The numbing affect from the cool water temporarily reduced the pain in her legs, but it also lowered her core temperature causing Arya to become lethargic. She hobbled over the tracks to the other side of the road to see if Carl had popped out the other side. Darkness made it difficult to see much, as she tried to make out any objects moving or floating down stream. She did not have the strength to keep pursuing him and the likelihood was that Carl drowned in the drainage tunnel regardless if he came out the other side or not.

Arya made the decision to start walking towards Fort Knox in hopes that a car would come by much sooner than her completing the mile walk.

After a few hundred yards, she was starting to feel nauseated from the pain in her shoulder and legs. All she wanted was for Lou to hold her tight and make her feel better. The thought of being in his arms made her keep taking each painful step until she could hear what she thought was a car coming.

Currently, Arya was walking on the side of the road and the train tracks were about 20 feet to here right. When the pain in her legs started to increase quickly and she could feel a slight tremor, she knew it was not a car approaching. The noise turned out to be a train coming and as it made its approach she waved the only thing over her head that would catch the conductor's eye, her gun. She fired a few shots into the ground between the road and the tracks.

As the engine started to pass, the train sounded its horn that sent a vibration through her body. Each flatbed car that passed on the rails was carrying two armored desert Humvees. At least 50 Humvees had passed before the pattern broke to M1 Abrams battle tanks.

She started to wonder if someone would fire back at her. Perhaps discharging her weapon to get the conductors attention was not a great idea.

Arya was sure the train was making a stop in Fort Knox and hoped that the sound of the horn was the conductor's way of saying 'I see you, crazy lady.'

It did not take long to find out though. After walking for a few more minutes, she could see the flashing lights of several police cars approaching. As soon as they started pulling up close to her, she placed her gun on the ground, started backing up and held her cuffs above her head in her right hand. Without her credentials on her, she was hoping this would go smooth.

"Ma'am, stay right there and do not move," the first officer called out. She could see his gun was pointed at her.

"I'm Special Agent Arya Shah with the FBI. I'm hurt and unarmed." As she made this announcement a vehicle came crashing out of the woods from behind her.

It looked very much like the Humvees on the train's cargo bed, but this version was camouflage instead of desert tan. The front bumper and debris guard had gathered torn brush from the ground from the journey. It also had a man attached to a .50 caliber machine gun in the roof turret.

This was turning out to be more exciting than it needed to be. The vehicle came to a sliding stop between the tracks and the road, just 15 feet from Arya. She could feel a wave of hot air come off the engine and pass over her giving her goose bumps. She guessed the Army did not like the idea of an armed person close to their base or precious cargo.

"Put your hands on your head." the officer shouted.

"My shoulder is badly-injured, I cannot lift my arm." Arya said. She could hear footsteps sloshing through the mud behind her.

"Back away soldier!" the officer demand, but it was too late. Arya felt a hand sliding up her raised arm until it reached her wrist. She turned her head and was face to face with a soldier who looked all business in his gear, an M4 submachine gun pressed to his chest with his finger ready to action the weapon. He slowly started to lower her hand.

"Who are you?" He asked

"Special agent Shah with the FBI."

The officer was running over to them now.

"Is that your only weapon?" the soldier asked as he made a head nod towards her gun on the ground.

"Yes, Lieutenant, other than my asp in my belt." She noticed the rank and felt that if she used it, he might show her the same professionalism in return.

"Are you deaf? Back away, soldier?" the officer said.

"Sorry, Officer, she is already in the custody of The United States Army, and it's Lieutenant Steven Taylor for when you write up your report." This led the Officer to mumble a few curse words to himself.

"My credentials are in my car about a mile back in a ditch. Honestly, I don't think I can take another step. I'm pretty sure I fractured both my legs and ruined my shoulder."

Another soldier came up on Arya's left and positioned himself between Arya and the second police officer that had followed his partner up to the scene. After a few minutes of debate and the officer taking down the lieutenant's name, the police took Arya's statement and gun and gathered around their cars to discuss their next move. For some reason, the soldiers seemed very protective of Arya once they discovered she was not a threat.

"May I take a look?" the Lieutenant asked as he started to kneel.

Arya nodded and the Lieutenant lifted her pant leg and looked at her right leg and then her left. He shook his head before standing back up.

"I'm surprised you are walking at all. Your legs are in bad condition. We should carry you to the Humvee and get you to Ireland." One of the soldiers helping carry Arya let her know that Ireland was the name of the Army Community Hospital.

She figured as much but thanked him for explaining. The Lieutenant had the Sergeant go retrieve Arya's gun from the police as part of the Army's investigation into the shooting of Army Cargo entering the base. The police were reluctant at first, but finally handed it over to the Sergeant.

The soldiers took the road back to Fort Knox, sparing Arya from the rough terrain route they took to get to her. She learned on the ride to the hospital that a few soldiers had a run in with local police the other day and things were a little on edge in the area. She also learned that the Army takes any apparent threat in the immediate area as a threat worth addressing, which is why the police and the Army at times find themselves in these positions. Normally, they are very supportive of each other.

Lieutenant Taylor dared not deny Arya his cell phone when she asked to make some calls. He just handed it over and smiled at her with amazement as she was all business with the agents on the other end.

He listened to her recap the crazy events that unfolded earlier. He thought it was interesting that she was also advising her team to call the Internal Affairs Division to liaise with the Army's Criminal Investigation Division to retrieve her gun and start their process of investigation.

They were carrying her through the E.R. double doors while she was still talking to her team. At the request of a doctor, the Lieutenant had to take the phone, but not before Arya demanded to make one more phone call.

CHAPTER 36

Lauren and I were chatting it up the whole way back to Quantico. We knew Hogan's Alley was coming up and she was nervous about the live tactical training in the FBI created city.

Several different law enforcement communities shared the mock town for teaching civilian and military officers, as well as local and international agencies investigative and tactical techniques.

She had good reason to be nervous. Lauren had never really been exposed to violence up close and personally, recent gunshot wound excluded. She had never been in a fight to defend her name or character or whatever reason people get into fights. Nor had she been responsible for protecting the person next to her. She was more nervous about letting down the person next to her than anything else.

I reminded her that if we were to make mistakes, Hogan's Alley would be the place to do it and learn from it. That did not comfort her as much as I hoped it would. I don't blame her, because I was intimidated by Hogan's Alley and I have been policing for years.

She was right, though, you don't want to let down the person next to you. However, you have to control your fear and keep your wits about you to be any good to your partner, team and self.

People that have never been in a combat situation don't understand how personal it is. Civilians don't typically walk down a street wondering from what direction someone may try to shoot them, or every time they approach a bank they are not assessing the outside for threats, and the same as they walk in, or wondering if the package left on the foot-steps of a business you are walking by is innocently awaiting the owners arrival, or if it is seconds away from exploding. Hogan's Alley has all that and more.

Marine officers train for urban warfare going door to door wondering if a bomb or bullets will meet them as they check each house on the street.

No question about it, the coming weeks would be in-tense. As we walked down the hall to Lauren's room, I cracked a few jokes to take her mind off of it. I knew she would be fine and that she would settle in after her first run. She has the street smarts and analytical sense to see potential scenarios before they happen and her athleticism would prevail in phys-ical altercations or times when running for your life came in handy.

She unlocked her door and gave me a hug before going in. It had been one hell of a weekend. It was definitely not what we all had planned, but in an uncanny way the weekend that brought us all closer together. As she was closing her door, my phone rang.

"Hello?"

It took me by surprise that Director Cooley was calling me after just getting back to Quantico. Unfortunately, it was not to ensure that we had arrived safely. After sharing with me the news of Arya's run in with a serial rapist and her being hospitalized just minutes ago, I felt powerless being states away. He assured me she was in good hands and that nothing was life threatening.

Cooley wanted to be sure I would stay focused at Quantico this week and wait for the weekend to visit Arya. I know he had pulled a major favor already for me and I did not want my emotions clouding my judgment or performance this week.

It turned into the longest week as I worked towards the

Friday night-flight I had booked that would get me to Louisville. She was released from the hospital mid-week and her team relocated with her to long term hotel suites in Louisville to keep her comfortable as they wrapped up their investigation.

Arya's vision turned out to be helpful. The FBI and local police searched Carl's house, not find anything. When relaying this to Arya, she had them explore surrounding farms in the area until they found the abandoned farm she saw in her vision.

From her hospital bed she walked them through the scene and found a trap door to a cellar. They found the missing college girl chained to a bed and in bad shape. Thankfully alive, she would recover physically in a couple of weeks. The mental torment she endured would take much longer.

◆ ◆ ◆

As I entered the hotel room, all was quiet. A light was on over the kitchen table and a note lay visible in the center.

Arya wrote that she tried staying up for me, but the medication she was on forced her to go to sleep. Her team had the adjoining rooms, so I knew she was safe, but I would not be satisfied until I held her in my arms.

When I entered the dark bedroom, there was enough light coming from the bathroom to see how she looked. Her arm was strapped to her chest in a shoulder harness that kept it immobilized. One leg was in a cast to her upper thigh with the words "FBI Track Star" written in marker on it. The other was in a pressure wrap. She was laying on her back sound asleep as I joined her.

When morning came, I was having coffee in the kitchen when Arya was awakened by her phone ringing.

"Hello?" she answered. She had a clear line of sight to

me and when she saw me sipping coffee, her face lit up.

"Yes, sir, I'm here. I...well...hold on." She put the phone down and removed her arm from the harness. She was staring at me smiling as she rotated her arm and shoulder like a baseball pitcher warming up.

"Yes, I'm all better." She said smiling as she spoke to the Director. They talked for a few minutes before she hung up and walked over to me.

"When did you sneak in Lou?" She said as she leaned over and kissed me.

"Last night."

"You know, it is even more awkward walking in a leg cast when your leg is perfectly fine." She was trying to figure out how to sit at the table and finally gave up, retreating to the sofa.

"I'm glad you are feeling well." We caught up over coffee and she filled me in on Director Cooley giving her time off to keep her injuries clear from suspicion. We enjoyed the weekend together at the hotel before traveling our separate ways Sunday evening.

CHAPTER 37

Lauren and I completed Quantico, graduating in the top five of our class. Her parents came in to town to see Lauren get her credentials and afterwards invited Arya and me out to dinner with them. They were good people and very impressed with Lauren's accomplishments. That was very evident when we talked about Hogan's Alley and some of the live exercises we were put through, Lauren's parents looked amazed and proud that their little girl grew up into such a self-confident, talented, and independent woman.

Understandably, they were upset to find out that we did not get a vacation or a month off. They wanted more time with Lauren before her career swept her away. That is not how it works though. We already had assignments waiting for us. In fact, our new team was meeting up with us two days from now in Atlanta.

We blinked and two days passed. Lauren was staying with us at Arya's apartment in Atlanta until she located her own place. We all drove into the field office together to check in with the Director in morning.

On the drive into the office, Arya hinted that she heard an outsider was transferring in and the Director was putting him or her on our team. It wasn't until we were approaching the Directors office that we started to figure out who was possibly being assigned to our team. He was sitting with his back to the door. The mystery man must have said something to send the Director into his well-known boisterous laugh, typically reserved for his own college stories.

The Director waived us in and the mystery was over. USMS Tom Holliday turned around with a broad smile on his face.

"Hey! How's the shoulder, Shah?" Holliday asked. Everyone seems to go quiet for a second before Arya spoke up.

"It would seem the left is accident prone, but a fast healer."

"Good to hear that you rebound quickly. Hopefully you have met your quota. It's good to see you both again."

"You, too." Arya replied.

The Director regained control of the conversation and made formal introductions of Lauren and Holliday.

The US Marshals were beefing up their liaison efforts with the FBI. Their extensive jurisdiction matching the Bureau's made it ideal to collaborate on matters crossing state lines. As the Director continued to explain to us the purpose of the team, we all started to take seats where we could in his office.

Come to find out, it was no coincidence Holliday was meeting with his old buddies in DC. They were already working with the FBI on a cyber case that seemed to jump around from state to state.

What made this case so different from thousands like it that the Secret Service and FBI handle, was the obscure nature of the coding used on the dark web, how it moved around and how it was used.

We had our work cut out for us on this one, but I was thankful for Lauren being on our team. Team work drives results. With Lauren tracking the criminals through cyberspace, Holliday providing his network of knowledge and Arya getting visions, we had more of a chance than most of the best teams assembled combined.

The Director knew this and was pleased to have such a team under his authority. He knew the results would come with some risks though. There were variables at work out of his control, supernatural variables. How would Holliday react when the truth reveals itself? How long could he keep my abilities a secret?

Today, he brought us together. Tomorrow, we would be hard at work tracking the online murder for hire syndicate. The most recent crime was in North Carolina where a man was murdered and his 12-year old girl was missing.

As we left the briefing, Holliday gave me a nudge. "Lou, is there something you want to tell me?" he asked.

I immediately started to get nervous and could not help to wonder just how much Director Cooley had shared with Holliday. I knew it was only a matter of time before we found ourselves in a situation that raised questions or concerns, but I did not expect the Director to just openly advise Holliday of my gift.

"What do you mean?"

"You know, how did you pull this off? How did you and Arya get the Director to hand craft this team?"

"Oh." I likely sounded a little relieved. "He must have been impressed with how we all worked together. Plus, Lauren really made a name for herself with her computer skills, analytics and determination to be an agent. Not that I had any clout, but Arya and I really pushed for the Director to pull some strings to get her assigned here. What's your story?"

"I was apparently volunteered by some old friends, you met them up north. They volunteered me to be...how did they put it...'more useful'." He laughed and put his Stetson cowboy hat on his head as he started to walk away. "See you bright and early, Lou."

The next day would come too soon and we were all about to find out just how difficult this next case would prove to be. Not just to solve, but rather how hard it would be on us physically, mentally and spiritually. We had no idea what we were getting involved in.

REFERENCES:

www.ashiwi.org, Pueblo of Zuni, 2014, April 28

www.legendsofamerica.com/na-zuni.html, The Zuni Indians – Still a Mysterious tribe. 2014, June 15.

www.churchofcriticalthinking.org/indian.html, Star Beings Gods and Sky Spirits. The Gods and Goddess's of Native American Indian Cultures. 2013, September 20.

http://m.fbi.gov/#http://www.fbi.gov/about-us/training/sat, The FBI Federal Bureau of Investigation, New Agent training. 2013, December 18.

www.newworldencyclopedia.org/entry/zuni, Zuni. 2014, February 20.

http://www.native-languages.org/zuni-legends.htm, Researched Important Zuni Mythological Figures. 2014.

TURN THE PAGE FOR AN EXCERPT

Book 2

ONLINE MURDER SYNDICATE

The Paranormal Mysteries & Adventures of Special Agent Lou Abrams

ONLINE MURDER SYNDICATE

CHAPTER 3

"Hey, you see that vest on the seat next to you? That's for you to put on. Let's not take any chances." She hoped it would not be needed, but better to be vigilant. Charlie fumbled around with the Kevlar vest for a few minutes but managed to complete the task.

Holliday was making good time in the borrowed government vehicle. They were a few minutes away from turning off highway 70 on to Slocum drive, to the west gate into Marine Corp Air Station (MCAS) Cherry Point North Carolina.

Lauren was back on the phone with Arya getting an update on the manhunt. They found Justin's abandoned car about 20 minutes ago by the Cherry Point Inn, which formerly served as the BOQ's many years ago. As soon as they ordered the search team to the area, Justin Mercer popped up a few streets over in a retired Brigadier General's backyard.

Lauren was in midsentence with Arya when the conversation was interrupted with a sequence of loud metallic thumps on her passenger door.

TINK, TINK, TINK, TINK, TINK, TINK

She heard the window break just behind her right ear. Simultaneously all the air in her lungs instantly left in a split second. She was wincing in pain as every muscle from her hip to her jaw were tightening with relentless force. But it was her lungs she was most worried about, as they were squeezed down to the size of two peas and unwilling or able to let any air in. She felt a hand thrusting her head down towards her knees, making the pain worse and allowing no chance for air to return to her lungs.

"Shots fired!" Holliday yelled.

Lauren turned her head slightly to see Holliday's hand leave her and return to the wheel. The engine was whining in response to the accelerator being jammed to the floor. She started to sit back up just in time to see their car slamming into another and the passenger side airbag deploy into her face.

Lauren could feel her grip on consciousness slipping away. A split second after the airbag exploded into her nose and eyes, darkness started to quickly consume her vision. Her lungs felt like they were pushing a million hot needles through her chest, in hopes to pierce her skin to let air in.

Perhaps it was the facial trauma that distracted her diaphragm, but a few seconds later it released the choking grip on her chest and lungs, and she was taking in what seemed to be the biggest and longest breath of her life. She would not let it be ruined by the thick smell of gunpowder from the airbags exploding.

As her vision came back, she realized Holliday had released her seatbelt and was climbing over her opening her door. Holliday fell out of the car, pulling Lauren to the ground with him.

She could hear rounds from a fully automatic rifle tearing into the driver side of the car. Lauren was laying on top of Holliday when she felt a bullet tug at her vest. It must have come clean through the door. She rolled off Holliday and kicked the passenger door closed to provide more shielding. That is when she noticed all the bullet holes on her door and the door behind hers.

Holliday was already firing back over the hood when Lauren pulled her gun and started looking for a target. She shook her head to free her sight of the dancing black dots scattered in front of her. The pain from her side was apparently still overwhelming her, but she knew she needed to push past it for now in order to avoid being shot. Being shot! She couldn't help it, she started to quickly feel her right side for a bullet wound. Her left hand came back wet and crimson colored.

As she took in the scene, she kept thinking how insane this was. The highway was at a standstill as cars just stopped and people watched the horror unfold from within their vehicles. She peaked over the window and saw that Charlie was lying in the backseat with a hole in his neck, lifeless.

"Shoot anything running towards you Lauren." Holliday shouted at her as he reloaded.

Lauren started to raise her gun over the trunk only to be met by a policeman running at her with his sub machinegun pointed at her. This is the first time she ever saw a Policeman holding an Uzi. Without hesitation, she squeezed the trigger twice on her 9mm Glock.

POP POP

The first bullet may have missed her target, but the second entered the man's chest an inch below his neckline causing him to crumble on the street just feet from the rear of the car. Unsure if she just killed a police officer or a criminal, she started to have second thoughts about what Holliday just told her to do.

PHTHHHH

What could only be a bullet whistled by her head caused Lauren to drop for cover again. The trunk of the car was now being heavily riddled with bullets. She started to scream out of fear, but it was interrupted by the opposite side rear tire exploding and the car jolting.

Lauren was crouched behind the other rear tire when a bullet traveling underneath the car took the heel clean off her shoe causing her leg to twist awkwardly, sending her firmly onto her rear.

As she tried to regain her position, she could see that the few seconds were about to cost her dearly. Another assailant had already rounded the car with his gun pointed at her. She saw the muzzle flash at the exact same time the spray of hot lead sent her backwards into the pavement.

Neatly sliced banana, granola, yogurt, and orange juice. Lauren's breakfast flashed before her as if she were starting the day over. Then that feeling returned and woke her to every muscle tensed, and she could not breathe. She was sure she was dying. No such luck on starting the day over.

As Lauren lay there gasping for air, waiting for more bullets to pinch the last remaining life from her, she saw her would be executioner explode into red dust.

The gun fire became heavy sounding, like quick deep thumping of a drum, and very intense for about 20 seconds. She still had not taken a breath and those damn red-hot needles had returned in her chest. Lauren could feel the tears running from her eyes to her ears as she lay on her back on the asphalt in excruciating pain.

Holliday's face came into view and she started to grasp at everything, anything, just to get some air.

"Relax Lauren! Relax. You got the wind knocked out of you. Trust me, you are okay." He said smiling over her. Holliday waved someone over to her and pointed to her arm as he holstered his side arm and started to remove her vest.

She could feel his hands quickly sliding over her chest, ribs, sides and then her back, gently rubbing the areas. His face was all business, his smile had left when he was removing her bulletproof vest.

Someone else's hands were lifting her hips by pulling her up from the front waist band of her slacks. It did not feel good. She would have swatted their hands away had it not been for a third person holding her left arm down, wrapping it with something. Her lungs started to take in a depth breath, but the pain in her chest made her wince and cut off the effort. This repeated several times before she got a full breath, and then the mystery hands set her waist down and left her.

There were three soldiers standing around her now offering to help her up. Holliday was now getting the laptop off the floor of the car and examining it. He made a face that signified he was shocked to find it in one piece. As she stood with the help of the soldiers, she took in the scene.

There was a traffic jam on I-70 for miles. Bullet shell casings everywhere. Their car had a hundred holes in it and thick black smoke was leaking from the front hood. Three other cars were involved, and they were torn up from the Marines unleashing their assault rifles and heavy machine gun mounted on one of the Humvees. One car was on fire. Six men lay dead in the highway, not counting poor Charlie Houghton in the back of their car. There were a few Humvees in the area now and the men that accompanied them took over the highway.

Three of the assaulters were dressed as police and the car on fire was what appeared to be a police car, with markings that looked like Greenville PD. It seemed like the West End Fire Department and EMS pulled up seconds before the Havelock Police. A Gunnery Sergeant stepped forward to give his account to the police while EMS ran from one body to the next. They tried to hold back the horrified looks as they approached the two bodies almost cut in half by the .50 caliber the Marine unleashed from atop the Humvee.

Holliday was again by Lauren's side helping her towards the paramedics. A Marine stopped them for a second and bent down to place Lauren's shoe back on her foot. She thought, "It's a fit" and laughed in her mind that she just had a Cinderella moment. The heel was missing, but it was still better than nothing. He didn't even look at her for a 'Thank you' as he spun around and rejoined his buddies getting orders from the Gunnery Sergeant.

Made in the USA
Coppell, TX
13 November 2020